# VAMPIRES,
## *Hearts*
## & OTHER
## DEAD
## THINGS

# VAMPIRES,
## *Hearts*
## & OTHER
## DEAD
## THINGS

Margie Fuston

Margaret K. McElderry Books
New York   London   Toronto   Sydney   New Delhi

MARGARET K. McELDERRY BOOKS
An imprint of Simon & Schuster Children's Publishing Division
1230 Avenue of the Americas, New York, New York 10020
This book is a work of fiction. Any references to historical events, real people,
or real places are used fictitiously. Other names, characters, places, and events
are products of the author's imagination, and any resemblance to actual events
or places or persons, living or dead, is entirely coincidental.
Text © 2021 by Margie Fuston
Jacket illustration © 2021 by Jeff Östberg
Jacket design by Sonia Chaghatzbanian © 2021 by Simon & Schuster, Inc.
All rights reserved, including the right of reproduction in whole
or in part in any form.
MARGARET K. McELDERRY BOOKS is a trademark
of Simon & Schuster, Inc.
For information about special discounts for bulk purchases, please contact
Simon & Schuster Special Sales at 1-866-506-1949 or
business@simonandschuster.com.
The Simon & Schuster Speakers Bureau can bring authors to your live event.
For more information or to book an event, contact the Simon & Schuster
Speakers Bureau at 1-866-248-3049 or visit our website at
www.simonspeakers.com.
Interior design by Jess LaGreca
The text for this book was set in Adobe Garamond Pro.
Manufactured in the United States of America
First Edition
2 4 6 8 10 9 7 5 3 1
CIP data for this book is available from the Library of Congress.
ISBN 9781534474574
ISBN 9781534474598 (ebook)

*For my parents.*
*And for anyone who has hoped for impossible things*
*just to make it through the day.*

I don't know how to live in this world
if these are the choices, if everything just gets
stripped away. I don't see the point.
—*Buffy the Vampire Slayer*

# One

*e strong like Buffy.* I repeat the mantra in my head as I glare into the garish fluorescent lights. But all I can think about is the episode where Buffy's mom dies, and they keep showing the body, eyes wide and staring, and I imagine what Dad would look like. Eyes open or closed?

I bite the inside of my cheek. *Be strong like Buffy.*

Plastered smile in place, I look down at Dad, just in case he's watching. He's not. He slouches on the arm of an extra-large wheelchair, the only one still available from the hospital lobby. He's always been tall and thin, but now three of him could sit in the wide seat.

When he first got sick, the hospital offered an insurance-bought wheelchair for us to take home, but back then my dad shook his head and smiled. *You can't show cancer any bit of weakness,* he said, winking at me so we both laughed. Mom tried to take it, but we overruled her.

No one jokes now.

The paper covering the exam table crinkles as I squirm to get comfortable. My left leg's gone dead. Numb, I mean. Not dead.

Mom turns her hard blue eyes on me, and I stop. She wanted me to stay home—told me I didn't need to be here for this. I don't know if she's worried about me or how my emotions might affect Dad, but she should know by now that I can hide my feelings as well as she can.

Dad catches my eye and runs a hand over the stray tufts of hair the chemo hasn't stolen yet. "Do I still look like Count Dracula?" he asks, lips parting into something like a grin.

Before cancer, Dad had a round face and thick brows and black hair he kept slicked back in an out-of-fashion look my mom constantly teased him for. But he loved it. He looked exactly like Bela Lugosi, the original Dracula. We always joke Dad is Lugosi's long-lost relative.

"You might be sliding into Christopher Lee territory now." Lee played Dracula after Lugosi, and his hair wasn't quite as great.

Dad snorts, and the sound is soft and weak. "Even Gerald looks better than me now. I've got more in common with Count Orlok." And then he grins, really grins. His eyes crinkle in the corners like they do when he's told a joke he's already laughing at and he's waiting for me to catch up to his wit.

I laugh. Dad and I are vampire connoisseurs. We've seen every vampire movie and television show and documentary ever made at least ten times. Joking about the undead feels normal. He even mentioned Gerald. I thought he'd forgotten what today is, but maybe not. It's not like he could wake up this morning and make his usual vampire pancakes with sliced strawberries as bloody fangs. But we could still be celebrating later.

I search his face for some indication he remembers. Nothing.

I realize I'm still laughing and stop. My eyes are wet, and I don't even remember letting the tears sneak in.

Dad stops laughing when I do. His face slackens and his eyes drift away. He does that a lot now. I wonder what he's thinking or if he's trying to exist without thinking, like I do sometimes.

Mom shifts her gaze between us like she doesn't get us at all. Her brow creases as I wipe at my eyes, but she doesn't need to worry. I'm still in control.

What would it be like without Dad here? Just me and Mom—two people who don't understand each other. Dad's always been the one thing to connect us. Sometimes Mom smiles at one of his corny jokes or even laughs at one of mine if Dad goads her into it. He's a fraying thread between us.

I tilt my head back and blink into the lights again.

The door clicks open, and Dad's oncologist comes in. He's young and looks like a professional tennis player, and it never ceases to bug me. Seeing him next to my dad doesn't seem fair. I want an ancient doctor who should have retired ten years ago.

"David, how are you?" He reaches out and shakes Dad's hand without waiting for an answer. It's such a ridiculous question. The whole world knows how he is.

The doctor shakes Mom's hand and then mine. At least he's nice. He always acknowledges that I'm here and I'm an adult and

I can handle whatever he throws at us—unlike my mom, who's always staring at me like she's waiting for me to break.

He pulls up his rolling stool. "The chemo's stopped working," he says. No prelude, no staring at his papers before speaking, no pre–bad news sigh. He blurts it. Leaving us no time to brace ourselves.

Silence stretches, and if nobody breaks it, then maybe we can stay in this moment forever and refuse to acknowledge what the doctor said. But then Mom nods, making the words real. My parents are holding hands, fingers interlaced like high school sweethearts.

My treacherous heart speeds, beating faster than I thought possible. Adrenaline rips through me, yelling at me to fight this, but what am I supposed to attack? I pull in breath after breath, calming my body, telling it not to be afraid. Dad's still here. He's right in front of me. Nothing's over until it's over. Dad taught me that.

I shake my head, but nobody notices. "What's the next step?" I ask.

Everyone turns to me. Mom's eyes are vacant, but a muscle in her jaw twitches, and she can't hold my stare. Dad's eyes are harder to read. Sadness lurks in them but also relief. The relief kills me. How could he possibly feel that? Doesn't he understand what this will mean for us? We'll never get to travel together like we planned—visit the places our favorite movies were filmed or the places where vampire myths were born. We won't go to anymore midnight showings of the latest vampire movies. We won't get to have chocolate shakes afterward at the twenty-four-hour Denny's and dissect how well the movie vampire's traits matched up with vampire lore. I won't do those things without him. I won't. He must realize this. I catch his eye, and he gives me the smallest nod. He knows, but he looks so tired. Like a man who can't keep fighting no matter how much he's losing by giving up. My eyes sting, and I can't look at him anymore.

I turn to the doctor's smooth, patient face. "We're out of options," he says.

"What about clinical trials?" I ask.

He shakes his head slowly. "We're too far advanced for that."

His use of "we're" pisses me off. *We're* not the ones going through it. He gets to go home tonight and have his tennis match, or sit in front of his television with a beer, or kiss his pretty spouse. He doesn't see the pain that my dad's in all day every day. He's not a part of this.

I drag in a deep breath and try to force down the fear leaking into the hollow of my stomach. Dad's not dead yet. I put those four words on repeat in my mind.

"How long?" Mom asks.

"A month. Maybe less."

If pancreatic cancer were a vampire, it wouldn't be well-groomed Lestat, and it definitely wouldn't be sparkly Edward. No, it'd be the vampire horde from *30 Days of Night*—merciless, bloody, ravaging a whole town until nothing is left.

But no, even that's not right. Cancer is so merciless that even the cruelest of vampires can't compete. Cancer takes its time. At least the townsfolk in *30 Days of Night* died quickly—a few moments of terror and then boom, nothing. That's got to be better. Anything's got to be better than this.

Two hundred and forty-six days and counting.

"Do you have any questions?"

Why? The word's been running through my head again and again. Nobody ever answers. Not even God, and Dad says he has all the answers. I'm sure the doctor can't, either.

Dad grips the doctor's hand, thanking him. I'm not sure what he's so thankful for, but he's always been like this, seeing reasons to be grateful where I see none. I used to admire that in him, but now I want to grab his shoulders and shake him until he admits we have nothing to be thankful for at this moment.

I wheel Dad out of the hospital, trying to avoid the sharp corners with his chair. I bump his feet into the wall more than once, and Mom asks me to be careful. Dad doesn't seem to notice.

When we get home, Dad ends up where he spends most of his time now: the hospital bed set up in the spare bedroom. He insisted Mom's snoring kept him up at night, and we'd laughed about it, but I know he did it for her. He moans a lot in his sleep now. Probably didn't want her to hear. I thought she should have argued with him a little, but she let him go.

She lets things go too easily.

Mom gives him his morphine drops the second we settle in. She never forgets a dose. She cares for him with the efficiency of a well-programmed robot, but today she slows down and tucks my old *101 Dalmatians* comforter under his chin. He claims it's the most comfortable blanket in the house. He stopped her from throwing it out at least a dozen times.

She rests her hand on one of the faded puppies and leans down, touching her lips to his forehead.

I stare at the empty television. This isn't the routine. It means something has changed.

"Anna," Dad says softly as Mom pulls away from him. "Do you want to talk about it?"

Mom leans back in slightly, like she'll collapse against his chest with the smallest nudge.

My stomach clenches, and in my head, I recite all the Dracula movies from oldest to newest. I cannot watch my mother break. She never gets emotional, and if she loses it now, everything will be too real, but I can't leave the room either, or that will be my admission that this is actually happening.

But she sucks in a deep breath, and her back goes rigid. "I'm fine, love." Her fingers squeeze the comforter before she pulls away. Her hard eyes find mine, and she nods. We're together in this then. Nothing has changed. We're not going to curl into sobbing balls of grief while Dad's still here.

Mom leaves, and I don't give Dad a chance to ask me if I want to talk. "Do you want to sleep?" I ask.

He shakes his head even as it droops toward his chest. "I can sleep when . . ."

He doesn't finish the sentence, but I know what he stopped

himself from saying. *I can sleep when I'm dead.* He used to sleep six hours a night and still be the chirpiest person in the house every morning, frying up bacon or eggs and flipping blueberry pancakes with unnatural energy. When I was little, I thought he was a vampire because I never saw him sleep. When I was older, I'd still ask if he was sure he wasn't one of the undead, and he'd chuckle and lift one of his bushy brows in the classic Dracula look. I'd laugh hard enough to lose some of my orange juice down my chin, Jessica would roll her eyes, and Mom would sigh. But there would be a hint of a smile on Mom's face as she ate her scrambled eggs.

Dad's not a vampire. If he were undead, he'd still be able to make jokes about dying. I wish he would say the words, so we could laugh like it means nothing.

Leaving it unsaid takes up an impossible space inside this too small room.

I swallow, pick up the television remote, and click on the guide. Every station has some sort of vampire-related special airing.

Today's the tenth anniversary of the day Gerald Durand announced to the world that he was a real-life vampire. And I don't mean one of those blood-drinking humans. I mean an immortal creature of the night.

Gerald was short and thin with stringy black hair that hid his gaunt cheeks when he wasn't tucking it behind his ears. His clothes were mismatched—modern slacks, a brocade waistcoat with faded gold stitching, a yellowing white shirt with ruffles at the neck and wrists—a collection of pieces from different eras with little care for how they went together. But despite all that, he held himself like a prince as he sat in a chair across from Lester Holt and smiled coyly when asked how many humans he'd killed. He said the number didn't matter. What mattered was he didn't kill them now, and it was well past time for vampires to live openly and peacefully with people.

Dad, Jessica, and I cemented ourselves in front of the television for weeks, witnessing it all unfold with our mouths hanging open, ignoring Mom's protests that we were too young to watch that nonsense. But nothing could tear us away because we were already vampire lovers in our house *before*—minus Mom, who never liked anything she deemed fantasy. Dad had always been obsessed with vampires and had classic movie posters hanging in his office with Bela Lugosi in various menacing poses, usually with his eyebrows drawn together or a hand around a woman's neck. Jessica and I would sneak in and stare at them—sometimes making up stories to go with the images. Her favorite was of Lugosi with his arms in the air like he might reach out and grab you. I always thought he looked funny in that one, not scary. My favorite was *The Lost Boys* poster though. I liked the way David smirked at me as if he had a secret. I wanted that secret.

We begged Dad when we were little to let us watch those movies with him, and sometimes he'd let us watch a clip, but most of the time we stuck to *The Little Vampire*.

I wanted vampires to be real, so Gerald didn't scare me. I was a kid who already believed in ghosts and fairies and impossible things, so all I felt watching Gerald was fascination. The world was what I'd always imagined: huge with possibilities.

Not everyone felt that way. Most people thought he was performing an elaborate prank. But then he stabbed a knife into his chest on live television and the world watched the wound heal. Everyone wanted to meet him and ask him questions, even though he never quite gave answers. A few other vampires joined him in the press, and it seemed like everything would change.

But then a child went missing in Paris near where Gerald lived. Fear took over, and when that happens, people look for the unknown to direct their rage at, because that's easier than facing fear and pain head-on. They blamed Gerald. He disappeared. Vampires vanished into the night as swiftly as they had come.

In theory, the existence of vampires broke the world open. For years, I daydreamed about a vampire kid moving next door. The two of us riding the bus together, studying math in the cemetery after dark. Would they start offering night classes at my school? Would an eternal being even want to attend school? Probably not. But it didn't stop my imagination.

In reality, nothing significant changed.

But Jessica and I did. I became more obsessed with vampires, but she stopped wanting to make up stories with me. She said it wasn't fun anymore. Back then I didn't get it, but now I think it scared her as much as it excited me—the fact that every story we made up could be real. Eventually she started saying Gerald was a hoax, like Mom did from the start. She'd roll her eyes and share a look with Mom whenever I'd talk about him.

But Dad believed. We started watching more vampire movies. There still weren't many I could see at eight years old, but we started doing Fangtastic Thursdays as soon as I could handle some of the classics, and every year on the anniversary of Gerald's reveal, we watch the marathon of documentaries, listen to researchers talk about their continued efforts to find them again, and make our own speculations about where they might be, all while munching on my famous white-painted sugar cookies drizzled in red frosting.

Only I didn't make the cookies this year. Dad's on a no-sugar diet, and Mom gave me a look when I started pulling out the ingredients last night. I was so worried he'd be disappointed, but he doesn't remember—not even now, with the special running in front of him. He probably thinks it's one of our many recordings.

A cameraman who worked Gerald's original interview is answering questions.

"Did he seem evil to you?" The interviewer leans forward a bit, like this is the question she's been waiting to ask.

His brow creases. "How could anyone tell? Most of us can't tell with the people closest to us."

An uncomfortable moment of silence stretches as the interviewer swallows. "In your opinion, should we still be looking for them?"

He shakes his head. "Why risk it?"

Dad coughs a little, and I glance toward his half-closed eyes. He looks like he needs to sleep, but I don't say it.

"Let's watch a movie instead," he says. "Something with a happier ending."

I click the interview off before fanning a few choices in front of him. "What will it be?"

His lips quirk, and he stares off like he's thinking, but it goes on for too long. Maybe he can't remember the names of all our favorite movies anymore. We used to quiz each other on what year an obscure vampire movie came out, and now he can't name a single one. A ball of pain forms in my throat. This should be easy—this is our thing. But he's tired. I push my pain away—it's nothing compared to his.

"Dad?"

He turns back to me, clearly fighting to remember what we were talking about. "Your choice, kiddo."

I smile, and it hurts. I hope it doesn't show on my face, but his eyes are glazed, and I doubt he would notice anyway.

"Bold move," I say. "You know what that means."

I want to make him laugh. It doesn't work, but one corner of his mouth rises, and I'll take what I can get. I finger my go-to choice: *Underworld*. Gotta love Kate Beckinsale kicking ass in a wicked leather coat. I try to force myself to focus on the trivial things I used to think about: cool coats and fast action sequences. Dad always gripes that all the action scenes are gunfights. What's the point of having a vampire and werewolf war if you give them all guns?

"Would you rather be a vampire or a werewolf?" I ask the question like we haven't debated this topic at length. I always choose vampire, but Dad always argues that as much as he loves vampire stories, he wouldn't give up sunny days. Werewolves get speed and superstrength and enjoy the sun and the moon. But I should win by default since werewolves don't exist. At least I don't think they do. The beauty of life after Gerald is we can't write anything off.

Dad's gaze flicks to me, and he leans forward. "Still a werewolf. Not going to switch sides just because I'm drugged." He drops his head back on the pillow and closes his eyes. "Nice try, though."

"But vampires are immortal." My consistent argument. Dad always countered that nobody wanted to live forever, but that was *before*. When was the last time we watched a movie where a vampire died from cancer?

Never.

He doesn't even open his eyes. I need him to switch sides. I need him to say he'd choose vampires now because he doesn't want to leave me behind. I need him to erase the relief I saw earlier. To keep fighting.

"Dad," I whisper. His eyes stay closed, and I should let him sleep, but sitting here, analyzing how much his round cheeks have sunken in the last two weeks, creates an overwhelming ache in my chest. What if he closes his eyes and never opens them again? The thought makes my heart pulse too hard and too fast, and I can't breathe or think about anything else besides making sure his eyes open. I reach out and touch his hand. "Dad," I say a little louder.

His eyes crack open. "What, honey?"

"You still have hope, right? You're not giving up. I know you believe in miracles." My voice breaks, and I bite my tongue to give myself a tangible pain to focus on. I put all my strength into making my voice strong and steady. "You taught me to believe in them."

"Of course I do, honey. And I always have hope, but sometimes what we hope for changes, and sometimes we can't hope for the thing we really want." He holds his hand out for me, but I don't reach for it. The gesture feels like acceptance, like he wants me to give up and hope for something else, but what? Maybe I had other hopes before, but right now I can't think of a single one that doesn't include my dad being there. "Do you understand?" he asks.

I nod but refuse to meet his eyes. When I look back, they're closed again.

"Dad?" I say.

The front door slams, and I flinch. My sister's voice rises and falls from the front of the house until it rises and doesn't come back down. Relief unwinds the knot in my stomach. She's angry, too. Mom told her they're giving up, and Jessica will talk some sense into them. Mom listens to her.

When Jessica left for college two years ago, it was almost a relief. We'd grown so far apart after the vampire reveal that we barely spoke. I mostly avoided her because I couldn't stand the condescending glances she shared with Mom whenever I spoke about anything vampire-related—even if was just a new movie.

But when Dad got sick, I needed her. I wanted the big sister from before vampires were real, the one I held hands with to fall asleep on those rare occasions Dad let us watch something too scary. Well, *she* was scared. I pretended so she wouldn't feel alone. I'd squeeze her hand and she'd repeat *vampires don't exist* over and over again until she fell asleep while I lay there and secretly dreamed they did.

I needed someone to be strong for again, but I also wanted her to squeeze my hand and tell me cancer wasn't scary. It might exist, but it was an easily defeated monster.

And she did.

Jessica showed up with color-coded binders full of research and options and clinical trials. She had statistics for Mom. She had hope for Dad. She even knew the best diet—the one Mom's been diligently following ever since. I've been eating cruciferous vegetables with every meal for months, and I haven't complained once. I know Jessica will have another plan for us now. A new routine will be nothing I can't handle.

But then she bursts through the door, cheeks wet with tears. "Daddy." She sniffles, pausing steps from the bed. Dad opens his eyes, and she falls into his arms, weeping.

The hardness in my stomach expands to my throat. This isn't the version of her I want.

The one ally I thought I could count on has fallen prey to my greatest enemy: statistics.

I stare at the blank television and listen to her sniffle. I wish I could walk in here and weep and then go back to my dorm and not worry about how Dad would feel after I left. But I'm here all the time. I don't get to escape—not that I want to.

Dad rubs her back as she wipes at her eyes.

He doesn't need this. It's not fair to him.

My throat aches like it might burst open if I don't release a few tears. I want to curl up against Dad's chest and let him comfort me too, but I place my hand around the front of my neck and squeeze. I'm in control even if I can't control Jessica. You can't take care of others when you can't keep a grip on yourself. Why can't she realize that? If she would get it together, we could figure out a different plan. Scientists come up with new cures every day—we just need to research more.

But all she does is cry.

My face gets hot and stuffy, and I need to leave the room.

"I'm sorry, Daddy," Jessica mumbles into his chest.

"It's okay," he says. But it's not. Everyone knows it's not.

I back toward the door.

"Victoria." Dad says my name softly, stopping me. He's still holding Jessica, but he looks at me over her shoulder. "Draw me a picture?" he asks.

I try not to cringe, nodding instead. He's made that request a hundred times before—sometimes when he senses I need a distraction, sometimes when he needs a distraction, and sometimes just for fun.

But he doesn't know that it's been months since I've drawn anything.

I head to my bedroom and pull out the tub full of art supplies from under my bed, smudging the thin layer of dust on top. Pulling out my sketchbook, I flip to the first picture—a landscape of the forest behind our house done in stark charcoal with none of the vibrant chalks or watercolors I usually favor. The shading's so intense I can barely make out the silhouettes of the trees. It looks like I drew it at midnight, not noon when it really happened. But I did it right after Dad got sick, and I couldn't stop shading. Shadows usually shape the picture, make it come alive, but too many drown it in darkness. I flip to the next one and the next, but they're all the same—a mess of shadows and hurt. Until they just stop. I couldn't try anymore. My sketches wouldn't let me lie about how I was feeling.

I dig out an older sketchbook, but all the pages have already been torn out and handed to Dad so I could pretend to be okay. Show him I could still draw with the same joy I had before.

Some lies are okay—especially the ones that keep a smile on his face—but I'm out of old drawings, and I desperately don't want to know what will happen if I let myself try again right now.

I shove everything back under my bed and head down the hall to the office my parents share. On one side is Mom's stark white desk with a single chrome lamp on it and a calendar taking up the wall above it. On the other side is Dad's mahogany beast he found at a yard sale because he likes the history of used things. So do I— they tell stories like paintings. Tacked to the wall above his desk, spread out in the spaces around his movie posters, are twenty or so of my drawings—from one of our family that I must have done in preschool, where we look more like trees than people, to one of Lestat I gave him on his birthday last year. I know he has more tucked away in his desk drawer, and I consider pulling one out and regifting it, but I don't want to risk him remembering it and catching me.

I turn to Mom's desk instead. It's not like I've never given her any—she just doesn't like clutter. I pull out her bottom drawer and fish through the bland documents until my fingers hit the texture of real paper—the kind meant to hold everything. I pull out a watercolor of a lavender rose I gave her a couple of years back. It's a bit plain, but I thought she might actually hang it up if it was more her style. The funny thing is, Dad's always talking about how Mom used to be this fabulous artist, but she gave it up when she went to law school. I asked her once if I could see some of her work, but she got quiet and said she didn't keep it. She doesn't have time for it because she has a real job.

She's less than thrilled I'm going to art school in the fall—that is, I am if I can draw again by then. Maybe she'll get her wish after all, and I'll study accounting like Jessica.

I stare down at the vibrant petals, melding subtle shades of purple. I want to create like that again. I need to, but I need Dad to be okay to do that, and I'm running out of old pictures to give to him. At least this one won't go to waste.

When I get back downstairs, Jessica hasn't come out yet, so I head into the kitchen instead.

Mom's cutting onions into unrecognizable slivers when I pull myself up onto the stool on the other side of the island. Her eyes are dry. My dad and I always joke that she's so composed even onions can't make her shed a tear, but it's really because she wears contacts.

"Jessica's going full sprinklers in there," I say, placing my stolen picture on the counter in front of me.

She stops mid-cut to look up, her gaze pausing on the drawing. I wasn't sure she'd even recognize it, and I wait for her to mention it.

"Your sister's taking this hard. Go easy on her," she says.

Her words constrict around my throat, and I take a deep breath to shake them off. He's my dad too.

She glances at my picture again as she goes back to slicing. "Are you back to drawing?"

My chest tightens. She doesn't recognize the picture, and that stings, but I didn't expect her to notice I wasn't drawing anymore. I don't want to explain why I can't—she's too practical to understand.

"Are you?" Mom doesn't accept silence as an answer.

"No." I stare at the vibrant petals and hope she doesn't ask why.

"You'd better get over that if you want to go to art school."

I wince. I hate that she says *if you want to go*, like nothing's been decided even though I already accepted. But she's not wrong. She just doesn't understand that I *can't* get over this.

I need to change the topic.

"What are we gonna do?" I ask.

She doesn't look up. "About what?"

"Dad. Jessica had other options in those binders. Maybe a

new diet?" We already tried the diet with the highest success rate, but that doesn't mean the others aren't worth trying as well.

The knife clanks against the quartz countertop as she sighs. "Victoria." She pauses as if searching for the words. "It's over. We knew the odds. Only twenty percent make it past the first year."

Each short sentence is a stake in the chest.

Why does everything have to be odds and statistics with her? Why can't she ever hope for the best without analyzing whether or not it makes sense?

"You don't know that. We can't give up."

Mom's agnostic. Dad's religious. I waver between them both, but lately I've taken up praying again. It helps me voice everything I keep hidden from everyone else. I'm not sure anymore though—this is not the outcome I prayed for.

"Your dad is ready. He doesn't want to fight anymore." I'm staring at her pile of mutilated onions, and I think her voice breaks a little. I look up to try to catch a moment of vulnerability, but she's picked up her knife again and gone back to work.

"You don't know that."

"I do."

"How?"

"He told me, Victoria."

She punctuates the last sentence with my name—it's usually my cue that our conversation is over and she doesn't want to deal with me anymore.

"He wouldn't say that." Dad doesn't give up. I'm the same way.

"Victoria," she says, but her voice cracks again, and for a second we stare at each other. I lean toward her, praying she's going to tell me she still has hope too, or at least show me that we're both burying the same unfathomable pain.

But she turns away, her blade beating once again on the cutting board.

Jessica's high heels click into the room behind me. "Dad's going to sleep." Her cheeks are redder than usual, but she got Dad's olive complexion and black hair, and she always looks stunning, even when she cries—maybe that's why she feels free to do it so often. I got Mom's copper-blond hair and pink skin. If I cry, I look like someone scalded my face with boiling water.

"We're going to watch a movie together."

"You should let him sleep," she says, sparing me a glance before turning to Mom. "We need to start planning."

My stomach bottoms out. The chasm that used to be between us opens again in an instant. She's too scared to hope just like she was too scared to believe in vampires. She's not talking about a new diet. The determined quiver in her lips tells me she's thinking about his memorial, and I can't allow it. If we all think like Dad's dying, then it's over. We need to plan for him to live, and I need to show them how.

Dad's birthday's in a week and a half, and every year we invite all our extended family along with some friends for a barbecue and way too many rounds of charades. Dad looks forward to it.

I give my hands one quick clap, taking charge like I always do for special events. "Okay, I know Dad's still on a diet, and maybe we need to make his diet more hardcore given the negative news today, but I'm thinking he can cheat for his birthday and we get that German chocolate cake from the bakery downtown that uses way too much frosting."

For a second, the normalcy of planning a party makes me forget about anything else. I'm picking the cake, like I do every year. Dad will say it's the best cake he's ever had, like he does every year.

But their faces, strained and sad, won't let me pretend. They share one of those condescending looks I hate—the ones that make me feel ridiculous.

"Victoria," Mom whispers, her voice gentler than I've ever heard it.

Jessica reaches out and places her clammy hand over mine. "Dad's not up for a party."

I pull away. I know that, but I don't want to admit it. I can't. "Then what did you mean?"

Vaguely, I'm aware how cruel it is to make her say it, to keep pretending I don't know, but I don't want to stop. I don't want to let go of this one last thing that says everything's going to be okay.

"We need to plan a memorial." She says the words slowly and carefully, as if I need the extra time to let them register.

I tell myself to let it go. Instead, I jump up fast enough to knock over my stool, and it crashes against the wood floor so hard I probably scratched it. "You realize he's still breathing, right?"

Jessica gapes at me.

"Victoria." Mom's voice is a warning, her brief softness gone.

I'd needed Jessica to come in here and make plans, but not *these*.

Jessica's face goes soft with sympathy, as if she understands something I don't, and I hate that look more than any other.

"Don't you have exams or something? Why are you here?" Jessica barely visited after she moved out two years ago, but she's been here once a week since Dad got sick, usually sitting in the kitchen with Mom, drinking wine and going through her binders.

"Victoria," Mom says. "Why don't you go watch that movie with Dad?"

I glance between them. Jessica's crying again, and I feel bad, but then I remember she's given up, and I hate her enough to not care.

Snatching my painting off the counter, I leave the room without looking at either of them.

Dad's asleep, but I go in anyway, pull *Underworld* out of the DVD player, stick in *The Lost Boys*, and watch Kiefer Sutherland trick Michael into drinking blood and becoming a vampire. But Michael doesn't want to be a vampire and live forever. He spends the whole movie trying *not* to live forever.

He doesn't understand—staying human means inevitable death. What fool fights so hard just to die one day? Someone who hasn't seen what death looks like, I guess.

There is no escape.
No hope. Only hunger and pain.
*—30 Days of Night*

# *Two*

The loneliness of sitting in a church pew by yourself can be brutal. Church seems like a place where nobody should feel alone, but here I am, the only one in my row, trying to sing the hymns without choking on the words. I loved coming with Dad. His faith was contagious. Lately I come here mostly because when I get home, Dad will ask me how church was, and he'll smile as I recite the few key points I remember from the sermon. Dad hasn't come in two months.

Today I'm here for myself. I need some kind of sign it'll be okay. I can go home and hold Dad's hand and know a miracle is coming because that's what I asked for. I need a reason to believe. The doctor says science has nothing left to offer us, but God's still in the picture.

The preacher gets up and starts droning on about how God meets us in our grief and some nonsense about trials making us stronger, but I'm already strong. I don't need grief. I tune her out and pull my phone from my purse to check the Google alert I have set for vampires. I need some little tidbit to distract Dad with later.

A new Dracula movie is coming out. Cool—can't have too many of those. A man murdered a woman and left bite marks on her neck. Not cool, but I click on it anyway. I still keep tabs on the news, looking for signs of vampires showing themselves once more. But most of the time their existence feels like something we dreamed.

This guy wore fake fangs and black contacts. Definitely human, then. Too bad.

I click my phone off and make one more effort during the final prayer. I only ask for one thing over and over again—not to lose him. Maybe that's why God hasn't listened to me. I'm selfish. I'm worried about what I'll be without Dad—a girl who looks at weird vampire articles alone in her room with no one to share them with.

The thought turns my stomach. If I were a better person, God might listen.

Tears burn my cheeks, but I wipe them away as quickly as they come. Even without Dad here to see them, they're a betrayal. They mean I've given up.

A hand squeezes my shoulder, and I jerk. Great. Someone saw me. I twist and face Jessica, dressed in a posh black dress, and I know—I just know—she's my answer. Standing there, dressed for a funeral, she's God's no.

He won't help me. Or Dad.

Hope slips away from me like the last lifeboat on a sinking ship. And though I keep my face perfectly smooth, inside I'm drowning, grasping for anything to hold on to.

I almost reach for Jessica, but she's already made it clear she can't help. "What are you doing here?" I ask. Church is Dad's and my thing. Jessica always stayed home with Mom.

She bites her bottom lip and glances away. To her credit, she doesn't try to lie and say she's here for me. I know why she's here—to plan a memorial. Dad would want it to be here. She turns back. Harsh charcoal lines her eyes, but for me they're soft and warm, and they invite me to lean into her and cry. For a second, we're kids again. Close again. It's the same look she gave me when I tried to follow her up a tree that I was too small to climb and inevitably fell, scraping away my skin on the bark. It's a look reserved for an older sister comforting a younger one. But I don't want it anymore. Still, if she just reached out and hugged me, I'd probably let her. I'd pretend I was little again—that I trusted her to make it all okay. But I step back so she can't reach me.

"Dad would want you to help with the planning," she says.

I shake my head, and Jessica sighs, moving away to mingle with the crowds of people. If I'm not on board with her plans, then she's not going to bother. A few women gather around her. One pats her arm. Another rubs her shoulder. I try not to think about what she tells them, but I can't help it. Does she give them a date for Dad's death? Has she already reserved the church for the weekend after she expects him to go? My stomach rolls with acid. I need an exit—from this church, from Jessica, from the reality everyone expects me to accept.

A few people try to trap me and ask how my dad is on my way out the door. They do it every Sunday, and usually I smile and tell them he's doing well, he's a fighter, and we all have faith. But Jessica's here telling everyone the opposite. I won't be able to say those things without facing their pity. I mutter enough under my breath for them to let me go, and finally I'm outside, gulping down the hot summer air. I grasp the burning metal railing with one hand. My fingers tremble, and I lose my grip on my phone, sending it crashing against the concrete step below.

"Shit," I say, and then repeat it again when I realize I swore in front of the church. I bend down, but someone beats me to it. I straighten immediately, holding out my hand for the phone, staring impatiently at the fingers gripping it, but they don't budge. I reach for it, and the hand pulls my phone back slightly.

"Are you okay?"

I finally look up at his face.

Henry Nakamura's dark-brown eyes study me. I can't answer.

The memory of the last time we stood this close makes my knees shake. I want to pull myself into his familiar chest as much as I want to avert my eyes and run the other way. Every one of my muscles twitches in confusion—at least it feels that way.

Henry's family has lived next door to us since the third grade. We met for the first time in the woods behind our houses. Jessica and I were hunting for fairy rings after Dad read us a book about them—well, *I* was hunting. It wasn't long after vampires went public, and our closeness was already fraying. Jessica claimed she was too old to play pretend and stomped behind me telling me all the reasons I'd never find one. She'd convinced me to give up, to go back inside and play what she wanted, when Henry popped out from behind a tree with a broken branch in hand and a streak of mud across his face. He said he'd been exploring his new terrain and would help me keep looking. And we did. Jessica sighed and called us a few names, but we stayed out until the sunset came and lit the woods with its own magic, and we grinned at each other as our moms yelled for us from our homes.

The next day he knocked on my door and told me he found something he needed to show me. We tromped through the woods until we stopped at a clearing with a perfect circle of mushrooms in the center. Of course they were the prewashed kind from the grocery store. I knew he'd done it for me, but that made it special. We spent the whole day pretending it was real because we could.

We became inseparable—until about a year ago.

It's hard to look at him now for a lot of reasons. Some of them are still open wounds. But Henry's also a hoard of memories involving my dad, like the summer we built dueling water balloon catapults, and we'd duke it out every warm evening when Dad got home from work. We never battled by ourselves. Dad made it more fun.

I stare into the glaring sun, trying to burn the memory away. I don't need to focus on memories while Dad's still here. Memories are for the lost.

"Sorry." Henry admires his shoes. "Horrible question."

"Yeah. It was." I lock my knees.

His head jerks upward, and his eyes widen. And even though he grew out the bowl cut he had when we were kids and his black hair now kind of hangs in his eyes and hits the top of his cheeks, accenting the perfect angles of his face, the hurt, boyish look he gives me is still the same one he wore so many times before when I said something mean and careless. It hits me with the same guilt, too.

"Sorry," I mumble, dragging my hands across my face. Henry's not the enemy. Jessica's not the enemy. Cancer's my only true enemy, but it's hard not to look for something tangible to scream at.

"Don't be."

He gives me the same soft smile he used to, and for a second I am carefree again, standing next to my best friend, knowing he'll forgive me more times than I deserve, and I wish we could go back there, if only for a moment. He'd let me yell and rage and never judge me for it.

He waits, body leaning slightly toward me.

But where will we be when one of us walks away again? More hurt than before.

He rocks back on his heels, breaking the moment. Glancing away, he watches a woman walk by us in an over-the-top pink hat boasting an array of garish flowers. I half expect him to comment, make a cheap joke to lighten the mood, but that was always more my style than his. He just looks sad.

My phone still sits in his hand, dangling by his side.

"I thought you'd be in Tahoe." I push the conversation to safer territory. Some of our senior class left for Lake Tahoe this morning—a last hurrah before we all go our separate ways for college. I know Henry's friend group went because it used to be my group too. My friend Bailey—former friend, I guess—and I came up with the idea back when we were juniors, but I still didn't get an invite. Maybe this isn't safe territory.

"I didn't have enough money saved up." His eyes focus on some distant point behind my shoulder as he scratches his cheek absently. A lie. He's never been able to look me in the face when he lies.

"That sucks." I don't know why he needs to lie, but it's not my place to care anymore.

He nods—the same uncomfortable one I'm used to now. We've stepped back from whatever vulnerable edge we just tee-tered on.

I hold my hand out limply in the air, gesturing for him to hand the phone over. He hesitates. His chin tilts down, and he glances at the screen.

I freeze. The last thing I need is him seeing my creepy article about the fake vampire killer. He's never really gotten my fascina-tion, and I'm not in the mood for one of his snarky comments. But when he places it face-up in my palm, the screen's black, and anyway, I have more important things to worry about than what Henry thinks of me. That coffin's been buried.

I take a step down the stairs, leveling myself with him. Dad will be waiting.

"Victoria?" His voice is hesitant. He touches my shoulder for the briefest, softest second.

I stop. My heartbeat thuds in my throat.

He chews his bottom lip the same way he always has when he's thinking about something. It almost makes me smile.

"Yeah?"

He sighs and frees his lip. "If I can do anything . . ." He gestures outward with his hand, like this encompasses the entire world. "I don't know . . . I just want to be there for you."

My mouth drops open a little. We haven't said more than five sentences to each other in the past year. One of his grandmothers died, and I never reached out to him because I convinced myself he wouldn't want me to, and my silence became another gap between us. Then my dad got sick and the hole of Henry's absence was swallowed by a much greater abyss. Still, I'm ashamed I didn't try harder to be there when his grandma passed, but I don't think he wants to make me feel bad. I know him well enough to know he's sincere—at least I think I do. But a lot can change in a year. Maybe they're only words people say in these moments to fill the silence.

He turns toward me, and I'm so afraid he's going to hug me that I turn and bolt for the parking lot.

"Dad's doing pretty well today," Mom says as soon as I step through the front door.

"Great." I beam at her, feeling a little lighter, like I'm not sinking, but she deflates me just as fast.

"Don't let it get your hopes up."

I freeze in the middle of kicking off my shoe. "Why would you say that?"

"I'm trying to protect you." Her mouth turns down slightly at the corners. "I know you, Victoria. You like to pretend nothing's wrong for as long as possible, but it's time to let go."

"You mean of Dad? *I'm* holding onto Dad, so why aren't *you*?" My voice comes out hot and ragged.

Mom steps back as if I've slapped her. "That's not fair." Hurt turns her voice raw, and somehow I feel worse, but I don't have room to feel worse—I push it away.

"Please stop." I kick off my second shoe so hard it thuds against the wall.

I try to brush past her to Dad's room, but she reaches out and wraps her hand around my forearm. We haven't really touched since Dad got sick. There's something about touching another person who shares your pain that amplifies it—makes it impossible to ignore—and we both prefer not engaging. Avoiding contact is our unspoken rule.

She's breaking that. My eyes sting as pressure builds behind them. My anger gets choked off with the flood of our shared sorrow, and it takes all my strength to hold it together.

Mom clears her throat and looks away from me for a second, but she doesn't let go.

"I want you to leave for a few days," she says. "Go to Tahoe with your friends. You spend all your time in that room with your dad, and I know it's where you want to be, but you need to take care of yourself, too. Jessica and I can handle things here for a while."

"I'm fine." I don't know how she even remembers that trip.

I gushed about it a lot when we came up with it, but that was forever ago. I pull away from her, and she lets me.

My anger comes back to evaporate the sorrow. They want me gone so they can sit here and plan the memorial. But what will happen to Dad's strength if he's trapped in a house with people expecting him to die? "I'm not leaving Dad."

"It's not a request. I'm your mom. I need to look out for you, too."

I gape at her. She can't. I spin away and practically run to Dad's room.

He smiles as I enter. He looks brighter today, like he's operating at 50 percent of his normal wattage instead of the 30 I've gotten used to.

"Hey, kiddo."

"I'm not a kid, Dad," I say, even though I want him to call me that forever.

He brushes my protest away with a hand. "Yeah, yeah." He pauses to read my face. Pretending is harder with him. "What's wrong?"

"Just fighting with Mom." I give a weak smile. "She wants me to go to Tahoe. Get out of the house for a bit. Can you believe her?"

He beckons me closer and takes my hand. His skin is soft and paper-thin, like the old ladies at church who hold my hand the whole time they talk to me. I almost jerk away. Dad's only forty-eight.

"I agree with her." This time I do try to pull away, but his grip tightens. "We talked about it earlier."

"You talked about it?" Hurt strangles my voice.

"Kiddo, you've been here for me since day one. It's like you stopped your own life, and I don't want that. When was the last time you even saw your friends? This will be good for you."

I focus on the jumping puppies decorating the comforter and bite the inside of my cheek. "I don't even like Tahoe." Besides, none of my friends will even look at me now. My parents don't know that though. I told them that Henry and I had had a falling-out—I didn't mention that the rest of my friends went with him.

Dad's quiet for a long time. When I look back up, he's frowning at the television across the room. Brad Pitt's face is paused as he sucks the blood from a rat. Mom must have turned on *Interview with the Vampire* for him.

He finally looks back at me. "Then go to New Orleans instead."

"What?" Thinking about New Orleans opens a soft, vulnerable hole in my chest. It's the place Dad planned to take me as a graduation present. It reminds me of all the things I'm not going to have now. We'd been planning the trip for the last couple of years. We picked New Orleans because Dad's favorite movie, *Interview with the Vampire,* was filmed there and because the first North American vampire was spotted there at the Ursuline Convent in 1728, and rumor has it they still keep vamps locked in their third-story attic. Plus, one of the vampires that came out to the public after Gerald lived in New Orleans. We joked about finding him—about how we might come back home and Mom would be wondering how we'd gotten paler on vacation instead of tanner.

I shake my head. "That's *our* trip. We canceled it for when you got better."

"I never canceled."

"Dad." I mean to say his name like an admonishment, the way Mom says mine when I've done something I should know is ridiculous, but it comes out more like a question. My heart's pounding, and I'm not sure why, but then I realize this means he still had hope—even three weeks ago when Mom reminded him to cancel. He didn't. He still believed.

"Find us our vampire." He winks and tries to chuckle, but it becomes a dry rasp. He turns serious. "You'll need to get one of your friends to go with you, of course."

"I don't want to go with anyone but you. I'm sure we can still call and postpone the flights and change the reservations."

"Victoria." Firmness isn't something he's had the energy for lately. "I want you to go. Take pictures. Live it for me and come home and make me feel like I was there."

The small bit of joy propelling my heart vanishes, and it slows to a dull crawl. He may have had hope three weeks ago, but now he's speaking like he'll never see it except through me.

I want to refuse, run from the room, and bury my head under my blankets. But he's squeezing my hand too tight for me to pull away. "Promise me."

"I promise."

"Good." He lets go of my hand and leans back against the pillows.

I never thought a promise would kill me, but I can't breathe. This is acceptance. Going to New Orleans is me saying my dad will never get to come with me.

Because he'll be dead. I push away the truth as it tries to burrow its way through my lungs and into my heart. I fight it because I don't know how to stop.

Getting up, I move my heavy limbs to the bedside table, pick up the remote with clumsy fingers, and press play.

Dad cringes as I sit back down, and I touch his shoulder.

"Did you take your morphine?" My voice is strong, like it belongs to someone else entirely.

He opens his eyes. They're duller than when I walked in, but he shakes his head. "I want to be lucid."

I nod. He wants to enjoy what little time he has left with me. That thought tries to sink in as well, but I'm still pulling walls up as quickly as the truth can destroy them. It's a losing battle. I no longer have the thing that gave me strength before: hope. I try to get it back, racking my brain for any reason to still believe in medical science or miracles, but I don't. Those possibilities have been taken from me—they would have already worked.

Claudia's lying in the white canopy bed on-screen, unconscious with the graying skin of irreversible illness. And then Lestat wakes her, strokes her cheek as he leans over her and says, "I'm going to give you what you need to get well."

And then he turns her. Heals her.

She comes back from death right before my eyes. She dies later, of course, but not from the plague. Human disease doesn't touch the inhuman.

*Find us our vampire.* A joke. Nobody has seen one in almost ten years. After the reveal and disappearance, teams of researchers were formed to try to track them down again. People pored over myths and legends with new energy, trying to separate truth from fiction in an attempt to find one. Nobody has, but they're out there.

What if my dad's words weren't a joke?

Claudia's having her breakdown on-screen, crying and cutting her hair, despairing about never getting old. It's a tense moment, but I can't focus on it.

"Would you want to live forever?" I ask, bracing myself for the same response he always gives when we debate vampires versus werewolves.

Dad's eyes are closed. I think he's asleep, but after a minute he answers. "This is the wrong time to ask me." He winces around his words. I get his morphine and give it to him, and this time he doesn't protest. I note the time because Mom will want to know.

He didn't say yes, but he didn't say no, either.

Dad drifts off, but peace eludes him even in sleep now, and every so often his face twists into a grimace. Each time it does, my chest tightens until it becomes a painful throb I can't ignore, pushing me to do something—anything. I can't sit here and watch my dad die, but I can't just go have fun in New Orleans or Tahoe and pretend nothing's happening.

But what if I go for a different reason?

A new, tenuous hope builds in my chest like an expanding life raft, and I cling to it.

I'll make Dad happy. I'll go to New Orleans.

But I won't be going for fun.


In the morning, I stand in front of a turquoise door I used to pound my fist against—five quick knocks—our secret signal as kids so Henry would know it was me. I even did it long after we'd outgrown silly knocks. Henry thought it was funny, and I would have done anything to see his huge goofy grin when he opened the door. I almost do it now out of muscle memory, but I stop myself just in time and ring the doorbell like an adult.

Sam, Henry's younger sibling, opens the door. His eyes widen at the sight of me.

"Victoria," he says. "What are you doing here?"

I open my mouth and shut it again, suddenly awkward.

"Sorry. That was rude of me," Sam says. "Are you here for Henry? Or . . ."

"Yeah." I smile back. I always liked Sam, but he's three years younger than Henry, so naturally we spent our childhood avoiding him.

"Henry," Sam yells. He turns back to me. "Sorry about your dad."

"Yeah," I answer. Sam nods, but he doesn't insist on asking me how my dad's doing like most people do. He knows better. Only another person who's seen cancer firsthand can really get it. It's a secret club nobody wants to be in.

Henry rounds the corner, and his mouth pops open at the sight of me. He recovers quickly.

"Hey." He lifts a hand and waves, seems to decide that's awkward, and drops it to his side. "Come in."

Sam scoots away, examining us for just long enough that I am sure he knows all our secrets. He always was a perceptive kid.

I step into the foyer, still warm and cozy with yellow paint and a cherry wood entry table holding fresh gladiolas—his mom's favorite. It's a bit like coming home after a long vacation.

Henry towers over me, running a hand through his hair. He's been doing that since he was a kid, but the confident way he carries himself now always makes it seem absentminded. He does it a second time, and I know it's not.

*SpongeBob* blares from the family room, and I grin. "Grandma Nakamura's still got control of the TV?"

He laughs. "Cartoons all day every day. Sometimes my mom steals the remote from her in the afternoon and turns on *Dr. Phil*, but then my grandma gripes about having to watch a pompous old white man pretend he knows better than anyone else until my mom gives up and turns the cartoons back on."

"She's not wrong." I laugh, and my chest gets lighter. Both his grandmothers have lived with his family since we were kids— his white grandmother, Grandma Connor, and his Japanese grandmother, Grandma Nakamura. He always had the best pea-nut brittle and the best peanut butter mochi, and I was endlessly jealous, since I never knew my own grandparents that well. Dad's parents died when I was young, and Mom's live a vagabond life-style, traveling the world while running a company that makes all-natural cleaning products. Mom lived out of a suitcase most of her life, and sometimes I wonder if that's why she wanted to be a lawyer—something stable.

"I'm a jerk for not saying anything to you when Grandma Connor died. I'm sorry." I blurt out the apology before I can rethink it.

He shrugs. "You had your reasons."

The words sting unexpectedly. Maybe he was glad I vanished.

"Right." I glance back at the door. "I'm sorry. I shouldn't be here."

I step toward the door, but he steps with me. "I didn't mean . . . Please stay."

I pause. "Can we . . . ? Can we talk somewhere?"

He leads me along the familiar path to his bedroom upstairs. The room hasn't changed, and I wish it had. The walls are still dark blue and covered with posters of soccer players. He still has two bookshelves double stacked with books. The *Underworld* poster I got him for his twelfth birthday hangs on his wall. We weren't even allowed to watch the movie yet when I gave it to him. The familiarity is uncomfortable, like my bones want to stay in this safe place forever, but my muscles jump with nerves.

He notices me staring at Kate Beckinsale in her long leather trench coat, outlined against a full moon.

"Still the only vampire movie I like," he says.

It coaxes a small smile from me. I've made him watch many vampire movies over the years even though he's never been a huge fan. "It's Kate Beckinsale kicking ass in leather. What's not to love?"

"True," he says. "I can look past anything for that." He plops down on his bed and watches me.

I hesitate when he gestures to the space beside him.

"I promise not to bite." He attempts to laugh, but the strain of trying to be casual ruins it, and it fades into a choking cough when I don't join him.

The first fracture in our friendship happened here: eighth grade, sitting on the bed laughing as we read the same comic book together, and then everything shifted. He turned to me with something new in his expression, a look that caught my laugh in my throat, and when he leaned in slowly, I didn't move away. We kissed. Then I left. Just got up and ran into the woods, because even though I liked it, even though I wanted to do it again, I knew it changed what we had already. What if it wasn't perfect anymore?

By the time he found me, I'd told myself it would be okay. I wanted this change. But before I could say it, he blurted out apology after apology. He didn't want to ruin our friendship.

We made a pact not to even consider dating each other until after high school. Afterward, any time we shared the smallest moment that teetered past the edge of friendship, we brushed by it without looking back. Well, I looked back. A lot.

Things would have been so different if I hadn't panicked.

Or if we'd at least specified in our non-dating pact that we wouldn't date other people, either. That might have helped too.

I take the smallest step back. This was a mistake. Maybe I can convince Dad to let me go alone. I need to go alone anyway. My plan is for Henry to pretend to go with me and drive me to the airport. Then he can go on his merry way to Tahoe. I'll pay for him to go if he really can't afford it. Nobody will know I went by myself.

He leans forward on the bed and rests his elbows on his knees, staring up at me with an open expression. He was always good at disarming people. It got us out of more than one scrape as kids—and for him it wasn't even about manipulation. When he smiled, he meant it.

Even now his warmth is a hook in my chest pulling me toward him, but I fight it.

"Draw anything interesting lately?" His voice is light, conversational, like we're just two old friends catching up at a coffee shop.

My eyes shift to his collection of my drawings pinned above his headboard. He's the one who convinced me to apply to art school instead of doing something to try to make my mom happy for once. Henry and Dad—they were in cahoots on that one.

I thought he'd have taken them down by now, but I also thought he'd take them down when he started dating Bailey. He never did, and I kept telling myself it meant something. I was wrong. They're not together anymore, but neither are we.

"No." My answer comes out sharp, though I don't mean it to. I'm rigid with the effort of holding myself together.

I don't want to stand in this room that holds so many of *our* memories and think of Bailey. Especially since I miss her, too, even if it's not the same as losing Henry.

I befriended Bailey first. She transferred the beginning of junior year and ended up in my art class. It was self-portrait day, and I was drawing an open field with high yellow grass and blue sky with wisps of rain clouds. My teacher had just finished scolding me for not following directions when Bailey came up behind me. "Well, I think it looks like you," she'd said.

I hadn't even thought about it being a self-portrait—I just didn't feel like drawing my face. Bailey and I had been making friendly conversation for a couple of weeks, complimenting each other's work, but at that moment I knew we'd be friends. She saw me in that picture before I did. I invited her to eat lunch with me and Henry that same day.

To be honest, I thought she'd be mostly my friend. She was quieter and less adventurous than me, more like the brooding artist on the inside, with blond hair and a soft smile on the outside. But she played soccer, like Henry, and they bonded too.

Bailey and I would hang out and paint a sunset in the evening. But she'd also meet Henry before school to kick a ball around. We had other friends too, but Henry and I always felt like our own bubble within that group, and Bailey was the only one who ever made it into the bubble with us.

It felt different, but okay, until I started to notice less of those little awkward moments between Henry and me—those times when our fingers touched and we were slow to pull away, and that slowness said that eventually, when the timing was right, neither of us would pull away. I thought those moments were a promise.

I thought maybe he'd stopped so Bailey wouldn't feel like the third wheel in our inevitable love story.

I thought that up until the point they told me they were dating—that they'd been dating for a month without telling me. That hurt worse. They knew it would hurt me. I had worried so much about Bailey being the odd one out, and then I was.

I pretended to be fine, but it felt like spilling a cup of dirty brush water across a watercolor you've been working on your entire life. The picture you dreamed it would be is ruined—there's no going back from that.

You have to throw it away and start fresh.

I even tried dating a couple of times after they got together to try to make things less awkward, but it always felt like staring at a poster of one of Monet's water lily paintings when you know the real thing exists right beyond your reach.

It was so hard, and I didn't have a best friend anymore to talk to about it. Henry said over and over again that it didn't change what we had, but how could it not?

Henry's face goes soft as he watches me struggle through my

memories, like he can guess where my mind has gone, but he doesn't press. "Sit down," he says. The words are a gentle invitation. His eyes are focused on me, and every time I glance from the door to him, they're still watching.

Dragging down a deep breath, I unlock my knees and step toward him. I didn't expect this to be so hard. The bed bounces under my weight as I sit.

He sucks in his own quick breath.

I fold my hands in my lap so less of me touches his bed.

"So," he says. "What can I do for you?" He pauses and seems to rethink his wording. "I mean . . . what do you want? Or rather, how may I help you? Yeah. Let's go with that one."

I swallow and look for strength in Kate Beckinsale.

There's no easy way to tell someone you need them to cover for you while you go vampire hunting.

"You can tell me." The softness of his voice reminds me of when we were kids and we found a wounded bird that crashed into their sliding glass door. We built it a little nest in an old shoebox and Henry cooed at it until it died. I glance out his bedroom window into the backyard. The rock we turned into a gravestone probably still sits at the base of the giant oak tree we used to climb.

I hope this doesn't make him pity me. I couldn't bear it.

"I need a ride to the airport." I lead with the simplest thing. He doesn't need to know why.

"Oh." He almost looks disappointed. He probably expected one of the grand schemes I came up with as a kid. If only he knew this was my wildest idea yet. Part of me wants to tell him the real plan, and not because I need to tell someone—I need to tell *Henry*. I need to tell the boy who always backed me up.

"Well, I told you I'd be here for you," he says.

"So you'll take me?" I stop rubbing my thumbs together. If I know Henry's nervous tics, he surely knows mine.

Too late. He eyes my hands, motionless once more in my lap.

"Why can't your mom take you? Or Jessica?"

"Busy." Short, one-word answers are best for lies.

"Where are you going?"

"New Orleans." I should lie, but I don't. He'll remember the trip Dad and I planned. I talked about it enough, but I may have left out the part about looking for real vampires. Henry's never been a believer, but I want him to see through me.

He does. He knows I'm holding something back.

"Victoria."

It's the way he says my name. It's hard to explain, but someone calling your name for an order at a coffee shop is different from someone you know saying it. The way he says it opens up all the trust that used to be between us and promises that it could be there again if I reached out for it.

"This trip should have been me and my dad. It was a graduation gift. He wants me to take a friend and have fun." I make my voice as firm and confident as possible, but I stare at my hands when I say it. "But I'm going by myself to hunt for a vampire. And I need you to cover for me."

I don't know about you,
but I was raised to fight back.
—*True Blood*

# Three

**H**is face tightens. He knows I'm serious and doesn't know what to do with it. I want him to give me one of his solemn nods, accepting my plan without question. Instead, he gives a choked laugh. "Gotta find yourself an Edward, huh? I mean, I'm team Jacob myself, but you do you."

He wants this to be a joke. He's giving me a chance to laugh it off and back out of what I just said. I knew this would be most people's reaction. It's not like vampires are out there holding court and sending invitations. Teams of professionals haven't been able to locate them, so why would I fare any better? But I had this glimmer of hope Henry wouldn't write me off immediately. After all, he once helped me set a trap for Bigfoot in the woods behind my house based on my flimsy evidence of gouged tree trunks and snapped branches—some of which I broke myself to create more proof.

"My dad's team Jacob, too," I say, because I don't know how to cut through his doubt.

He laughs again, but it catches awkwardly in his throat.

I swallow. He doesn't even try to hide his pity.

I bite the inside of my cheek to stop myself from breaking down. "Stop looking at me like that. Vampires exist."

"Vampires *don't* exist." He says it slowly, cautiously, like I'm no longer a wounded bird but a feral animal he's trying to tame. "That was a hoax, Victoria. Why do you think they vanished so quickly? They couldn't keep it up."

I cringe. We've been through this debate before, but back then it didn't matter to me if Henry believed or not as long as he didn't look down on me for it. Plenty of people were incredulous when Gerald first appeared—even when he stabbed himself and healed on live television, people called it an elaborate illusion. They accused the news team of being in on it for the sake of ratings.

But I remember the look on the anchor's face when Gerald's pale, torn skin melded back together—the pure shock of being confronted by something you've been told is impossible your entire life. Nobody's that good at acting.

I twist toward Henry, leaning closer, forgetting for a moment about all the reasons to stay in my personal space. "Can you prove without a doubt that they don't exist?"

"No, but—"

"My dad's dying. The doctor said there's nothing left to do but watch him. Clinical trials won't take him at this point."

Henry reaches out and grabs my hand off the bed. "Don't give up yet. Miracles can happen."

I jerk my hand out of his. "I'm not giving up. I'm going to look for a vampire. I know it's a long shot, but it's something."

I'm used to slim odds. Science gave us slim odds the second they said pancreatic cancer, but it didn't stop us from trying. I don't know what the odds on miracles are, but it didn't stop me from praying. The odds are I won't find a vampire, but it won't stop me from looking.

I hold my breath, waiting.

He sighs. "I need to get dinner started."

"What?" I expected more. "Your mom always cooks." His mom makes elaborate meals every night. I've spent the last year missing her seafood Alfredo.

"Not anymore. Not after . . ." He trails off and stands, but this time it's me grabbing his hand without thinking, and he drops down beside me again.

"Tell me."

"She rarely ever cooks since Grandma Connor died from . . ." He stops, but we both know what word he left off his sentence.

"But that was over a year ago." I regret my insensitive words, but Henry only tightens his hand around mine.

"I know."

I can't imagine a world where Henry's mom's not already in the kitchen, wearing her white and blue paisley apron that somehow always stays bright and crisp even though I'm sure she's had it for as long as we've lived side by side. I'll walk downstairs, and she'll ask me to stay over like always.

I wish I could say I was only worried about him and his mom, but all I can think about is who I'll be in a year if my father is dead. If I'll be a pool of deep blue grief and no help to anyone. The thought makes me grasp harder at the wary hope inside of me.

I suck down a few short breaths. "Is that the real reason you didn't go to Tahoe?"

"Yes." He stares past me at the *Underworld* poster.

"You're still lying."

He sighs, rubbing a hand over his face. "Leave it alone."

But he should know better than to say those words to me. I've never left anything alone in my entire life. "Tell me."

"I didn't want to leave you."

"Me?" I jolt, moving instinctively away from him. The bed bounces, and a pained expression crosses his face. I open my mouth and close it again without forming a sentence. Why the hell would he need to stay behind for *my* sake?

A year of silence crushes the air from the room.

He runs a hand through his hair, muttering something under his breath.

"Listen," he says, finally looking at me. "I know what it's like to lose someone like this, and I don't know, I just thought you might need someone besides your mom or Jessica to talk to. . . ." He trails off and looks away. "I thought you might need me, you know, like you used to. Remember when you were, like, seven and your hamster died, and you came over here and hid under my bed, and your parents let you spend the night because you wouldn't come out? I know it's not the same thing, like, at all, but . . ." He stops and runs his hand through his hair again. "It was silly."

My throat tightens. "No, it wasn't. I'm here, aren't I?" My fingers shake, and I clasp my hands together. I thought he might help me, expected it, even, because sometimes when we tentatively smiled at each other across the hall I got the sense we could be friends again if one of us took the first step, but I didn't expect him to be waiting for me.

I wasn't there for him, but he is here for me now.

And even though the hurt he caused me lingers under everything, I still ran to him.

It seems silly that we stayed apart.

He's staring at me with a familiar look in his eyes. Too familiar.

"So what do you think?" He knows I'm asking about more than the ride. I want him to believe in me. I want him to build a trap for Bigfoot again if I asked him.

But he shakes his head, his face pinching as if he wishes he could believe with me.

I still need a ride to the airport.

"Please." My voice cracks, and I look away. Henry's approval meant more to me than I thought. "I can't sit and watch him fade away. All I need is a ride to the airport and for you to not tell anyone what I'm really doing out there."

He sighs. "Of course," he says. "Of course."

Dad looks genuinely happy when I agree to go on the trip, and it kills me.

"Who'd you decide to take with you?"

I hesitate before giving a half-truth. "Henry." It's not a total lie. I'm taking him with me as far as the airport at least.

"Henry?" He smiles a little, and a trickle of life shines in his eyes. "Good. I was hoping you two would reconnect eventually."

"Yeah." I smile back. It's not a lie. Henry does seem to want to reconnect, and maybe after this trip, we'll be able to. Still, I long to tell Dad the truth—that I'm only going for him, not to see the sights and have a good time with Henry. Dad would support me. He'd tell me to believe, no matter what anyone else thinks. Just imagining it strengthens me. But he'd also tell Mom. They don't keep secrets, and she would never understand this. Like Henry, she never believed. I can't risk her doubt stopping me.

People live inside a carefully constructed box they call reality and refuse to see anything outside of it, but unwillingness to look beyond that box doesn't make it any less real.

Dad's eyes close, and he drifts off as I stand there. The doctor said one month or less, but I have a week if I want to be back for Dad's birthday. I've already started making arrangements for an after-dark party and sent out invitations to family and friends with clear instructions that it's a surprise. I just hope they don't contact Mom instead of me to RSVP. She won't get it—she doesn't know Dad could be fine by then, and I don't want him to be disappointed on his first day of eternity. I know planning a party will make it so much more horrible if I fail, but I can't let myself think like that.

I leave that night, after he's gone to bed, because even normal goodbyes aren't easy anymore.

Mom's awake though, sitting at the kitchen counter with a mug of steaming tea. She's never up this late, which means she's waiting for me.

She gives me a tired smile, and I know it's not simply because it's way past the time she goes to bed. I recognize some of my own exhaustion in it. I wonder if I'm starting to let mine show too, if that's why she wants me gone so badly: my mask was slipping, and she doesn't want Dad to see.

But I have hope again now. I wish I could share it with her, but that would make her change her mind about me going, and now I *need* to go.

Her fingers curve and uncurve around her cup as we stare at each other.

"Be safe," she says.

I nod, relieved to stay in familiar territory. We won't get emotional. She'll give me the generic motherly concern, and I'll be on my way. I start to pull my suitcase toward the front door.

"Did you remember to pack your art supplies?" she asks, twisting in her seat to look at me.

I don't want to have this conversation. She's had all my life to encourage my art, but she's choosing now to care? When I can't draw anymore?

"You might feel inspired out there," she says.

"Yeah," I say, keeping my answer as vague as possible. My art stuff is upstairs under my bed where it belongs now. I don't want it. All I want is to escape this conversation. "Bye, Mom," I say before she can pry anymore.

She nods and goes back to her tea, and I finally make it out the door.

I tremble from both anticipation and the overwhelming desire to stay home and hold Dad's hand forever as I drag my suitcase down the sidewalk to Henry's house. But forever will never happen if I don't go. Another year won't happen. Maybe not even another month.

My suitcase wobbles up the uneven driveway to where Henry waits by his truck.

"Hey," Henry says, grabbing my bag and tossing it in the back.

I climb in the passenger side without answering, and we ride in silence until it becomes too weighted.

"You think I'm delusional," I say to the dark side of the road slipping by us.

"No." After a long moment he says, "I think you're sad."

I want to be angry at his words, but there's no hint of condescension in them, just honesty.

"I'm not," I say. "I'm determined."

Sadness only gets in the way. I have no room for it.

"Okay," he says.

We go back to silence until we pull up at the airport and drive into the economy parking lot. "You can drop me at the terminal."

"I'm walking you in."

I huff as I push open the door and step into the warm night. "You don't have to do that."

"I know," he says, pushing his own door shut behind him after clicking the lock.

He reaches into the back and lifts out my hot-pink rolling suitcase, pulling up the handle and passing it to me.

I turn to say goodbye, but he's not paying attention to me. He's yanking a dark-blue suitcase out of the back of his truck and popping out the handle.

"What the hell are you doing?"

"Coming with you." He starts rolling toward the shuttle pickup.

My mouth drops open. "You can't. You don't have a ticket."

"You told me what time your flight was. It wasn't hard."

"You said you were short on money."

"We established that was a lie to stay close to you." The way he says this makes us both pause and awkwardly look in different directions.

The moment goes on so long there's no good way to break it until Henry takes off for the shuttle—apparently deciding action is the best way to end the standoff. His long legs make him hard to catch, but I do, and my suitcase clips the edge of his, tilting it onto its side so he has to stop and right it again. "I don't need you to come with me. I can handle myself."

He eyes me. "Of that I have no doubt. You were always the brave one." He smiles a little, and I wonder if he's thinking of one particular memory, like the time I decided to live in the wilderness for a week when we were eight. He packed up some peanut butter sandwiches and came with me into the woods behind our houses. We lasted a couple of hours before our parents found us and made us come home for dinner. Later I found out he told his mother where we were going before he left. Definitely not the brave one.

"Did you really expect me to drop you off and let you fly to a state you've never been to by yourself?" he asks. "I want to come. We should be doing this together."

I should be doing this with Dad, but that's not an option. I told myself all I wanted was for Henry to drive me and be my cover, but what did I really expect? How many wild ideas did I come up with as a kid that he tried to talk me out of only to join me later so I wouldn't be doing it by myself?

I hesitate, which means I'm about to say yes because I never hesitate to say no.

"So is the team back?" he asks.

It feels that way. Even with the awkwardness between us and the things I'm sure neither of us has healed from, we still feel like a team, like we never spent a day apart. I guess ten years of friendship isn't destroyed that easily, and the truth is that I don't want to go alone. Henry's been by my side for all my greatest risks, including the time I jumped out of a tree thinking an umbrella would let me float Mary Poppins style. This past year has been safe and boring because I haven't wanted to go on adventures without him.

I eye him for a minute just to make him sweat.

"I guess," I say. I need him. I might have been the brave one, but it was always because I knew he'd be there when I hit the ground and ended up covered in my own blood.

"Sweet." He grins, and it pulls a warm, yellow brightness from me.

But I can't be warm and bright when Dad is cold and fading.

We pull our bags up to the shuttle pickup and wait together.

We don't get to sit together on the airplane—one of the disadvantages of not actually having invited your travel companion.

On the last leg of our flight, I'm stuck between a snoring woman and a chatty man.

"Are you visiting family?" he asks.

"No."

"Work?"

"Nope."

"Ahhh, fun then."

The last one's not really a question, which is great since I don't know how to answer.

"Well," he says, cracking open his second can of beer in the last thirty minutes, "you need to pace yourself. Everyone drinks all day long there. They even have drive-through daiquiri places."

It does not surprise me that he knows this.

"Always assume that everybody around you is drunk. The

pedestrians, the drivers, the bicyclists. The horses pulling those annoying carriages. All drunk. Remember that." He burps a little and chugs the last of his beer as the flight attendants come by to collect the drinks before landing.

"Even the vampires?"

He snorts. "You're one of those." He leans in, eyes focusing. "Especially the vampires. Nothing worse than a drunk vampire. That'll leave a mark."

My heartbeat quickens as I struggle to look nonchalant. "And where would one find these drunk vampires? You know, so I can avoid them."

He relaxes back into his seat. "With all the other drunks on Bourbon Street."

Bourbon Street is party central for the French Quarter and already high on my list of places a vampire would be able to enjoy a discreet sip from an unsuspecting tourist. But it also presents a problem: How do I stand out when there will be masses of other tender morsels to choose from?

He's closed his eyes, but I ask anyway. "Anywhere else?"

He cracks an eye open and shrugs. "I think there's some kind of vampire souvenir shop in the Quarter. Buy something and they'll give you the password to a secret vampire bar." He winks.

"Thanks." I try to hide my disappointment. I know all about the shop and the "secret" bar, but if I can find the same info on the first page of an internet search then it's not very secret, and I won't find real vampires in a tourist trap. Maybe, but I doubt it, and I've only got a week. I save the info for a last resort. I need something better than tourist traps and old legends.

The plane lands on the runway hard enough to jar me in my seat. Nobody panics, so I guess it's normal. I haven't flown much.

Henry's standing in the aisle, pulling down my bag. "Ready for this?"

I don't answer, but the man next to me slips out and lets me go on ahead of him.

"Don't forget what I said, little lady."

"Right," I say, grabbing my bag and maneuvering it down the slim aisle.

"What was that about? Making friends?" Henry asks once we're off the plane and into the overheated airport.

"Apparently this whole town is always drunk." I don't mention the vampire part of our talk.

His eyes widen a little. "Sounds interesting."

I punch his arm without thinking about it. And then decide to overthink it. Maybe I shouldn't be sliding back into familiar gestures, but it feels so easy to pretend none of the weird stuff happened and we're kids again.

I clear my throat way too loudly. "We need to stay sharp so we can catch a vampire, not end up as a first and second course."

"Yeah," he says, and I sense him holding himself back from telling me vampires don't exist one more time. "But I actually think I'd be the main course and you'd be an appetizer." He stares down at my pink rose-print sundress. "Or maybe you'd be dessert."

"Did you just say I look like dessert?" I raise my eyebrows.

He flushes. My cheeks heat as I do the same. This is the type of half-joking flirting we had before Bailey—when we definitely weren't kids anymore.

"So you arranged transport?" He scans the lines of cars picking up other travelers.

I guess we're back to ignoring any attraction, which is what I want. What's best for our friendship.

"Oops," I say. I can play that game again. We did it for almost five years before I messed it up.

He sighs and pulls out his phone. "We can take an Uber."

"They're probably drunk."

"It's nine o'clock in the morning."

"Not sure that matters," I say, and raise an eyebrow.

He grins.

Fifteen minutes later, we're cruising down narrow streets, the driver slamming on the brakes whenever pedestrians decide to jump out into the road, which is often.

"So how would it work?" Henry asks.

"What?"

"Turning into a vampire. What's the . . . procedure?"

I shoot a look at our driver. "Maybe now's not the time."

"I'm sure he's heard weirder conversations."

Our driver nods. "You better believe it."

"There," Henry says. "So tell me."

"Oh, you know, it's like a whole big sucking thing." I laugh. He doesn't. The driver snorts though, and I'm starting to think he'd make a better sidekick than Henry.

"At least someone's seen *Buffy*," I say.

Henry sighs. "I'm being serious."

"I'm not a hundred percent certain, but from my research, my best bet is I have to be bitten and then drink the blood of the vampire while my blood's in their system."

Henry grimaces like I've declared I'm going to lick the floor in a public restroom. "So you'll be a vampire too."

I squirm in my seat. I've accepted the fact that it'll be easier to get a vampire to turn me here than to get them to fly home and save my dad. I certainly don't want to count on a vampire's humanity. If I find one, I won't even mention Dad. It might ruin my chance. Plus, if I'm a vampire too, it will make it easier for Dad to adjust. I'd give up *anything* to save him. Besides, I've been dead inside since the moment they said "cancer." Maybe being undead will help me feel alive again, but I don't want to get into all that with Henry. He'd only try to make me feel better.

"That's the plan," I say lightly.

Henry stares out his window. His hands clench into fists periodically, and I hate to say it, but his reaction excites me. If he's upset, part of him thinks it's possible.

"I don't think you've totally thought this through," he finally says. "Be honest with me. No joking."

I cringe. He knows I joke when I'm nervous and don't want anyone else to see it. And of course I haven't totally thought it through. Dad and I talked about finding a vampire on this trip and being immortal, but we always said it with a grin, like we didn't mean it. Plus, Dad always chose werewolves. I chose vampires because I liked the idea in a hypothetical way, but in reality? I don't want to think about it. It doesn't matter.

"It's the only way," I answer, but he shakes his head in reply.

I can't be as open as he wants.

Our car stops on a narrow street, and I jump out onto the cracked and uneven concrete, lifting my pink rolling suitcase because there's no way it will roll anywhere on these sidewalks.

The hot, wet air immediately latches onto my skin like a film, and yet I don't care.

"Good luck," our driver calls. And when I look back at him pulling away, he winks like he knows something. I kick myself for not grilling him.

"It reminds me of Disneyland," Henry says.

I smile a little. I had been trying to place the familiarity and couldn't, but there's a quaintness to the buildings and the streets that makes you ignore the cracks in the sidewalk, the suffocating air, and the garbage cans lined up for trash day. Beyond all that, the buildings rise two or three stories high, each one butted against the next, each with its own personality, from a bright and cheery yellow with a white balcony railing to a brick with an ornate curving black wrought-iron balcony draped in rich green plants. My favorite one has a balcony of cascading flowers, wild and tangled without any sort of symmetry. Our building's a simple white with a single balcony off the second-floor apartment.

My fingers suddenly itch for a pencil and paper to capture the intricate curves of the balconies, and the feeling surprises me. I haven't felt the urge to draw for so long now I'd forgotten the rush that comes with seeing something beautiful and knowing you can capture that feeling and hold it forever. Nothing's been beautiful for so long.

Desire hits me, and I'm thinking in blues and greens and yellows like I used to, imagining the watercolors dripping on the page, but art without emotion is dead, so the second I let the colors flood my mind, the grief hits me too, turning me into a sea of blue, threatening to drown out everything else, including my hope.

Good thing I didn't come here to draw pretty pictures. And I definitely didn't come here to feel things, so I rein my emotions in and force the swirling colors into a well between my stomach and ribs.

I switch my heavy suitcase to my other hand to distract myself.

"Can I carry that for you?" Henry asks.

I hesitate. Carrying my bag is a very boyfriend thing to do, but I'm probably overthinking.

"Sure, yeah, thanks." I pass him the handle and awkwardly try to make sure our fingers don't touch, like we're strangers.

He pauses and squints at me. "You okay?"

He hasn't said anything about finding his own place, but I don't want to press the matter and make things weirder than they are.

"Totally." I hold open the door before following Henry up the three flights of stairs. He hasn't even broken a sweat at the top and relaxes against the wall while I fumble with the key in the lockbox and open the door.

I reach out and snatch my suitcase from him and roll on through into a wide living room painted a startling shade of bright blue.

"Wow," Henry says, walking in. "A little much."

He's right, but I don't say so. The place is quirky to the extreme, with an old-fashioned grass-green velvet couch as the center point in the room with a wooden coffee table scuffed up just enough to be charming. On either side of the couch sit mismatched chairs clearly stolen from different dining room sets. Huge oil paintings of flowers decorate the walls. Dad obviously picked this place for me.

"I like it," I say.

I roll my suitcase past the couch to the first bedroom with Henry at my heels.

"Wow," he repeats.

Deep green paint covers the walls, a darkened forest but for the four-poster bed in the center covered with a hot-pink comforter. A light, dusty-blue velvet couch is the only other piece of furniture in the room. The whole bizarre place welcomes me, and I let myself love it for one small second before reminding myself I'm not here to stay inside and relax.

Henry's practically leaning over my back to look in, so when I spin around, I'm pressed up against his chest.

He takes a quick step back—so quick I'm a little offended. "There's another room, right?" he asks.

I take a breath that sounds too deep. "Should be. It was supposed to be me and my dad."

Thinking about my dad steadies me. I need to focus.

We walk down the hall to a master bedroom, which has a huge king-size bed made of black lacquered wood and covered in a deep burgundy comforter. The walls are painted a blue so dark they're almost black, and they're bare except for a huge window with black curtains.

"Well, it looks like a vampire lives in here," Henry says.

"You can take this room."

"Don't you want the master? This is your trip."

"It was supposed to be my dad's room." I pull my suitcase back to the smaller room, the one that was always going to be mine.

Henry doesn't press it. I sit my suitcase on top of the hot-pink bed and try not to think of him unpacking where my dad should be. But it's all I can think about—how much I want Dad to be here, how much I want this trip to be a lighthearted search for vampires with the one person who believed with me.

Henry's not that person, so when I turn to find him leaning against the door, watching me, I snap at him before I can stop myself. "Why are you here? Because if you were hoping for a cool trip, this isn't going to be."

"I'm here to help you. I'm certainly not here for vacation." He snorts, looking out of place in his faded jeans and soft blue T-shirt.

"Help me with what?" I press. He made it perfectly clear he didn't believe in what I'm doing, so what help can he be?

His silence is my answer. He thinks he's here to protect me from myself, and now he's one more obstacle in my way.

"So what's the plan? Where do we look first?"

I analyze his face. He's not grimacing like he did whenever I came up with a plan he didn't like when we were kids. His lips are even, no condescending smile or judgmental frown. His brown eyes are wide and earnest. He's going to try if I let him.

I suck on my top lip as he waits for me to decide.

"It might sound a little strange."

His brows rise.

"Don't freak out."

"Now I am. Tell me. It can't be worse than what I'm imagining."

I wait for his composure to slip as I say the words. "We need to break into a convent."

For a moment he just blinks at me. And then, "I stand corrected. That is definitely worse."

The thing is, this is kind of
the whole reason you have friends,
so you don't have to do the terrible parts alone.
—*The Originals*

# Four

Jetlagged and tired, we stroll down the street, wiping at the humid air on our skin like we can somehow get it to disappear. No such luck.

"Why would a vampire choose to live here?" Henry asks, running a hand across his brow. "Anytime you tried to bite into someone, you'd have to go through a layer of sweat." He tugs at his white T-shirt and jeans, which appear to be clinging to his legs.

"Didn't you pack any shorts?"

"Nope. I didn't really check the weather report."

I sigh. I wear beige linen shorts and a pink tank, and the humidity still claws at my skin with each step. A pair of twenty-something girls strut past us in breezy dresses and effortlessly curly hair. We both turn to watch them.

"I guess people get used to it," he says.

I brush at the strands of sweaty hair around my face. "We can buy you some shorts later."

"But why New Orleans? If I were a vampire, I'd probably live in Alaska or someplace where it's dark all the time, and you can make everything look like some kind of animal attack."

"I'm glad you've thought that through, but you realize they also have full days of sunlight there, right?"

"Yeah, that's when you vacation in Paris. We could have gone to Paris," he grumbles, tugging at the collar of his shirt.

"Don't you remember? One of the vampires from ten years ago said he lived here."

Henry frowns. He doesn't have to say it. I know he thinks all those people were attention-seeking hoaxes.

"Besides, it's not about the weather. It's about the people. Night on Bourbon Street is one of the wildest party places in the world. Only a year ago a woman went missing here. Her fiancé said she was there one minute and gone the next. She showed up a week later and couldn't remember a thing. She thought she was drugged, but there were a ton of articles and news stories speculating about whether vampires were surfacing again and how many might be hiding in the French Quarter. Think about it. Every night tons of people get blackout drunk and can't remember huge blocks of time. It'd be a smorgasbord."

"Your general excitement and use of the word 'smorgasbord' concern me." He takes a dramatic step back from me.

I step after him and punch his shoulder. This time I don't overthink it—I embrace it. It feels comfortable, like I never really stopped. As if we're still best friends and he's going along with another one of my bizarre shenanigans.

"It makes sense."

He nods, his face deadly serious in a way that makes it clear he doesn't think it's serious. He just needs a little more convincing.

"Besides, look at this place. The whole town is vibrant and alive, yet somehow ancient and decaying all at the same time." I run my hand along the cold, old bricks of the building we're passing, blackened in some spots and faded in others—no two bricks exactly the same. I bet each one has a story to tell. Startling royal-blue paint covers the doors, which open to the sidewalk, letting smooth jazz and raucous laughter spill out. Across the street, what looks like a newly renovated building sits with fresh gray paint and curved windows trimmed in unblemished white. In another city, the buildings might clash, but here they make sense. The French Quarter's beautiful because nothing fits, so everything fits.

"Wouldn't you want to live here if you were immortal? Everywhere you look, something's different. It would never get old."

I can't hide my excitement. My steps are lighter than they've been in months—I have a plan, and I'm in control again, doing something instead of sitting around while everyone else decides Dad's dying.

I glance back at Henry, who's walking behind me as we thread through the crowded sidewalk.

He wipes sweat from his forehead. "It's great."

"Well, it'd be cooler for vampires, since they'd only be out in the evenings." Or maybe they don't even feel the heat if they're cold all the time. If everything goes well, pretty soon I'll only be out in the evenings—I'll never see the vibrant colors of this place in quite the same way. Never get to draw this place fully alive in the sun. I want to stop walking, to spin in circles and try to commit all of it in the daylight to memory. But I don't have time. A different kind of loss pinches at me, but I ignore it. Losing the daylight is so small in comparison to losing my dad.

The crowd thins, and Henry takes a few steps to catch up with me. "Why are we out now? Why don't we lie low until dark in . . . how about there?" He points to a quaint café painted a fading yellow with a blackboard sitting out front boasting fresh beignets. Sugar wafts in the air, attempting to coax us off mission.

"They might be in the attic. Attics are dark any time of day."

Henry groans. "Breaking into a convent attic is on my list of things I never want to do."

"You can wait outside."

"For you to be brought out in cuffs? Don't you have another plan we could try?"

I stop walking so I can look at him. "This one's my best bet."

"Okay." He folds his arms across his chest, his signal he's really prepared to listen to me. "Convince me."

I don't know how honest I should be. I didn't even have this plan two days ago. Yeah, Dad and I said we'd hunt for vampires out here, but we didn't do any real research. It was more like, maybe we'll run into one while touring these cool vampire-related sites.

I hesitate. I need him to prepare himself, though, in case this goes badly. "I was digging around on the message boards on the flight and someone posted about their friend coming here to try to get into the attic. They went alone and never came back—that was only five days ago."

"I feel like that would have made the news."

"Not if it was covered up—or if they didn't take the friend seriously."

"They could have left—run away from their life."

"Or this is the easiest hunting ground for a vampire looking for willing victims."

"An attic in a convent?"

"This isn't just any convent. Its name on the message board is what caught my eye in the first place because it was on my dad's and my list of places to visit. Do you know why?"

Henry raises a brow. He's only going to humor me so much. I know he can tell I'm gearing up to go off the "vampire deep end," which is what he used to call it anytime I gushed too long about some vampire legend or movie. He's still listening, though, so I'll take what I can get.

"Because this was the location of the first North American vampire sighting." I grin and jerk my thumb to the right.

The convent is large and unassuming, beige with dull gray shutters, about how you'd expect a convent to look, and yet it possesses a simple beauty that makes you want to whisper when you stand beside it.

"So the nuns are vampires?" I know he's trying to give me the benefit of the doubt and not let what he's really thinking show on his face—that I've lost my marbles somewhere along the way. I try not to blame him.

"Don't be ridiculous. I don't think there are vampire nuns."

He looks relieved until I continue.

"Once upon a time, the nuns locked the vampires in the attic."

"Of course. Of course." He keeps muttering the words as he stares into the sky like it will offer him some kind of relief.

"But the nuns don't live here anymore," I continue, talking to him like he isn't praying to the overcast sky for Jesus to save him.

He finally looks back down at me. "Then who does? Besides the vampires, of course."

I give him a glare for his sarcasm, but he's too distracted to appreciate it.

"It's a museum."

"A vampire museum."

"Of course not. A museum about the nuns, but it's a cover for the vampires."

He says something under his breath I don't make out.

"What'd you say?"

"You don't want to know."

"Fine. Please hear me out." I take a deep breath, steeling myself. I need him to hear the truth in this—one of the many stories of vampires that people tried to explain away before we got confirmation they existed. "There used to be a French colony here, but it was all men, and one day they decided they wanted some women to liven things up, so they sent a letter to the French king and begged him to send women. The king rounded up volunteers and sent them over on a boat. Only the boat gets here and nobody sees any women get off, only some suspiciously coffin-shaped boxes that they carry to the convent. Everyone assumes the women died, but then the women start showing up on the street looking extra pale and extra red around the lips, and the men who get close to them start disappearing. Historians tried to come up with explanations for this, like scurvy, which would make the women's gums bleed, and they claimed the missing men could have hopped a boat up to Baton Rouge or anywhere else, but that's just a lot of what-ifs to cover up the uncomfortable truth."

Henry stares at me like I'm an overly eccentric history teacher.

"Do you want to know what that truth is?"

"I'm dying to." He cracks a faint grin.

"Please take this seriously."

"Okay, okay." He holds up his hands in fake surrender. He drops his smile, but I sense it lingering around the edges of his lips.

I almost tell him to go home right then, but I need to finish the story. "Rumor has it the nuns realized the vamps were out there making the men disappear and decided to do something about it, like seal off the entire third floor. They say all the third-floor shutters have been nailed closed with nails blessed by the pope. But people still report seeing them open at night."

"Maybe they should have doused them in holy water when they blessed them."

I try not to punch him, but he's eyeing the rounded,

inconspicuous third-floor shutters, so maybe he believes me a tiny bit.

"Do you really think they're still there after all this time? Wouldn't all those vampire researchers that popped up after the Gerald debacle have checked this place?"

"Yeah—they did, right after it happened, and why would a vampire hang around in a place they knew they'd be looking? But that was ten years ago. People aren't bothering to search a place that's already been picked over. Plus, do you remember Jerome, the vampire from New Orleans? He got asked where he lived in the French Quarter, and he got all mysterious and quiet like he wouldn't answer, but then he said he had a very, very good view of this convent. He actually said *very* twice like that, like there was a hint in it. What if he lived here? What if he supported the convent, and they kept his secret? He would have had to move during the vampire heyday, but now? What better place to hide than a place that's already been checked a thousand times over?"

"And you're sure he's back?"

"No, but this was where that guy was headed the last time his friend saw him. Either he found someone here or he found something that led him somewhere else."

"So we're going to break in and get to the third floor, find a coffin, hope a vampire is inside and not some old bones, hope the vampire is nice, ask them to turn you, and then go home." Henry's tone is sarcastic, but an edge leaks into it—anger, maybe. He doesn't want me to risk this no matter how slim he thinks the odds are that I'm right.

"Yes," I say. My voice wobbles. I'm a weird mixture of doubt and fear, but I only really need to get rid of one of those emotions. Doubt poisons your thoughts until nothing seems possible. This is possible. "Yes," I say a little clearer. I reach into my back pocket and pull out my phone to show him a drawing I found online of the convent layout. Henry leans over me as I point. "There are two stories between us and the attic, but if this is right, then the stairs are to the left of the front door. Easy access. So are you going to help me or not?" I don't wait for an answer, just head across the street. When I turn around, Henry's standing along the stone wall, eyeing the decorative trim at the top.

"What are you doing?" I ask.

"This is going to be hard to get over, but I think I can boost you. I'm not sure how I'll follow."

I laugh—actually belly laugh—for the first time in a while. He may not believe the way I do, but he is committed. "How about we buy tickets for the museum instead?" His face flushes, feeding my laughter. "I appreciate your dedication though."

"Here to help," he mutters.

"Seriously, you're the best." I link my hand in the crook of his elbow and drag him along through the front gate.

The woman selling the tickets eyes us. "You know this is nothing but a museum, right? Not a supernatural tour. It doesn't even look like a convent anymore. It's a museum about the nuns."

They must still get some people snooping around trying to track down the legend. I open my mouth to try to set her at ease, but Henry beats me to it.

"I love nuns," he says.

The lady and I both stare at him.

He flushes. "I mean—not like that—the history. I love church history."

The lady hands us our tickets with a scowl.

"Sorry," I say. "He's not great with words."

I tug him out of there and into the convent's garden.

"If she wasn't suspicious of us before, she sure is now," I hiss.

"Sorry. I'm not great at being a spy or a vampire hunter or whatever it is I am."

"Well, you're certainly no Buffy."

He laughs. "Fair enough." He goes quiet. "This is beautiful."

Low, immaculately trimmed hedges start in the center of the courtyard and jut out, lining the many brick paths converging in the center. I wonder if they carry some significant meaning. Instead of the one way, there are many. Dad would love to see this. It should be him, standing here with me, talking church history while I wait to get upstairs and look for vampires, but someday we'll come back together.

A black metal gazebo sits in one corner. A metal cross adorns the top. I let Henry wander down each of the paths even though I itch to get inside. The longer we enjoy the gardens, the less suspicious the woman at the entrance will be. I catch her watching us more than once. She must know the truth—a guardian of what's inside. I bet they pay her well.

Goosebumps rise on the back of my neck, and it takes all my self-control not to run inside and dart up the stairs.

After enough time has gone by, I wave at Henry to follow me through the front doors.

The first thing to catch my eye is the ancient wooden staircase right where I wanted it to be. Roped off.

Henry comes up behind me. "Well, that's inconvenient."

"Nothing I read said the second floor wasn't open to the public," I whisper, but he's gone, perusing the stuff on display as if we're actually here to learn about the nuns. Maybe on another day I'd be a little bit intrigued.

I trail him into a room that finally catches my eye—an old wooden trunk sits against the wall. I grab his arm and squeeze. "What's that look like to you?"

"Too short to be a coffin."

"Yeah. Yeah." I drop his arm. "I need to get upstairs," I say, but he doesn't hear me. He's moved on already to another doorway.

"Wow. Come look at this."

Thinking he's found something, I hurry to his side, but it's only the entrance of the church with its high beige ceiling and ornate stained-glass windows, various statues of angels and religious figures lining the rows of simple wooden pews. The floor, a deep green tile with a soft brown cutting through the middle, gleams as if polished every hour.

The altar at the front is nearly impossible to look away from—the biggest I've ever seen, with beige and gold columns and a curved top peaked with a golden cross. Angels dressed in pastels trumpet from the top.

Henry steps through the door and beckons me to follow. "Have you ever seen anything like this?"

"Nope." I don't follow. Nothing about it reminds me of our church back home—my dad's church, I mean. I'm not sure the church belongs to me anymore or if it ever did. If I really believed in God, would I be out here hunting vampires or would I be home praying every day?

"Come look at this." He stands in front of the pulpit, mouth open slightly as he takes in the rich purple walls and garish amount of gold. It's too much. Too pretty. It lacks sincerity. Why present people with overwhelming beauty when real life is so very ugly? It makes my stomach turn.

"Come on, you're not a vampire yet. You can still enter a church."

His joking tone turns my skin hot.

"I don't have any interest in an overwrought church." I resent every bit of money someone poured into this. Why not spend it on cancer research? At the very least, why not feed the hungry? Isn't that what Jesus was known for?

He walks back to me, face drawn. "Don't talk like that."

"Like what? With honesty?" I sigh and look away. "I'm going upstairs."

"You can't. All the stairways are roped off."

I just shrug. "I'm *going* upstairs."

He frowns. "I don't think that's a great idea."

"I don't have a choice."

"We always have a choice."

"No. You have a choice. You can stay here in your cathedral and count the angels, but I need something an angel isn't going to give me."

I spin before I can see his reaction.

He doesn't follow, which tells me all I need to know.

I stop at the main staircase and try to see up to the second floor, but I can't. I don't hear anyone moving either. Nothing but a flimsy black rope between me and the stairs. And a statue of the Madonna and child. Wearing robes of gold and an overlarge crown, she seems to stare straight into my soul, and I can't move. The babe in her arms gazes up the staircase like a watchdog in a crown twice the size of his body. Perhaps their judgmental expressions were meant to admonish people like me who intend to break the rules.

I turn and head down the hallway to another staircase without any statues guarding it. I step under the rope with only the slightest twinge of guilt, but the old wood stairs creak louder than alarm bells as I climb them.

I pause on the second floor long enough to notice a lovely mustard velvet settee, something I could totally imagine Lestat sitting on, sipping from a glass of red wine mixed with the blood of his latest victim. A little shiver traces down my spine. I turn to the next rise of stairs, roped off again. I read a rumor that the base of these stairs is rigged to set off an alarm the second you cross. I found no other accounts of this, though, so I hold my breath and crawl under the rope.

No alarm bells, but that doesn't mean I didn't trigger a security system. Or something else altogether.

The first flight of stairs is polished, gleaming wood to match the ones before, but once I turn the corner, out of view from the second floor, the varnished wood ends. The last stretch hasn't been renovated—dull and worn, they cry out as I climb. My steps slow. Will I scream the moment fangs break through my skin? The thought pulses in my mind, heavy and demanding. Dark stains cover some of the steps—stains I don't want to investigate—and my stomach rolls. A tremor turns my legs soft, and I grip the railing, sucking in a deep breath of ancient wood and dust and something else more sinister. Or maybe I'm letting my imagination escape from me. But what if I can't get them to turn me? What if I just end up drained of blood, and Dad's final memory on this earth is hearing about my gruesome murder? Even worse, they could find a way to cover up the truth. I'd end up another comment on a blog dedicated to vampire research.

They never found the missing kid that got pinned on Gerald ten years ago and sent the vampires back into hiding. Nobody knows if vampires are inherently bad or if they're like people— bad and good mixed together so thoroughly it's hard to tell who is which until someone's ripping out your heart.

I'm panicking like prey about to get tossed into a cage with a predator. And prey gets eaten. I need to be bold and fearless to stand a chance. I take several shallow breaths, reminding myself who I am: a girl who takes risks. A girl who will do anything to save her dad.

I bound up the stairs and reach a dense, dark wooden door.

Two thick, black old-fashioned bolts lock it from the outside.

Only one reason exists for locking a door from the outside: you're keeping something, or some*one*, in.

I pull at the first lock. Metal scrapes metal and then gives up the fight. The second lock follows suit. I grip the handle, take a deep breath, and pull.

Nothing.

I yank harder. The door's jammed or double-locked from the inside or maybe nailed shut. I crouch and begin examining the edges for evidence of blessed nails holding it in place.

I wiggle my fingers under the doorjamb. That would freak Henry out for sure if he'd had it in him to come with me, but what's the worst that can happen? I get bitten? The icy air on the other side of the door chills my fingers so abruptly that my whole body trembles and not just from the chill. Why keep an attic so very, very cold? It should be brutally hot from the summer heat. Unless something *is* up here.

I pull my fingers back out and slap my hand against the door. Something scrapes on the other side.

"What are you doing up here?"

I jump and turn, pressing against the cold door. Abnormally cold. I make a mental note and add it to my list of evidence before acknowledging the slender older man dressed in a faded navy security uniform. His bushy eyebrows meet as he glares at me from a few stairs below. I don't know how I didn't hear him coming.

"I . . . I was . . ." I curse myself and my inability to lie.

"I know what you were doing."

I gulp. I bet he doesn't, but I'm not about to explain myself.

"You're one of those supernatural yahoos always trying to break in upstairs and make some grand discovery." Okay, maybe he does. "I hate to break it to ya, but there's nothing but a bunch of old records in storage up here." He looks tired, as if I'm the millionth person he's had to say this to.

"Then why's it locked?"

"Girl, don't push your luck." He motions for me to follow him, then turns and heads down the stairs without waiting to see if I do. I'm tempted to turn around and give the door one last tug, but I don't. I'm not the first one to try this, which means everyone else failed before me, or worse, *didn't* fail but didn't live to tell. Maybe these people aren't on some vampire payroll. Maybe they're actually keeping the worst of the worst locked away. As self-preservation kicks in, I follow him back down.

Henry's mouth gapes when we pass him, but I don't say anything. Best if I go down by myself. Besides, he was too much of a coward to do anything to begin with.

As we exit the front door, the humid air closes in on me like shackles, and I start to panic. I can't be arrested. I need to keep looking. I need to get back up there. Even horrible things can sometimes give you what you need.

"Sit here." The guard gestures to a stone bench in the garden. It burns the backs of my thighs when I lower myself onto it.

The guard walks over and starts talking with the woman we bought the tickets from. She does not seem pleased, to say the least.

The door clicks open behind me, but I don't bother to look up until Henry passes me, face grim, and goes up to speak with the two of them.

I can't hear what they're saying, but the old woman and the security guard glance in my direction more than once. Henry keeps his back to me.

The next thing I know, Henry's leading me by my elbow off the hot hell of my stone seat and through the front gates of the convent. As we exit, I glance back at the woman and the security guard, expecting to see fury. I don't. What I do see is much worse: pity.

Henry tugs me along until we're across the street, standing underneath a flowering tree.

I yank my elbow away from his touch. "What did you tell them?"

He looks up at the white blossoms draping over the side of a high stone wall. "The truth."

My face gets hot. "Which is?"

"Don't." He finally looks down at me, and the problem is, it feels like he's looking down on me not just because he's ridiculously tall, but because he sees me as a child chasing a fairytale, or a nightmare, or something between the two, and I want to slap the look from his face.

"I hate you."

He jerks back a little, then reaches for me.

"Don't touch me." I shrug away from him and start down the street, but his long strides pace right behind me. "You shouldn't have come," I holler over my shoulder.

"Victoria, wait." His pleading reminds me of when we were kids and he needed me to slow down so he could catch up to me—before one of his steps equaled two of mine. Now he could overtake me at any moment, but he doesn't. He lingers behind me and waits for me to turn. I do.

"I'm sorry," he says.

"For what?"

"Listen." He runs his hand through his hair, stalling, like he didn't expect me to turn around and let him speak. "I can't apologize for not believing in vampires. I don't, but I do believe in you. I believe you're doing everything you can to save your dad, and nothing's braver than that. I want to help you. I was only trying to help you."

He's telling the truth. He always did when we were kids, even when it got us both grounded. I used to hate that about him, but now I cling to it.

Honesty's a difficult thing when someone you love is sick. How do you balance it with optimism and hope? Sometimes honesty just feels like brutal pessimism. But Henry knows how to wield it.

"Okay," I say simply. I don't ask him again what he said. I don't need to hear it. I already know.

He smiles and steps closer to me as the wall of ice between us dissipates, leaving us standing in chilly water, but that's easily ignored.

"What do we do now?" he asks. "Where else can we look?"

"I'm not sure." My throat throbs as everything piles up inside of me—disappointment, fear, lingering anger at Henry and at myself for not being more prepared. I could have fit a crowbar in a large purse. Why didn't I think of something so basic? "That was my best lead," I whisper. I want to melt into the cracks in the sidewalk. "I don't know why I came here. What did I think would happen? That I could roll into town, break into an attic, and get some vampire blood? I'm ridiculous. I've watched too many movies. Professionals have been searching for vampires and haven't found one. How can I expect to do better? I can't believe you didn't talk me out of this." I keep babbling as all the doubt I buried rises to the surface.

Henry's eyes widen as he witnesses my breakdown.

"Let's go home," I say. But that doesn't feel like an option the second I say it. Go home and do what?

I can tell by the look on Henry's face that this is the moment he really came with me for. To scoop up my pieces when I realized what a fool I'd been and return me home to watch my dad die.

I open my mouth to take it back—I can't give up this easily—but Henry beats me to it.

"No," he says. He looks as shocked as I feel. "You've never been a quitter. Remember that time in fifth grade when we had the school Olympics and you sprained your ankle during the mile and refused to bow out gracefully?" He smiles a little. "You limped around that track and made everyone else wait until you crossed the finish line. We didn't even get to do the fifty-yard dash because you just *had* to see your race through."

"You were pissed," I remind him.

"It was my best chance at a medal!"

"You didn't talk to me for a week."

"I think it was two."

"You forgave me eventually."

"Yes, but you wouldn't have forgiven yourself if you'd quit, and you won't forgive yourself now." The expression on his face says he's surprised to be the one talking us into staying.

How can he know me so well? I guess some bonds don't go away with absence. They're easy to find again if you need them. This feels easy, standing here in the street with Henry—my emotions swinging from anger to forgiveness. When you have enough memories to lean on, differences can be overcome.

Hope expands in my chest again. I almost let the pity and disbelief of the security guard, the ticket woman, and Henry take it away from me. But it's there. I can't let it go so easily. I'm stronger than that. If I don't keep believing, then I've already failed, and that's not an option.

"You're right, but I don't know what to do." The words aren't easy for me to say. They've never been easy for me.

"I know what will help."

You'd better get yourself a garlic T-shirt,
buddy, or it's your funeral.
—*The Lost Boys*

# Five

utter. An unnatural amount of butter is Henry's idea of help. We sit at a local seafood and burger shop—everything in this town is seafood and *something*—with a huge plate of thin-fried catfish and wedges of garlic fries covered in so much butter it drips onto the plate as I free a fry from the pile.

"Wow," Henry says for maybe the hundredth time. "These fries are amazing. Who would have thought to put butter on fries?"

"Probably not a cardiologist." I bite into another rich, buttery, garlicky fry and decide Southerners know how to eat. The fried catfish is just as amazing—crisp, without a trace of grease on the light breading, the perfect complement to the dripping fries. Besides, if I'm going to become a vampire, this may be my last chance to eat garlic. Garlic's been used forever to ward off supernatural evils. People still believe in it today—as recently as the seventies, a church handed out cloves of garlic to test its congregation—if you didn't eat it, you were a vampire. Might have made sense if they cooked it, because what rational human hates garlic? But raw garlic? No thanks.

Dad loves garlic. If I didn't think she'd be suspicious, I'd call Mom and tell her to make him his favorite roasted garlic potato soup.

I love it, too. It's not something I think about on a daily basis—my love for garlic—but how many foods have garlic in them? Dad and I always talked about going to the Gilroy Garlic Festival one day and trying garlic ice cream. Even Mom was excited for that. How awkward will it be going now when Dad and I can only go at night and all the food repels us? It's almost funny to think about. And sad.

But I don't want to think about the things we'll give up as vampires. Nothing matters as much as being alive. Or kind of alive, I guess.

"We should probably get some sort of vegetable with this," I say to distract myself.

Henry stops chewing for a second, eyes narrowing as he examines my face. Somehow the tiny trace of sadness in my chest leaked into my voice. He knows me well enough to hear it. I will him to ignore it, to not confront me on something I'm trying to avoid.

He gives me a light, easy smile—a gift. "No way. It would ruin the flavor combination."

"For once, you're absolutely right," I say as I rip off another piece of catfish and dip it into the jalapeño tartar sauce.

"For once?" He raises his eyebrows as he pops another fry in his mouth.

I grin before turning serious. "I need to get back in that convent."

This gets Henry to pause and wipe his hands on a napkin. More fries for me.

I wait for him to snap. To show me he doesn't really believe in me at all.

"Okay." He stares a little too intensely at the fries. "Don't you have other leads?"

"No," I answer, but I do. A club in the Quarter's been mentioned more than once on the message boards—a couple of people said a vampire holds court in the VIP section. Plus, they found a body outside the club six months ago—stab wound to the neck was the official story. It made the news. I showed Dad and said we should check it out on our trip. He said no way, that we weren't going to hunt killers—be they vampires or humans. He made me promise I wouldn't go near it before I left, and Dad and I don't break promises.

Besides, something's in that attic. I felt it.

He chews his bottom lip. "It just seems like going back is a good way to end up in jail."

"I'm not asking you to come with me." But I want him to, more than I care to admit. He got me off the hook last time, even if I didn't like how he did it. I know he would try again.

"But I'll be the one you call to bail you out of jail?"

"What's the point of you being here if you won't at least be my get-out-of-jail-free card?"

Henry's face tightens for a moment, and then he loses it. He snorts and drops his forehead to the table. His shoulders shake with laughter.

I'm tempted to kick his shins under the table, but when he raises his head, this boyish grin sits on his face, and it unwinds a little of the tightness inside of me.

"Maybe we should take it easy tonight and regroup in the morning. I'll help you do some research—come up with a better plan."

His eyes are wide and sincere and invite me to lean on him, to let him help me, and I desperately want to. But his plans will be safe, and you don't find vampires playing it safe.

"Yeah, great idea." I give him a wide smile, because if he's anything like he was when we were kids, he'll be asleep hours before me and not even a werewolf howling in his ear will wake him up.

I leave Henry curled up on his side, knees dangling off the edge of the too-small couch where he fell asleep watching *Interview with the Vampire*, which he's never once stayed awake for, and I creep into the night that I tell myself I want to belong to.

This city is a vampire—beautiful and old and seductive, living off the energy of the people it attracts. I do love the night already, the way the neon bar signs contrast with the old gas lamps and make the puddles of water from the summer thunderstorms glow like portals to another place and time, but nobody steps in them because nobody wants to be anywhere but here. Life pulses up and down Bourbon Street, and I imagine anyone without a dying dad wouldn't be able to walk down this street without grinning.

I bet Mom would hate it though—nothing's organized, nothing has a place. I imagine us on a mother-daughter trip and cringe.

I turn onto a quieter street with fewer people and darker corners for lonelier creatures to hide in. This city offers places to fit almost anyone's mood.

Even at night, the heat and humidity refuse to let up. It's like lying in bed sweating under a comforter, but you can't kick it off because some cruel person nailed it to your bed frame—probably what a coffin feels like. I shudder. Small spaces are not my thing. I really, really hope the coffin thing's a myth. My skin feels too tight just thinking about it.

I wore a gray sweatshirt and jeans. For some reason I thought it would make me less conspicuous, but given what the other women I've passed on the street were wearing, less is more, and I would have been better off in my white miniskirt and flimsiest top. Now I stick out like someone up to no good, which is accurate.

A few men give me a sideways glance, and I tug my hood up. When you're already in a furnace, what's a few more degrees?

The streets around the convent aren't empty like I'd hoped, but of course I'm not the only one intrigued enough to come here. This place is a must-see for supernatural tours, and even though tours end at ten, I suspect the group of twentysomething women holding drinks and taking selfies are leftover from one. An older man with a cane walks back and forth in front of the entrance as well, scowling in their direction each time they laugh.

A single streetlamp gives one corner of the wall an eerie yellow glow. The streetlight on the other side of the road sends the shadows of a scraggly tree across the wall like skeletal fingers trying to tear it down and set whatever's inside free. I tuck myself in the shadows.

This part of the plan is simple: wait.

The women leave first, losing interest when their cups run dry.

The man is more diligent. I count the beats of his cane as he moves until my mind numbs and I lose track of the number, but eventually he stops and stares up at the third-floor shutters. He's a believer. I can sense it in the way he holds his position for so long, the way he leans forward like he'd fly up to those windows and rip through them with his bare hands if he could guarantee what he needed was there. He *needs* something—not just wants. People that want give up easier. I wonder what he needs, but I don't want to think about it too much. My own need is all I can handle. At least an hour passes. Maybe more. When he finally glances down, his head swivels in my direction. He gives one slow nod as if resigning his duties to me and then retreats into the dark.

I want to call out to him not to give up, but being alone and vulnerable out here is more likely to attract what I'm looking for.

I cross the street to a small gray door in the wall, a good

twenty feet down from the side entrance. Chipped black bars in the center let me peer through at the empty convent inside. Almost empty. A single light is on in the second story. Interesting. I examine the third-story shutters for any movement, but they're all sealed tight.

I grip the bars, cool compared to the warm night air, and press my face against them.

So many people have reported strange experiences out here at night: the third-story shutters flying open, strange black animals lurking in the shadows, a creeping coldness across the back of the neck, lost time they can't account for. Perhaps the most terrifying story is of two paranormal researchers who camped outside through the night after failing to breach the upstairs attic—just like me. In the morning, their bodies were found exsanguinated. This story is well-known among those who follow the supernatural, even though the police claim there's no official record of it.

More recently a few people have reported strangers approaching tourists and holding odd conversations, but I didn't find many details, and the stories were secondhand.

But maybe all I need to do is stand here and wait. Let the vampires come to me.

Then try not to die.

I don't know how long I stand there. Nothing changes. But I also don't see my friend the security guard. I lean back and eye the door I'm holding onto. I might be able to pull myself up, but then what? Surely they keep their doors and windows locked.

Am I going to stand outside and toss pebbles at the third-story shutters like a fool in love?

At this point, I'm considering it.

"Waiting for something?" The man's voice is high and light and doesn't quite break the silence.

My heart rate speeds, half from terror and half from excitement.

I turn slowly, preparing to be disappointed or terrified or both. I keep one hand gripped on a bar of the door like I can somehow scurry up it if this goes south.

He's thin and taller than me but not as tall as Henry. His blond hair passes his shoulders, and he keeps it tucked behind both ears, showing off a delicate face and full, pouty lips. In dark skinny jeans and a powder-blue tank top, he looks more like an errant punk elf prince than a vampire.

I can't tell if he's what I'm looking for or not, but he is standing here in front of the convent despite being dressed for the clubs a couple of blocks over.

"Maybe I'm waiting for you." My pounding heart pushes the words from my mouth—bolder words than I've ever spoken.

He smirks. "I doubt it." His gaze drifts above my head—to the third-floor shutters or the stars? I can't tell. "Or maybe you are."

His smirk widens into a full-toothed grin.

I eye his teeth with all the enthusiasm of a dentist, even though a real vampire wouldn't be out flashing their fangs willy-nilly. What real vampire wants to draw that kind of suspicion to themselves?

I'm not even sure real vampires have fangs. Gerald never showed his on camera despite every interviewer asking him for a glimpse. Maybe he didn't have them. Maybe he didn't want to make the public more scared of him than they already were. Either way, visible fangs would be a sign of a vampire-wannabe, not a real one.

The dark makes it impossible to tell anyway. I take a step toward him.

"You're very brave," he says.

His words chill my warm, pumping blood.

"I'm Victoria." My name sounds odd, uttered in the dark, and I'm not sure why I say it, but I feel like I need to give him something of myself.

"Carter."

His name cuts through the night and pierces my heart, making it stall out for a moment before speeding forward, urging me to jump toward him and beg him to turn me.

The name cannot be a coincidence—not in this town, on this street, at this time.

Wayne and John Carter were brothers living in New Orleans in the 1930s. They seemed normal until a bleeding woman escaped their home one day and led authorities to countless bodies and other survivors who were still alive and being drained of blood for the Carters' nightly supper. One of the survivors went on to do the same—probably having been turned before the rescue.

The story's enough to turn even my stomach. This is the part I don't like to think about—who I would become as a vampire.

But surely all vampires don't need to be killers. I can be a vegetarian like the Cullens—at least I hope so.

Carter stares at me with his head slightly cocked, probably reading every thought crossing my face.

He smiles. "Scared yet?"

Feet pound behind us. His head swivels, and then he's brushing past me, so close my racing heart freezes, and then he's around the corner, long legs carrying him down the sidewalk in a blur.

"Wait," I yell, moving after him.

Someone else grabs my arm, sending a shock through my already electrified system. I turn and swing upward with my fist, connecting with a nose.

Henry's nose.

"Dang." He bends over and cups the lower half of his face. "Where'd you learn how to do that?"

"My dad got me self-defense classes for my eighteenth birthday."

"Your dad's awesome."

My still speeding heart slows to a crawl. "I know."

He unfolds himself and wipes his nose. His hand glistens slightly.

"You okay?" I ask.

"It's not broken."

"Great." I spin and tear down the dark street before he can lunge for me again.

I check half a mile of road and side streets before giving up and turning around. When I do, Henry's trailing behind me.

I wander back in his direction. "I lost him." I don't add *thanks a lot*, which is what I'm really thinking. If Henry had left me alone, if he'd never even come at all, I might have what I want this very moment.

*Or I might be dead.* I try to shake off the other, still terrified, voice inside me. Even if he wasn't a vampire, human monsters exist too.

"Who?"

"Who do you think?" I snap. I can only compose myself so well after all.

"Well, from where I was standing, he looked like some punk-ass creep, so you tell me."

I don't want to say the words out loud. I know how he'll react, and I want to live in my own bubble of conviction without Henry's doubt poking holes in it.

He won't leave it alone, though. He stares at me, waiting.

I start the sentence a million times in my head. *He might be . . . I think he's . . . It's possible . . .* I consider framing it for him to make it easier, but in the end, I don't need him to be comfortable or to believe me. I need him to support me, and he already promised that. "He was a vampire."

Henry doesn't laugh like I thought he might. "Okay. Why do you think that?"

He's taking me seriously, or at least pretending to.

"There was something about the way he showed up there, and he kept glancing behind me at the third floor like he knew why

97

I was there." I can see Henry struggling not to show his disbelief on his face. I decide not to mention his name and the connection to serial-killing vampire brothers. "Plus, he was super fast." Speed's a common trait in many portrayals of vampires.

"Well, I'm super fast too, but it's because I'm in good shape, not because I'm dead."

I ignore his joking. "He hinted at it."

"How? What exactly did he say?"

"He said he might be what I was looking for."

Henry loses his ability to keep a straight face and frowns.

"I know how that sounds," I say.

"Do you?"

"Yes," I hiss, but my tiny thread of hope frays under his scrutiny, and I struggle to hang onto it. "This is my best lead." I hate the hint of desperation in those last few words.

A tiny voice in my head reminds me of the club, but it's not an option—not if there's any other way. Dad would kill me for going back on a promise. We'd only be vampires for a day before he found out and staked me.

I know Henry senses my desperation because his frown eases.

"Then we need to find him again tomorrow." He nods like we can do this.

I worry my one lead just slipped away like a bat after dusk.

What twisted kind of mortal are you?
    —*The Little Vampire*

# Six

The next day, we wander the French Quarter, peeking into every odd little novelty shop as our skin soaks up the humid air, turning our steps slow even though urgency gnaws at me. But if I want to find Carter again, I'll need to wait out the sun. Vampires don't come out in the daylight.

Still, I decide we need to keep an eye out just in case I'm wrong. The thing about vampires is every story's a little different, so I can't be 100 percent certain about any one trait. Gerald and the other vampires who showed themselves never answered any questions about their skills or weaknesses, like they had some rule about giving humans something to use against them, but I've sorted through all the myths and stories to come up with a list of likely characteristics.

They drink blood. (One of the only traits I'm certain about. Even though vampires who live by stealing energy instead of blood are said to exist, most myths revolve around the consumption of blood.)

They only come out at night. (This trait's been key since the beginning—Sumerian texts mention creatures of the night who drink the blood of sleeping humans.)

They hate garlic. (Garlic wards off the supernatural. This trait has been repeated in too many stories to be ignored.)

They can't go into churches, and they fear crosses. (I desperately want this one to be untrue. Dad would hate it.)

They have no reflection in mirrors. (This stems from folklore and the idea that mirrors reflect the soul. Bram Stoker took it one step further and said painters could not paint them.)

They have no heartbeat, and they're colder to the touch than a normal human. (I read a lot of scientific explanations on this—all arguing a different side—but I'm keeping it on the list as a possibility.)

They may possess other unusual abilities like immense strength, mind control, manipulating the weather, and healing. (We know the healing thing is true thanks to Gerald stabbing himself on live television. The weather thing is less known, but it comes from the draugr in Norse mythology.)

I'm looking for five out of seven since I can't count on everything being true.

I run through my checklist to keep my focus, occasionally sharing a detail with Henry as he attempts to get me to enjoy myself. He drags me into more than one art gallery, and the work is rich and vibrant and makes me ache with the knowledge that I may never have it in me to make something like that again. Even if I become a vampire and save Dad, how long until I forget what the sun glinting on water looks like?

He's trying to be nice though.

We play tourist under the pretext of looking for the vampire, but as other tourists laugh and smile and soak in the experience, I shut down and feel nothing. I'm not here to feel things. I'm on a mission. I'm definitely not here to feel happy.

When we reach the grand white St. Louis Cathedral, Henry suggests going inside, but I shake my head. God had his chance, and if I went in there, if he gave me even the smallest sign, I might use it as an excuse to fly home early and wait for a miracle that won't come. Instead, we sit outside on the benches with the church looming in front and the street artists lined up behind, displaying their wares along the wrought-iron fence enclosing Jackson Square.

I sit, caught between two things I can't risk loving anymore, trying not to let it pull me apart.

"We need to keep walking," I say.

"It makes more sense to sit for a minute. This is a high-traffic area." Henry stretches his legs out in front of him, flexing his feet up and down. We have covered a lot of ground.

"I doubt we'll find a vampire taking a stroll in front of a church."

"I thought we wouldn't find one in the daylight," he mumbles.

Fair point. Why'd I share my list of traits with him? What I really want is to keep walking—movement allows me the delusion of progress.

But I know I'm losing this argument.

Henry stretches his arms across the back of our bench until his forearm rests against my bare back. His hand hangs loosely next to my shoulder. It's not like he's got his arm around me. If he put his hand on my arm too, that'd be weird. This is just two friends not weirded out by touching. But for a second it's all I can focus on even though I'm not supposed to feel anything right now.

I try watching the rotating cast of street performers. My favorite is a tap-dancing boy who's so good he almost makes me forget about Henry's arm. I toss money I should probably be saving into his bucket, but he deserves it, and it gives me a chance to get up and break contact.

Finally, the sun slips behind the cathedral and dusk approaches. And then I wait even longer, until the sky finally starts to turn to ink.

Henry is leaning back on the bench, his eyes closed. I kick his shoe.

"Wake up. The sun's gone, and we need to check back at the convent."

He grumbles under his breath but pulls himself to his feet and trails me to the convent. I hold my breath as we walk, like Carter will be standing there waiting, but of course, when we get there, we find nothing.

"Maybe we should wait here," he suggests.

I shake my head. "He might not come back here if he suspects I'm hunting him. Plus, I'm tired of waiting."

"Hunting seems like a strong word choice," he says.

I ignore him and drift down the street in the direction Carter headed last night.

I turn down a busier side street with restaurants and bars and people talking too loudly and taking up the sidewalk while others weave around them.

Henry stops in front of a candy shop. "I want to grab another praline. Want anything?"

"I don't know how you're still eating those things," I say, keeping my focus on the street. This is like his fifth praline of the day.

"They're just too good," he says.

"Fine. I'll wait out here and keep watch."

He starts to turn.

"Wait." I fish a twenty out of my pocket. "Pick me up a package of them for my dad's birthday next week. You know how my family loves sweets."

Henry stares down at the bill. "Next week?"

"Yeah. Don't worry. We'll get back in time."

He keeps staring like the money's booby-trapped, and I have to shake the bill in front of him to snap him out of it. He plucks it from me and heads inside without another word.

I lean back against the brick exterior, still hot from the sun, and run through everyone on the street again: two girls in sundresses walking arm in arm, a homeless man sitting outside the building opposite me, a group of men laughing too loud, a woman in a VAMPIRES EAT FREE T-shirt—a choice to be sure— and I'm wondering if I should try some sort of bold advertising like that when I spot a flash of blond coming out of a club and heading in the opposite direction.

I move without hesitating, without even thinking of hollering for Henry.

I can only see his back, but he's tall and dressed in black skinny jeans and a dusty rose tank top.

He turns a corner too quickly, and I'm stuck behind a family with three kids gawking at cats in the window of a tapestry shop. I dart around them, stepping into the street and earning myself the blast of a car horn. Ignoring it, I race around the corner, tearing through puddles that somehow never dry up in the heat. Warm water splashes my legs.

An empty stretch of broken sidewalk greets me. I twist in the other direction, but I'm sure he came this way. I keep going, away from the tourists on the main street and away from Henry. He'll be mad when he comes out and I'm gone, but I can't let him slow me down.

The streets running perpendicular to the river get more of a breeze, but somehow they're always almost empty. A couple passes on the other side, each carrying a full plastic cup.

At least someone's having fun.

"Why are you following me?" Carter's breath moves the back of my hair, and I spin so fast my toe snags on a raised piece of concrete and I stumble, closing the already tiny gap between us and face-planting into his chest.

He grabs my arms and rights me, quickly stepping back like I'm the dangerous one.

As I smooth my hair, he folds his arms over his chest.

"I . . . I'm not. I'm lost. I'm trying to find my friend." I swivel my head around like I'm looking for Henry. Really, I'm looking for anyone, but the street is vacant.

He smirks.

He knows I'm lying. I don't even know why I did. Of course I'm looking for him. But standing alone with him on a darkened street makes my skin tingle with warning. My basic animal instincts say *Lie, run, get back in the light where things like him can't go.*

That feeling's exactly what I need.

*Be strong like Buffy.* I straighten. "You said you might be what I'm looking for."

His eyes narrow, and he runs his tongue over his bottom lip in a way I might find sexy in a movie, but in real life it makes me want to turn around and bolt.

"You don't look like the type," he finally says.

"The type for what?" I glance down at my hot-pink tank top with the white lace overlay. One of my favorites.

He smirks again. "If you don't know what, you probably shouldn't be looking for us."

My heart pounds, and not because I'm afraid, even though I know I should be terrified, but because he said *us.* He all but admitted he's a vampire.

I struggle to get my breathing under control, but it's like standing in front of a wild animal, hoping you don't scare it away while also hoping it doesn't eat you.

I put what I hope is a sexy purr in my voice as I take the

smallest step toward him. "I know exactly what I want."

I'm not sure I'm pulling it off, but at least he doesn't laugh.

"Okayyy," he says, dragging out the *y* at the end like it's my last chance to turn around and pretend this never happened. I don't, and he grins in answer, reaching into the back pocket of his impossibly tight jeans to pull out a crisp white card. He hands it to me. An address is written on it in elegant black script. Of course a vampire would have a calling card—Lestat would definitely approve. I tuck it into the back pocket of my jean shorts before he can change his mind.

"Be there by midnight and wear something different."

I nod, too nervous to be offended.

"Victoria!" I turn my head and lock eyes with Henry striding down the street. He looks pissed.

I turn back around to confirm I'll be there tonight, but the street is empty.

"Damn it, Victoria." Henry jerks to a stop beside me. His chest heaves like he ran a mile to find me. "Shit. Wait for me next time."

My mouth pops open a little. Henry never loses his cool.

He tucks his hands into his jeans and looks past me. "You scared me."

"Oh." The moment hangs between us, giving me a chance to step into it, wrap it around myself like an old familiar blanket.

But it's too damn hot still, so I take the easy way out and change the topic.

"Did you see him?" I turn around and scan the empty street again.

"Who?"

"He just disappeared," I whispered.

Henry snorts. "The blond guy? He literally walked away and went down an alley while you were turned around."

I sigh. His mode of transportation doesn't really matter. Vampires can walk too. They don't need to morph into bats or something ridiculous to be real. This isn't a Bela Lugosi film after all.

"He's what we're looking for."

"What *you're* looking for," Henry corrects.

I pull out the white card Carter gave me. "I'm going here at midnight."

Henry takes the card from my hand and examines it like there may be some secret code hidden there. "I don't like it," he says. "This guy told you he's a vampire?" The cynicism in his voice is killing the rapid beating of my heart, drowning out the tiny trickle of hope sneaking through me.

I yank the card back from him. "Obviously he didn't come right out and say it."

"He's probably a serial killer."

"I'm going."

"Or a drug dealer."

"Still going."

He rolls his eyes toward the black sky. "*We're* going."

Welcome to my house!
Enter freely. Go safely, and leave
something of the happiness you bring.
—*Dracula* by Bram Stoker

# Seven

I procured a fake ID from a shady dude I found on Craigslist for just this type of moment. I hope the thing holds up. I repeat my birthday in my head again and again as I smooth out my white eyelet sundress.

"You're gonna have to sit this one out," I tell Henry, who's walking beside me, looking surprisingly suave in dark-wash jeans and a plain black T-shirt. The black hair usually draped over half his face is slicked back. "You look good, but they're still going to card you."

"I look good, huh? That may be the nicest thing you've ever said to me."

"Don't let it go to your head."

He smiles, and I swear it's sexier than usual. Dimples with high cheekbones is an excellent combination.

I smooth my unwrinkled dress again.

"Don't worry about me. I'm covered." He flashes his own ID.

I give him a hard stare. I know he didn't have one of those before.

He shrugs. "A friend convinced me to get one when I turned eighteen."

I can't believe I missed his eighteenth birthday. He missed mine too. His was right after his grandma died, and mine was after Dad got sick. I didn't have a big party, and I doubt he did either.

Neither of us needs to apologize for that. Other things maybe, but not that.

Being reminded of the year we lost opens a small ache in my belly that I thought went away when Dad being sick became my priority. But the way Henry's arm brushes mine as we walk pulls it wider and wider, and I don't have room to deal with that hurt right now. I'm about to walk in the street to get some breathing room when I stop.

I recognize the slanted cursive of the neon red sign hanging in the walkway up ahead: JOSEPHINE'S.

"Please tell me that's not the address on the card."

"What's wrong?" Henry doubles back for me as I hold up the white card and the address. Crap. I hurry forward to confirm what I already know: this is the one place I promised Dad I wouldn't go.

"Victoria?"

Henry's standing beside me again, waiting for me to explain, but I don't quite know how to feel. This is one of the places I thought I might find a vampire, and now I'm here at the invitation of someone I suspect is one. But someone died here. Where I'm standing.

My heart pounds from a weird mixture of fear and hope.

I've never broken my word before—not to Dad. But he told me to find him a vampire. In the moment I thought he was joking, but what if he has the same wild hopes that I do? Wouldn't he tell me to go inside if he knew how close I was?

Henry's hand is on my arm, and I didn't even notice.

"Someone died here."

His hand drops away from me, and I kind of want it back. Probably should have eased into that bit of information.

"Yeah, it's a place people look for vampires—people who do enough digging on message boards, at least. Someone died from a stabbing to the neck out here. At least, that's what it looked like."

"I thought you had no other leads? Not that I'm anxious to visit actual murder sites."

"I told my dad I wouldn't set foot in this place. He made me promise."

"Then we shouldn't go in," Henry says, like it's that simple. He knows I take my promises seriously, especially to my dad. He steps back, looking relieved to have a reason to escape this scenario.

But it's not that simple. Dad's life never hung in the balance of me keeping my word or not. I could call and explain, try to get him on board with my plan, but deep down I know what he'd say. So I won't ask. I'll pretend he might have said yes. Plausible deniability and all.

"We're going," I say.

Henry shakes his head. "Your dad wouldn't want this."

"Don't speak for him." I stride toward the entrance. I don't want to hear it, especially when I hear truth in it. Why can't Henry lie to me when I need it?

At least he follows me.

The guy at the door frowns, glancing between me and my license a couple of times, then shrugs like he knows it's a fake and doesn't care. He waves Henry through with barely a glance.

"Don't say it," I say, but the noise swallows us, and all I get is Henry's half grin in reply.

Lights pulse and flash from the ceiling, spotlighting one writhing body for a second before moving onto another. There's no smooth, soft jazz in here, just a DJ on a high circular platform in the center of the room, bobbing his head with his eyes closed like he doesn't want to see the mass of bodies beneath him. Two long, packed bars line both sides of the club.

"Well," Henry says. "Not what I expected."

"Yeah." Even though I'm standing on the edge of the crowd, occasional body parts brush up against me. More people enter, and we're slowly getting pushed deeper in. For a moment I get cut off from Henry by a throng of grinding people. Then a hand settles on my waist. "It's me," he shouts against the music.

I turn and am pushed too tight against his chest as more people struggle around us to get to the bar. His hands splay out across my lower and upper back.

The smell of alcohol, the music so loud it drowns out my thoughts, the people pressing too close around us—all of it reminds me of the last time we kissed. The fatal mistake in our already strained friendship.

I tilt my head up to look at him, and he's already staring down at me—lips parted, eyes conflicted, and I know we're reliving the same memory.

It was just over a year ago. Henry's grandmother was already really sick, and Bailey and I had teamed up and convinced him to get out of the house for a little bit—go to a small party at a friend's house that ended up a little wilder than we planned.

It seemed like it was helping, and when Bailey had to leave to make curfew, Henry and I stayed. We danced with everyone else, and if we got a little closer than usual, so what? I missed the way we casually touched each other before—an absentminded hand on the shoulder, legs brushing from sitting too close, a squeeze of a hand. We were best friends. It didn't *have* to mean anything.

But then I saw the tears rolling down his face, and I didn't think—I reached up and brushed them away, and when my hands stayed on his face, he didn't protest or stop me, so I pulled his face down closer to mine, and when I kissed him, he kissed me back, and it wasn't the soft peck we shared before—it was years of pent-up feelings. At least for me. It felt right and wrong and confusing, and then he pulled my hands away from his face and stepped back.

I still remember his expression perfectly: an odd mix of longing and confusion, but also disgust.

I'm sure we both thought about Bailey. Bailey, who was my friend too.

He turned and ran, and I didn't follow him the way he followed me five years before.

I hated myself a little too much.

And maybe if I'd apologized, it would have been okay. But his grandma died a few days later, and I didn't know how to bring it up but also couldn't pretend it didn't happen either. Plus, a ton of our mutual friends saw it, but they waited until after the funeral to tell Bailey. And everyone turned on me—not that I didn't deserve it. I kissed him. Henry got a pass—he was grieving and confused. Bailey still dumped him, though. And for a second I thought he'd reach out, but too much damage had been done.

But here we are, and all the damage between us feels electrified, like we could shape it into something else.

But that's not what I'm here for.

I look down, even though it smashes my nose into Henry's chest. When I look back up, he's scanning the crowd.

"I say we go up," he says.

I nod. He weaves us through the crowd, arms still tight around me until we get to one of the twin staircases framing the entrance that lead to a balcony surrounding the entire dance floor below. A velvet rope blocks the stairs along with a burly gentleman flaunting a receding hairline.

"I'm really sick of all the roped-off stairs in this town," I mutter to myself. To the man I say, "How do I get up there?"

"Invitation."

I frown. It's like I'm already a vampire, and I can't get invited in anywhere.

"How do we get one of those?" Henry asks.

"If you're asking that, then you don't have one."

"Wait." I break away from Henry, who seems to have forgotten how tightly he's holding onto me, so I can dig into my purse and find what I'm looking for. I hold out my white card with the address, grinning when he begrudgingly unlatches the rope and waves us through as I tuck the card back in my bag.

"Thank you, kind sir." I smile at him but get nothing. Not even a flicker of annoyance.

"Not you," he says, clicking the rope back in place as Henry tries to follow.

"Hey," I say.

"One card, one person."

"Can't I just loan him mine?" I ask.

The man doesn't even look at me, so I guess that's a no.

Henry's fingers wrap around my elbow. "I don't like you going alone."

An unexpected rush of warmth hits me. He worries about me. It's clear now in the way his eyes shift up the stairs toward whatever I'll find up there and then back to me. It was clear earlier when he found me after I'd disappeared, chasing after Carter. But I don't need his worry holding me down. The weight of his fingers becomes too much, and I pull away.

"I don't remember needing your permission." My stomach clenches as I say the words, but I turn without waiting for his reaction and take the dark wooden stairs two at a time. Henry calls my name at least once, but I don't look back.

When I reach the top, my white kitten heels sink into plush red. If the downstairs is like any other rowdy club in a big city, the upstairs is like an old-fashioned English mansion, at least how I imagine one. The bright strobe lights don't reach up here. Dim light comes from stained-glass wall sconces that cast dull patterns on the deep blue wall behind. People lounge on burgundy velvet sofas and chairs gathered around gleaming mahogany coffee tables.

The first group I pass sneers at me in my sundress, which feels suddenly childish. I don't fit with their black-on-black attire and slick hair. But I don't care. I raise my chin and keep going. I don't stop until I reach the other end of the balcony—the part that curves around the back of the club. This section boasts a velvet couch with a huge wooden frame, the back so high a giant could sit there and rest their head. Multiple people lounge on it and in the chairs artfully strewn around.

My blond maybe-vampire leans against the elaborately carved arm on the far side of the couch. I walk up and stop by a chair that holds a man with a woman draped in his lap. His head is at her neck, teeth probably nibbling. I stare, but with her long curtain of hair, I can't tell if he's kissing her or drinking from her. But her eyes are closed, and the arm she has draped across his shoulders seems a little too limp.

Nobody notices me. I study them: their expensive clothes, the way their bodies relax across the furniture like they own everything that ever existed, the boredom tugging at their faces. Part of me longs to draw them and all their dark shadows. I could capture their essence with charcoal alone—no color. Carter leans forward and picks up a glass of wine from the table, slowly raising it to his lips. The liquid moves sluggishly down the glass and into his mouth. Too thick to be wine.

I try not to shudder—that could be me one day. I'll cope with it when I need to.

I wish I could think of a way to make a good impression. I'm not sure what that looks like, though. How do you introduce yourself to a possible den of vampires?

"Hi," I say.

The guy in the center of the couch, who had been leaning forward and watching the throbbing mass of people below us, turns and narrows his eyes. He's undeniably handsome, with warm brown skin and black hair hanging in loose curls down to his chin. His nose is large and hooked and gives him a sharpness only softened with his wide, heavily lashed eyes. His age is hard to guess—he appears my age or a few years older, but he could be hundreds of years older if he's immortal.

"Who are you?" His deep voice gets everyone else to turn their focus on me—except the woman in the man's lap, who I'm hoping is asleep. The man pulls himself free of her though, licking his lips as he takes me in.

I swallow, overly aware of the pulse in my neck.

116

Carter's eyes widen as he finally sees me. "I didn't think you'd come."

"I'm full of surprises."

Carter smirks. The one beside him, the guy everyone else seems to watch, stares at me with his dark-brown eyes. The leader. I get the sense he's taking in every inch of me even though he appears disinterested. He swallows some of the liquid from the wineglass he's holding, and when he lowers it, a faint smile graces his lips, stained red from his wine or whatever else he's drinking.

"What did you do now, Carter?"

Carter glares for a moment before he composes himself. "I thought you might like her."

I really don't like his tone.

"Oh?" the handsome man says, placing his glass on the table.

I fist my hands into my skirt. I wish Henry were here.

"Come around this way, then." He beckons me.

As I walk around to stand in front of the table, I take in each cup—all with the same thick, matching liquid. A few bottles of open red wine sit in the center of the table, but Mom loves red wine, and I've never seen her drink anything as thick as what's in those glasses. I clench my hands tight enough that I'm sure the eyelet print will be ingrained on my palms forever. But this is what I wanted—proof. So far I've got two on my list: out at night and drinking what I assume is blood. My stomach turns at the thought of taking a sip to confirm that last one without a shadow of a doubt, but if I get the chance, I will.

"She's not his type, Carter." A man with dark-brown skin

and a shaved head leans forward to shoot Carter a condescending look, then straightens his midnight-green velvet bowtie and relaxes with his own glass of red liquid.

"What do you know, Marcus?" Carter stretches back in his chair and swirls his drink, the blood sticking to the sides and then slowly pooling at the bottom of the glass.

I fight a gag. I need to stop thinking about the blood.

"She's a marshmallow," says a woman with black braids that reach her waist. "Look at her dress."

I shoot her a glare, and she catches it with a smile. She's wearing white too, but where my dress flares, hers clings. Her shimmering gold lipstick even gives her a pop of life I don't have, which is truly unfair if she's undead.

The leader rubs his chin.

I need to do something, anything, to regain control of this situation.

I unclench my aching fingers and reach across the table, offering my hand to him. "I'm Victoria."

He takes my hand immediately, his long fingers cradling mine with a gentleness I don't expect. He stands and bends over, glancing up through thick lashes. "May I?" he asks.

I give a nod that probably looks a little like an involuntary twitch. His hands are cold, which I anticipate, but his lips are warm when they graze my knuckles. When he rises, he keeps my hand. I let him. Half because I need him to like me and half because I don't mind the feel of his fingers beneath mine.

They ground me in the moment. Otherwise, I might believe I'd stepped into a movie scene or one of my dreams that always border on nightmares.

"Lovely name," he says. "I'm Nicholas."

We stand for a second, and I'm not sure what I'm supposed to say or do, but everyone seems to be waiting on me.

I catch Carter's eye, and he cocks his head like a cat watching a wounded animal and deciding if it's still worth playing with or if it needs to be put down. That's what I am in this scenario—a mouse.

Be entertaining or die.

"Are you going to ask me to dance or just stand there holding my hand?" I ask Nicholas.

Carter lets out a sharp, delighted laugh.

Nicholas's eyes widen slightly. Good. I've surprised him, and most people love surprises. Vampires even more so. Eternity would get monotonous otherwise.

His answering chuckle is low and throaty. "I never say no to a beautiful woman."

Heat races from my chest to my neck to my cheeks. Hopefully, the dim, reddish glow from the sconces covers it.

He walks around the table without letting go of me and leads me down the stairs and into the throng of bodies. Somehow, they part for him, maybe from the instinctual shying away from a predator, or maybe from his commanding presence. He carries himself like a king, and I drift behind in his wake, which I can't have. I need to be on equal footing. Need them to part for me, too. I let go of his hand and grab his arm instead, pressing up against his side as I make the crowd bend to my will.

It's a stark difference to struggling through with Henry. I already feel more powerful.

I fight the urge to search for Henry in the crowd. I hope he's not watching.

I catch Nicholas glancing down at me.

"What?"

He shrugs, shifting his biceps beneath my fingers. "Impressive."

And then, when we reach the middle of the mass, he pulls me into him, grasping the center of my waist. My hands instinctively land on his chest like I'm one second shy of pushing him away or latching on and pulling him closer. We move together, my body embracing the sharp beat and his hands holding me. His touch is simpler than Henry's—no complicated history, only this moment. When the song shifts and slows, he spins me around so my back presses against his chest. I feel every shift of him behind me. His fingers spread across my belly, and though his hands felt icy before, my skin flares hot beneath them.

I fall into the heat until one hand trails up my arm, drifting across my bare collarbone and trailing gently across the front of my neck. Suddenly I'm the naive girl in every bad vampire movie—the girl Dad and I would yell at to get out of there before it's too late, and then we'd laugh at her inevitable demise.

I never understood why they didn't come to their senses and run before their throats got ripped open.

Now I do.

I shiver from the heat. The music swallows me and spits me out again until I'm nothing but another human vibrating to the pulse in the beats, mind completely, blissfully empty.

His head bends down to mine, his hair brushing my cheek. "Tell me what you want."

To keep forgetting, to stay like this in a haze of touch. That's why the victims so rarely run. It's not about feeling at all. It's about *not* feeling.

"To be like you," I say.

His hand tightens ever so slightly on my neck. "Do you know what that means?"

"Yes. I want it." And in that moment, I'm not thinking about my father at all. I'm thinking about myself dressed in black leather like Selene, able to stop any threat against my family. I'm thinking about being eternally gorgeous and fierce and always in control—my own romanticized version of vampires with none of the horror. I'm thinking about how Nicholas's cold fingers against my warm throat makes me want more of him. I let myself sink into that empty, emotionless want and spin to face him. His hand slides from my stomach to my back without losing pressure, and I end up with my face against his chest and his other arm pressed tightly between us because he still hasn't let go of my throat. My pulse rages under his thumb, but not from fear.

It is free to beat without consequences in this dark club where nobody can see me. An addictive feeling for a girl whose heart's been pumping lead for months.

My fingers mindlessly count his ribs.

Perhaps being a vampire gives you the power to seduce anyone, even someone who should be thinking about other things. Norse mythology mentions mind control as one of their powers, but I know my mind's still mine—it just wants to forget for one second, and focusing on all my quivering physical senses lets me.

And then Ariana Grande sings a line about having no tears left to cry, and it breaks through my heat and turns my skin cold. I stop moving, and he stops the second after I do. His hand leaves my throat and pulls my chin up with one finger.

What kind of daughter am I that I can forget about my purpose here and get distracted in the arms of a handsome guy? Not a great one.

My emotions, locked safely in my well, begin to spill over, and a deep, sorrowful blue leaks through me.

He sees it as he searches every inch of my face.

"I can't give you what you want."

"Why?" My voice cracks.

"It's not right for you."

He lets go of me and pulls away.

I latch onto his sleeve. "Please help me."

"I can't."

I don't know when he called them over, but the next thing I

know, one of the bouncers is guiding me to the door, and I'm out on the street, disoriented and alone.

No. Not alone. I spot Henry leaning against the building where the line of waiting people ends.

My stomach flips. How much of that did he see? I didn't just forget about Dad—I forgot Henry and the way his hands felt pressed into my back. His fingers did not make me lose myself like Nicholas's. They made me feel too much—all the past and all the future I thought we'd have together eventually. The future I'm trying to change.

I walk cautiously over to him. He doesn't look at me, so he saw enough.

"Hey."

"Hey," he says, scratching the side of his head, glancing down at me and then away again. I wipe at my dress like shame can leave a stain, and the movement makes me angry.

I'm allowed to feel ashamed at myself for forgetting about my dad, but Henry certainly doesn't get to feel it for me. I bite my tongue to keep myself from yelling at him.

"I found them," I say instead. "They're real."

Henry spares me a condescending look I want to smack off his face.

"I'm not kidding."

"Right," he says. "So you got all their secrets, did you?"

"I got kicked out."

He taps his foot against the pavement.

"I need to get back in, but I can't go back as myself—the bouncers know me now."

Henry pulls himself off the wall so he can stand and face me. Folding his arms across his chest, he says, "It's getting pretty late, and I'm tired."

"I have to do this tonight. Who knows where they'll be tomorrow."

"Well, it looked to me like you could handle yourself. I'm not sure you need me at all."

A judgmental silence stretches between us as fresh hurts pile onto old ones.

"Fine," I say, brushing past him and moving down the street. He doesn't follow.

I need a new look. Something that says I'm a creature of the night and can spend an eternity in clubs, pulsing to the music and never caring about anything again. Turns out, most clothing stores close before ten, but lingerie stores tend to get a nighttime clientele.

When I strut back toward the table of vamps at 2:00 a.m., I wear a black lace top with thin, solid triangles covering my boobs, but see-through lace is the only thing covering my stomach. It's tucked into a short, white pleather miniskirt. I pulled my hair back from my face in a tight, high bun, rimmed my eyes in black, and covered my lips in red.

Who knew the power of an outfit? As I glide through the club,

I hold my head higher and my shoulders squarer. I'm not even a vampire, but I feel like I could break anyone with a single look.

Carter actually cracks up when he spots me. "Look at this. I win."

Everyone swivels around to stare. Nicholas raises his brows and sips his wine as if on a scale of surprises, I'm about a two.

The girl with the long, gorgeous braids eases out of her chair and somehow glides toward me in her six-inch gold stilettos. She holds out her hand and gives me a sly smile. "I'm Daniella, and you just got interesting."

"Um, thanks." I smile and strut back with her in my equally high silver pumps. I may prefer flaring sundresses, but I am no stranger to rocking a towering heel.

Marcus looks bored as ever.

I swagger over and stand across the table from Nicholas. "Well?"

"Well what?" He rolls the blood-red liquid in his glass, an uninterested movement, but I'm not blind to the way his gaze keeps catching on my bare thighs.

"Will you reconsider?"

He draws out the silence with a slow sip. Finally, he sets it on the table. "Leave us," he says to nobody in particular. Carter and Daniella share a quick look and stroll away without a word, but Carter winks as he brushes by me. Marcus grumbles under his breath but leaves as well.

When we're alone, Nicholas gestures to the empty space beside him. I force my feet to move without hesitation even though the common sense inside of me tries to turn them to lead. Sitting, I tug at my skirt, but it wasn't really meant for this position, and the cool velvet cushions tickle the backs of my thighs. I cross my legs and make one more attempt to drag it down. It refuses to compromise.

"Comfortable?" Nicholas asks. A trace of amusement tugs at his lips. He knows I'm not.

"Never been better."

He smirks.

"Will you change your mind now?" I reach toward the table, casually lifting the wineglass Carter abandoned like it's no big deal. I lift it, bracing myself.

His fingers close around mine, guiding the cup back to the table but not before I get a faint whiff of something coppery.

He lets go of me and leans back as if I didn't just try something. "It was never about how you looked." He searches my face, and I don't know what he finds there under my black-rimmed eyes and blood-toned lips, but his eyes narrow. "Why do you want to be a vampire?"

My heart pounds at the admission coupled with the smell of copper still lingering in my nostrils. I can't believe he said the word. He must plan to kill me—one way or the other. I swallow, trying to get my dry mouth to work. "I told you. I want to live forever."

"I don't believe you. You're too sad—a change of clothes can't cover up the kind of sadness you carry in your bones. I know that kind of sadness. I've danced with it before." His voice suggests he still knows it. "People who know that kind of sadness exists in the world never really want to live forever, and if they do, they're fools. Are you a fool, Victoria?"

He's right, of course. I *don't* want to live forever with all the pain and sorrow simmering inside me. Containing it is a constant, exhausting battle I keep losing, but that's the point. All my pain can be linked back to one thing: death. If Dad and I escape it forever, I won't be sad. I'll escape. But I don't know how to explain that to him without laying myself bare.

"Can't vampires turn off their emotions?"

"You've seen too many movies." His voice is tired. He rests his head against the back of the couch and closes his eyes. "So that's what you really want. That I can believe, but I can't give it to you."

"No." I scramble to regain control. I've let him see too much of me. "I want to live." I dive through my well of sorrow and try to find the part of me that once loved living. I know it's there somewhere even if I don't feel it anymore. I turn away so he can't see all the pain I have to dig through to find a sliver of joy to share with him.

"I want to stand in the moonlight on a summer night. I want the bite of fall to nip at me through my sweaters. I want to dance with the snow under a full moon. I want the spring breeze to blow my skirt so hard I have to keep it down with my hands. And I want to live those moments forever."

My voice shakes at the end, and I have to swallow hard to keep the aching sadness inside of me from bubbling up and drowning out my words with sobs. Because that's the problem with emotions: It's all or nothing. You can't pick and choose which ones you want to feel.

His eyes snap open and stare into mine for a moment.

"Prove it to me," he says.

"How?" How do you prove you love life? Especially when life has gutted you in the worst way.

He picks up his wineglass again and swirls his last sip around for a moment before downing it. Finally, his lips curve into a small smile, and he turns to me. "I'll give you a challenge—a game if you will. How long are you in town?"

"Until Tuesday morning."

He nods. "That'll work. Each day I'll present you with challenges—little things you can do to show me you enjoy life. Each time you complete a challenge to my satisfaction, I'll give you a piece of the clue that will give you what you're looking for."

"What kind of challenges?"

"Oh, I haven't decided yet." His smile turns wicked.

I want to say no. I don't have time for games, but if I need the prize, do I really have a choice?

"Deal," I say. I hold out my hand, and we shake on it. "When do I get the first challenge?"

"In the morning. Go and get some rest," he says, as if that will happen.

I reach for my bag with my phone in it. "Will you call me then?"

"Gracious, no. I don't own a phone."

I freeze with mine halfway out of my bag. "You're kidding me."

He flashes an unnaturally white smile. "I'm old-fashioned."

"How are you going to give me the challenges?"

He fishes a black leather wallet out of the back of his slacks and passes me another white card with a different address on it. "This will get you to a bookstore in the Quarter. I'll leave you a note in one of the books—you'll know which one."

"Will I?"

"Don't underestimate yourself."

"I rarely do," I retort, and push myself to my feet, even though my stomach is heavy with doubt. "You know, this would be a lot easier if you'd simply give me what I came for." And faster. Each second is one more second gone from my dad's life—that's true for everyone, but you're more aware of it once someone gives you an actual deadline.

"Ah, but where would be the fun?"

"It doesn't sound like fun."

"My dear, that's exactly the attitude you need to work on." He gives me a lazy wink as he pours another glass of red for himself. "Enjoy the game."

I'm scared that if I let myself be happy for even
one moment that the world's just going to come
crashing down, and I don't know if I can survive that.
—*The Vampire Diaries*

# *Eight*

When I wake up in the morning, Henry's gone. I wonder if he's blowing off steam or if he went to the airport and found an early flight out. The last thought stings, and I tell myself I don't care, but when I spot his bag open on his bed, tension I didn't know I was carrying unwinds inside me. I'm washing off the mess of black under my eyes, which makes me look more like a zombie than a vampire, when the door creaks open.

He comes in and leans against the doorjamb of the bathroom, holding two paper coffee cups.

He watches me struggling to remove the black layer of makeup under my right eye.

"Are you trying out for *The Walking Dead*?"

Normally I'd laugh, but I spare him only a quick glance before going back to rubbing the delicate skin under my eye. I'm going to give myself a real black eye trying to get this off.

He shuffles, awkwardly straightening and then leaning back against the door again.

"I'm sorry about last night. I had no right to treat you like that."

I glance at him in the mirror. "Continue."

"I saw you with him and I got, I don't know . . . worried, I guess." He stares up at the light fixture above my head, jaw clenching and unclenching. "But you don't want me to worry about you, right? It's not my place."

He meets my eyes in the mirror. His question hangs between us. Of course a friend can worry about another friend, but his worry holds something else, something heavier and yet fragile, and what I say next might break it.

"Right." My hand tremors ever so slightly as I casually dab at my eye again. "No need to worry about me." I push down the twinge of regret trying to bloom.

I try not to look at Henry's face, but I still catch the brief fall before he smooths out his expression. Perhaps I'm not the only one capable of hiding my emotions.

"Forgive me?" His question is too light, too cheery.

I match his tone. "Depends on what you've got in those cups."

His face relaxes. "Café au lait."

"Done." I turn around and lean against the sink, holding out my hand.

The creamy coffee cuts through my haze, and I spend the next fifteen minutes updating Henry on the conversation I had with Nicholas and what we have to do now. All the while pretending nothing significant happened between us.

"I don't like it," he says when I finish.

"I'm not asking you to."

"He's probably just some creep messing with you."

I glare. The thought has crossed my mind, but the thick red liquid in their cups? I'm sure I smelled a whiff of blood, and that's pretty elaborate for "just some creep."

Henry holds up his hands. "But I'm here to support you."

"Good," I say, but I'm wary. I don't need to worry about Henry's emotions when I'm busy wrangling my own. "Now get out so I can change."

Before we leave, I call Mom. Scheduled check-ins were part of the deal. I wanted to call Dad, but she convinced me to call her in case he's asleep.

She answers on the first ring. "Are you safe?"

Mom's not big on chitchat.

"Yeah. I'm fine. Henry's here. We're both fine." I glance at Henry, watching me from the couch. "Is Dad awake?"

"Let me check." Mom goes silent, and I hear a door open on her end. "I'm sorry. He's asleep."

"Oh. Okay."

"Are you having fun?" she asks.

I know she wants me to say yes—that I'm suddenly myself again out here, that the physical distance somehow makes everything okay—but I can't. I can't even answer.

"Find anyone cute dressed in leather with too-sharp teeth?" There's a forced, joking lightness to her tone. I can't tell if she's making fun of me or trying to be like Dad. It's a Dad joke, and I don't want it. I have Dad for that.

"Stop," I say.

It's her turn to go quiet. We sit there for a few awkward seconds before she sighs, like she's giving up on something she didn't feel like doing anyway.

"You should call your sister," she says. "She needs someone to talk to."

"I thought she had you."

More silence. "You have me too," she says in her firm, no-nonsense voice. No forced lightness. No jokes. This is my mom talking, and she means what she says.

My chest tightens with longing, but I don't know how to take what she's offering.

I've been quiet for much longer than I meant to be.

"Please call Jessica," she says again.

Back to Jessica.

"Sure," I say, and end the call, but I don't plan on following through. I can't handle Jessica's grief when I'm trying to avoid grief altogether. I can't explain to her why she doesn't need to mourn Dad. She'd never believe me.

"You okay?" Henry asks.

"Yeah." I pull the door open. "Let's go."


We find the faded yellow bookstore with sea-green shutters down a quiet side street where nobody ventures at eight in the morning. The damp from the nightly thunderstorms still clings to everything, including my skin. Maybe Dad and I would get used to it if we lived here, but then again, we wouldn't be out in the daylight. I get the urge to stop right here and paint the staggering, colorful skyline of the city against the perfect blue sky. I'll miss the blue sky. The sun. But I'd miss Dad more.

When we push through the weather-worn blue door, an elderly woman glances up from a desk in the center of the room and sets the yellow teacup she was about to sip back on the saucer.

"Oh my," she says, standing and straightening her tan pantsuit. "I usually don't get customers this early. Can I help you find anything in particular?"

I glance around at the floor-to-ceiling bookshelves. This looks more like the library of an incredibly rich individual than a bookstore.

"We're just looking." I smile brightly. Asking the elderly lady running the shop if she's seen any vampires or, if not, what books they might like seems like a bad idea. From what I've read, locals will shut down immediately if they think you're fishing around for things you've got no business looking for. Or worse, they'll feed you stories that leave you chasing tourist traps like "secret" vampire bars.

Henry nudges my arm like he wants me to tell her why we're there.

I shake my head slightly.

"Okay then. I'll be here with my morning tea and a little Dickinson."

"Thank you, ma'am," Henry says as we move to the back of the shop. When we're out of earshot, he says, "Do you have any idea what we're looking for?"

"Yeah—a book."

"You could have asked her if someone fitting his description came in here before us."

"I didn't want to make her suspicious if she's not in on this. We may be able to get information out of her if we do it the right way."

He sighs. "Fair enough."

"Start looking for anything vampire related."

Twenty minutes later I've checked every Anne Rice book in the place and several vampire histories, and of course, good old Bram Stoker.

Henry's buried in the graphic novel section because, as he said, you never know what a vamp might like.

I head for a small room off the side of the main area, where I identify a large amount of poetry, which seems like something a person who lives forever would be into. Some poems might take an eternity to understand, but I've always had a soft spot for them. The precision with which poets use words reminds me of drawing.

I scan Lord Byron and Dickinson mostly because they're the only ones I recognize, and then spot a small, unassuming volume with a simple brown cover titled *Poems for the Dead and the Barely Living*. My heart speeds as my fingers close around the cover.

I flip through the pages and land on one with a small slip of paper tucked between.

I unfold the note and read Nicholas's elegant script.

Nobody writes like this anymore, so I chalk that up to one more piece of proof he's legit.

*My lovely Victoria,*

*I am pleased you've accepted my challenge. This book will be our main form of communication and the source of all your clues. Each task I assign you will be designed to bring a little excitement and joy into your life, two things you'll need in abundance if you truly wish to live forever. Your first task will be:*

*Eat beignets at Café Du Monde while dressed in all black.*

*This may sound simple, but I take my joy seriously. Take a picture of yourself to prove you've completed the task and return it to this book. Each time you're successful, I'll leave you with a word or two underlined in one of my favorite poems. Collect all the words, say the correct phrase to me, and I will give you what you desire. Fail, and you'll never see me again.*

*Sincerely,*

*Nicholas*

*P.S. The shopkeeper has a gift for you. Show her this note.*

This sounds easy enough except for one small problem: I don't own a lot of black clothing. It doesn't go well with pink, which I look best in. Maybe he assumed anyone looking for vampires already owned a wardrobe worthy of Selene, but I've always been more a fan of Buffy's style. This means one more thing to buy, and while I saved up over the years thanks to my rich grandparents who are always traveling and try to make up for that with money, my funds aren't unlimited, and the getup I wore last night cost me a nice chunk of what I budgeted.

I'm about to close the book and place it back on the shelf when a poem catches my eye. A scribble of writing above the poem says *To get you started*. The poem itself has three words underlined.

**Alone**

From childhood's hour I have not been
As others were—I have not seen
As others saw—I could not bring
My <u>passions</u> from a common spring—
From the same source I have not taken
My <u>sorrow</u>—I could not awaken
My heart to joy at the same tone—
And all I lov'd—*I* lov'd alone—
*Then*—in my childhood— in the dawn
Of a most stormy life—was drawn
From ev'ry depth of good and ill

The <u>mystery</u> which binds me still—
From the torrent, or the fountain—
From the red cliff of the mountain—
From the sun that 'round me roll'd
In its autumn tint of gold—
From the lightning in the sky
As it pass'd me flying by—
From the thunder, and the storm—
And the cloud that took the form
(When the rest of Heaven was blue)
Of a demon in my view—
　　—Edgar Allan Poe

The poem sends a small shiver across my skin. I'm not sure who the poem's supposed to be about—me or Nicholas—but the line that says he can't awaken his heart to joy sticks out to me. Is this a warning? Nicholas wants me to prove I am not the empty, soulless creature in the poem.

But I wasn't always like this. Once upon a time, I laughed easily, felt pain easily—knowing it was only temporary and joy waited for me around every corner. I can pretend to be that person again.

I grab my phone out of my pocket and take a picture of the poem.

Then I'm on the move, heading to the front of the store, calling a little too loudly for Henry to follow, but who cares?

According to my note, the shopkeeper is in on this.

She smiles slyly when I approach with the note.

"I thought you might be her," she says with a wink. Setting her teacup down with a *clink*, she reaches below her desk and brings out two boxes wrapped in shiny white paper with black satin bows. One's a perfect square and the other's a rectangular garment box.

"A little much," Henry says.

"He does like to go overboard," the woman says.

"You know Nicholas well?" I ask.

She smiles. "I'm Ruth."

"Victoria," I answer.

"I know."

"Is Nicholas who he says he is?" No point in being subtle. She knows something, even if she doesn't know he's a vampire.

She pushes the gifts toward me. "Open them. I do so love presents."

Could she be compelled to not answer? It's not high on my list of potential vampire traits, but it's still possible. I give her a hard look, and she winks. Definitely not compelled—she enjoys this.

The smooth satin ribbon slips through my fingers like a dream as I unwrap it. I open the square box and remove a baby-blue Polaroid camera. I hadn't even thought about how I would deliver the pictures, but apparently Nicholas did. I can't help but wonder how he planned all this in one night, but I push the thought aside as I unwrap the second box and find a pair of black shorts and a black tank.

"Wow," Henry says, handing me back the note I'd given him to read. "At least he's thorough."

"Indeed," Ruth chimes in. She points one knobby finger toward the back of the bookstore. "You'll find a bathroom there to change in." She claps her hands together. "This is so exciting."

Dressed in my black denim shorts and my new black tank top that's a tiny bit saggy in the armpits, I arrive at the famous Café Du Monde with Henry, who has more bounce to his step than usual.

I eye him cynically.

"What? We've been in New Orleans for forty-eight hours, and we're finally going to experience some of it. We might even have some fun with this."

"We're not here to have fun," I say, more for myself than for him. I had *something* last night—maybe not fun exactly, but I lost control and forgot why I came here. I almost slide back into my guilt for allowing myself one blissful moment, but I don't. After all, I'm one step closer to getting what I want.

"But." Henry holds up a finger. "Fun's been ordered." His face darkens. "Although I don't like that he's ordering us around."

"He's just ordering me, really. How would he know about you?"

Henry shrugs, scratching the back of his neck. "I don't know. I guess I'm not important."

"You're important to me." The words sound cheap even though I mean them.

"Right." He stares up at the green-and-white-striped canopy of the café. Tables full of happy, smiling people sit underneath, and a line winds around the front.

"Let's do this." I head toward the back of the line.

"That's the spirit."

I ignore his sarcasm. I can pretend to be happy for a moment if it means eternal happiness with Dad. I'll smile until my cheeks pop if it gets me what I want.

A thirty-minute wait later, we're sitting on the outdoor patio with fifty other people. Sugar lingers in the air. Every breath tastes sweet. People laugh and chatter, and there's no room here for anything but pure joy.

My chest tightens, but I focus on Henry's untroubled face and the way his eyes dart around, taking everything in. He sucks in a deep breath, and his smile widens. I mimic his expression as the waiter appears and sets three square pastries in front of me, each one covered in a mound—no, a *mountain*—of powdered sugar.

Henry rubs his hands together. I remember him doing the exact same move when we were kids and someone brought doughnuts to Bible class.

"I might not hate this guy," he says.

His excitement softens me. I let go of some of my lingering tension.

"You first," I say.

"Together." He picks one up and bites his lower lip as if he's stopping himself from diving right in.

"Fine." Doing something fun together doesn't make it any easier. Perhaps it makes it harder. It makes me want to be the carefree kid I was before. Still, I pick up one of my beignets, balancing the pile of sugar creating the two-inch mountain on top.

"One, two, three," he says, and closes his mouth over it. His eyes widen as he chews, and he gestures for me to take a bite. When he pulls his beignet away from his mouth, a trail of powdered sugar sticks to his upper lip.

I snort and send my powdered sugar flying, covering the table and my shorts.

Which makes Henry crack up. A spray of delicious white dust billows off his pastry and into my face. I cough as I inhale, and Henry laughs harder.

"Not funny," I choke out, but he only gets louder, and pretty soon my coughing morphs into a hard, deep laugh that burns the muscles of my stomach. Eventually, I gulp a breath, lick sugar from my lips, and brush at my black clothes now covered in white.

"Serves you right," Henry says.

"Hey, you never said to go on three."

"Try it." He waves his bald beignet at my bald beignet. At least it will be easier to eat without the loads of sugar. I bite into it, thicker than a doughnut and a little more fried. The pastry itself isn't sweet and perfectly complements the heavy dose of powdered sugar. I cannot lie—it's glorious. We fall into a pattern of sweet silence. So easy—too easy.

Henry finishes his first and then watches me chew with his arms folded across the table. "Remember that time my mom bought us a bag of powdered doughnuts and you ate all of them while I was in the kitchen getting milk?" he asks.

"No way. That's a gross exaggeration."

"You looked an awful lot like you do now." His long arm stretches easily across the table and brushes uselessly at some of the powder on my shoulders.

My all-black attire looks like I lost a fight with a bag of those powdered doughnuts. A little ache burrows into the moment, but I don't close myself off. The trade feels okay because Henry is laughing, and I love the boyishness in it. It's like we're kids and anything that happened past that point doesn't exist.

"Take a picture so you can stop staring," I say, digging the camera out of my purse and handing it to him. Our fingers touch, and if this were a real date, I'd meet his eyes and we'd share an awkward moment acknowledging we maybe liked it, but instead, I stare down at my plate and reach for my last sad bite of pastry that doesn't even have much sugar on it.

Henry takes the shot as I pop it in my mouth, surprised it still tastes good cold and sugarless.

"That should do the trick." He hands me the still undeveloped picture. "I think I caught a piece of the old you."

The old me—the me before my dad got cancer—who laughed

at silly things and never thought beyond the moment. The old me shouldn't be possible.

Last night was one thing—I got lost in feeling nothing. But this easy happiness with Henry feels like betrayal. It's just as bad as grieving while he's still alive.

The sweetness of my last bite turns heavy in my belly, weighing me down until I fear the chair won't be able to hold me any longer, and I welcome it. Being sick is such a concrete desire that it overrides my guilt and, most importantly, any lingering happiness.

Henry wipes his fingers on his napkin one at a time. "I could go for another three."

"I'm going to puke."

"Dang," he says, pushing his chair back and coming to my side. With one arm wrapped tightly around me, he weaves us through the tables to the open sidewalk. I bend at the waist and take in several deep breaths while Henry keeps a hand on my back.

"Can I get you anything? A water? Coke?"

I shake my head. He believes my sickness is from the sugar alone, and I don't correct him.

I stand up straight again, nausea in check. Everything else inside me roils unchecked and dangerously close to bursting.

The smell of fresh, hot dough and sugar makes my throat burn. Dad's probably waking up and eating scrambled eggs if he's up for it—sometimes he only eats half an apple. Sometimes he eats nothing at all.

"It's okay to cry," Henry says.

His words pull me back, away from my dad, to this uneven sidewalk.

"What?" I shake myself, blinking away the sting in my eyes.

Henry bites his lip. His hands tighten on my shoulders, and I'm not sure if it's to comfort me or to steady himself—he doesn't look totally in control either. "When my grandma died, my mom did the same thing you're doing. She never cried. Not a single time that I saw anyway, and now she walks around like all those unshed tears are weighing her down." He looks away and takes a deep breath before turning back to me. "At first I thought she was strong for not crying. But I don't know, Victoria. I think she'd be better now if she had let everything out then."

The darkest blue, a mixture of pity and sadness for my friend, trickles out, and then an angry red follows, chasing away the sadness and leaving me a confused, hazy purple. I hurt for him, but I don't need someone to tell me how to feel.

Crying won't help. Nobody ever got anything done while crying—and this is not the same. My Dad's alive, even if he barely looks like it.

I step backward, out of his grip. "I'm not your mom. I don't need you to save me from her mistakes. I'm fine. I can do this."

Henry cringes, and I soften my expression, reaching for his hand.

"I can do this if you're with me," I say. I could do it alone if I had to, but friends make each other feel needed.

145

On the way back to the bookstore, Henry keeps glancing at my powder-drenched black clothes and chuckling until he catches my mood and turns silent. He doesn't ask me if I'm okay, and I appreciate him for it. It's good to be with someone who knows what not to ask.

When we get back to the bookstore, more people are browsing the shelves, and Ruth is helping another customer, but she turns in our direction and winks as we pass by on our way to the poetry section. I nod in return.

I pull the book off the shelf and tuck the picture inside without looking at it. If Henry did catch the old me in that picture, then I don't want to see it. It will only make me feel worse.

I head to the bathroom and change, tossing the evidence of my sin in the trash and putting on my old, safe clothing.

When I come back out, Ruth is alone at her desk again, and Henry waits by the front door.

"How long until the next one?" I ask her.

"I'd give it a couple of walks around the Quarter," she says, checking her large gold watch with a cat's head decorating the center.

"But it's daylight out. How would he get here?" I lean one hand on her desk, leaning forward and lowering my voice as a few customers drift toward us. "You know, if you're leaving the notes for him, you could just hand it over now. I won't tell."

She opens a book and slowly flips through the pages. After a second, she looks up over the top of her glasses. "Oh, are you still here?"

I groan and head for the door that Henry's already pulling open.

With all the cracks in the sidewalks, walking around the French Quarter is an exercise in remaining on your feet. I like it though. The sheer concentration it takes to avoid stumbling pulls me out of my mind so I can go back to carefully feeling nothing.

I don't bother looking in any shop windows. The only thing I stop for is to put five dollars in a sleeping homeless man's cup with ANY-THING HELPS written in faded ink on the front. Henry frowns at me but doesn't say anything. Dad always kept care packages with food and money in his car in case he saw anyone in need. Mom frowned at him, too, but never asked him to stop. Dad's a person who helps anyone. He always has been. I want to be that too, but I'm sometimes a bit more selfish than he is. He definitely has more to teach me.

When I push through the bookstore door again, I'm determined to do whatever Nicholas has set out for me even if I need to fake joy and excitement to do it. Feeling it for real is too much—too risky when Dad's still sick. If this all goes wrong and I spent my dad's last days sucking down sugar and laughing until it hurt, the guilt alone will end me.

Nicholas might control the task, but I control what I feel. No more slipups.

Ruth's chowing down on a bowl of something that smells spicy and delicious when we come in.

Henry stops and takes a dramatic breath. "That smells amazing. What is that?"

My mouth waters too, but I plow through to the poetry

147

section, find my book, and pull it off the shelf as they chatter out front.

The picture's gone, replaced by another note next to a marked-up poem. I take a picture of the poem with my phone.

**Because I could not stop for Death**
Because I could not <u>stop</u> for <u>Death</u>,
He kindly stopped for me;
The carriage held but just ourselves
And <u>Immortality</u>.

We slowly drove, he knew no haste,
And I had put away
My labor, and my leisure too,
For his civility.

We passed the school where children played,
Their lessons scarcely done;
We passed the fields of gazing grain,
We passed the <u>setting sun</u>.

We paused before a house that seemed
A swelling of the ground;
The roof was scarcely visible,
The cornice but a mound.

Since then 'tis centuries; but each
Feels shorter than the day
I first surmised the horses' heads
Were toward <u>Eternity</u>.
—Emily Dickinson

I've read this one before in freshman English. I should have paid better attention. Then again, maybe the interpretation is obvious. Nicholas, the gentlemanly death, will stop for me and lead me toward eternity. For a moment, I close my eyes and cling to this promise. No matter what his trials entail, or how hard it is to complete them the way he wants, this will all be worth it.

I read the note, grab Henry, and say goodbye to Ruth.

"What have we got this time?" Henry asks. "Dancing to street music?"

"Um, not quite."

"What then?"

"You're not going to like it."

You do know that it's very bad luck
to cross a threshold without being invited.
—*Only Lovers Left Alive*

# Nine

Henry and I ride the St. Charles Streetcar line. It's the oldest streetcar line in Northern America. The trolley is painted puke green with red-accented windows and doors, yet somehow manages to be quaint and charming. We sit together on a small wooden bench that isn't quite comfortable for two with the window down beside us so the breeze will occasionally wipe the sweat from our faces. Of course the oldest streetcar line does not have air-conditioning. Some of the trees growing along the line need trimming and occasionally scratch along the side of the tram and make me jump back, pushing harder into Henry.

One actually comes all the way in and nips my upper arm.

"Ouch." I rub my skin a little dramatically. "Who's in charge of trimming those things?"

"I'll switch places with you," Henry says for the third time.

"It's okay. I like the window seat." And I do. The threatening trees are worth putting up with for the view. This street is full of huge mansions with grand columns and gigantic porches and balconies. Each one is unique and special in its own way. One is pure white with delicate Victorian details, another is over-the-top with columns the size of ancient tree trunks, and another is all uneven stones and curved archways.

I unfold the note, now damp with sweat, to read it one more time.

It contains an address on St. Charles Avenue with instructions below it.

*Break into this house. Steal a cross and a clove of garlic.*

I'll admit the last part is kind of funny. Breaking and entering is not.

I gulp as we pass a smaller house that's no less exquisite in its quaint storybook details, like shuttered windows painted teal and a double staircase leading up to the porch.

None of these houses look like a place you should break into. If you can afford a mansion, you can probably afford a security system or at least a big dog.

Henry runs his hand through his hair for the ninety-seventh time, bumping me with his elbow as he does. My arm will bruise if we don't arrive soon.

"At least it's not a convent." My fake cheeriness turns my voice tight and awkward.

I wait for him to laugh. He doesn't. At least I don't have to worry about feeling any kind of joy with this challenge. I wish he'd give me something though.

"You don't have to do this," I say.

"Neither do you."

"I wish that were true."

"Victoria." He turns to me, trying to get me to look straight at him, but I can tell by the way he says my name that I don't want to. I stare out the window instead. "Victoria," he tries again, but I don't take the bait. He sighs but keeps going despite my ignoring him. "Eating beignets was harmless. I didn't like him ordering you around, but it didn't cost us anything. This is different. This is . . . wrong. Who knows how far he's going to push you, and for what? You don't know anything about him."

I turn to him so I can lower my voice. "I know he drinks blood."

"You think you do. It was dark. Fake blood's easy to make."

"I smelled it." How do you fake that smell? My stomach rolls just from remembering it.

"You could have imagined it. You want this so badly." He tries to reach out for my hand, and I yank it away. Am I supposed to *kind of* want this? Like, just be here to have a good time, and if I happen to save my dad, then that would be a cool bonus?

So much for the support he promised earlier.

"Henry." This time I say *his* name in a way that makes him refuse to look at me.

He rubs his hands on his jeans, then runs his damn hand through his hair again. We've already played this conversation out three times since I read the challenge to him, and it always ends with him going silent and adjusting his hair one more time and me fuming silently beside him.

We both turn to watch a jogger running down the center of the opposite track. A tram's coming, and the woman waits an obscene amount of time before moving over. The tram never slows for a second.

"Close one," Henry says.

Maybe the joggers are making him more nervous than the task before us, but everyone runs on the tracks here, moving over only when the tram's a real threat. I admire their boldness. I'm going to need some of it.

We jerk to another stop.

"This is us," Henry says. "Are you sure you want to do this?" He sounds hopeful, like now is the time he's going to ask this and get the answer he wants.

"Of course not." I stand anyway and walk down the center aisle, and Henry thankfully follows. As we exit, I reach back and squeeze his forearm, trying to thank him, but his eyes are already drifting past me, taking in the street.

It's noon and hotter than ever. Without the breeze from the tram, my shirt sticks to my skin as we walk. Thank goodness for the large trees giving the sidewalks a heavy cover of greenery. Faded beads leftover from years of Mardi Gras parades dangle from the branches, the cheap plastic at odds with the old-world elegance of the mansions.

Henry tries to leap up and grab one but misses.

"Don't draw attention to us," I hiss.

"Right."

He straightens and walks beside me as I read the addresses.

I stop.

"No way," Henry says.

"Yep," I say.

"People who try to rob houses like these don't make it out alive."

"Or they become vampires."

"Dead either way," he counters.

No comeback to that. It *is* a kind of death, but I've only been thinking of it as a way for Dad to live. But I'm not the one dying already, so it's different for me. I am giving up what might have been a long human life. The thought freezes me for a moment. My mouth dries out, and I stare at Henry's profile as he scans the house. I thought I'd grow old with Henry. Even though we were on the outs, deep in my bones I still knew we'd come back to each other—that one day we'd be sitting on the back porch on our tenth wedding anniversary, watching our kids play the same games in the woods we used to. I'm taking all of that away from myself and maybe from him, too. Did he have the same dreams? I thought he did—before Bailey. But maybe part of him still does, and that's what keeps pushing him to try to make me doubt this. Bringing him into this was selfish.

The realization guts me.

"We're still going through with it, aren't we?" Henry asks as he continues to scan the house.

"No," I say.

He turns to me, looking surprised that I've come to my senses.

"*I* am. I want you to sit this one out."

"No way." He doesn't even look a little bit tempted. "I go where you go."

Until I actually become a vampire—he won't follow me into that.

I swallow. "Okay." My voice is weak. I don't want to push him away yet. I want more memories of him to cling to when this is finished, but I need to stop thinking about a future that doesn't belong to me anymore. I need to focus. I pull myself out of my head and stare at the house in question. It's easily one of the most impressive on the street, composed entirely of large dark-gray stones and accented with curved windows and stone arches that lead into a shadowed front porch. Multiple stone birdbaths all in varying states of decay and rusted wrought-iron lawn furniture, none of which matches, cover the front lawn. Everything about it is haphazard and ancient and suggests someone inside is too. Probably someone who never leaves the house. To make matters worse, a beat-up chain wraps around the black gate leading up the hedged walkway to the house.

It's terrifying, but at this point Nicholas could ask me to swim across the Mississippi and I would try it. Of course, knowing him, he'd ask me to do it while wearing a sequined prom dress and a tiara, all while smiling like I was crowned homecoming queen. It's that last part that kills me. I can run through the actions—even robbery. At least that's what I'm telling myself. But feeling what he wants me to feel is a different story.

"Okay, then." Henry starts walking, and I have to jog to catch up with him.

"Where are you going?"

"We can't just climb over the fence on a busy road."

Well, *I* was going to, but instead, I follow him down a street running along the side of the house. Henry stops at another, smaller black gate, casually leans his arm over the top, and unlatches it from the other side. I guess it pays to have long, gangly arms. I almost feel bad for teasing him about them as a kid. Almost.

He holds the gate open. "My lady." His face is grim, like a knight walking me to my beheading, not the hero saving the day.

I step onto a narrow brick path leading up to the back of the house. The backyard mirrors the front but with dilapidated garden creatures and overgrown weeds. You'd think with a house this size you'd spring for a gardener. I tiptoe past a bunny with no ears, what I'm guessing is a cat with no head, and several of those butterflies on poles missing one or both wings.

"This is where garden decor comes to die," I whisper to Henry.

"Yeah, hopefully it's not where *we* come to die."

I cringe.

We stop at the base of the back deck.

"How do you want to play this?" he asks.

I shrug. "Try the back door?"

He shakes his head like this is an outlandish idea, but we creep up the broken stones of the staircase, and Henry reaches for the burgundy back door at the same time I do.

"Let me go first," I whisper.

His hand brushes past mine and closes in on the handle. "I didn't come so you could take all the risks."

I straighten from my crouch and drop my hand to my side. He's breaking the routine we had as kids. I *did* take all the risks, and he cleaned up my cuts afterward.

"But . . ."

He holds my stare and slowly shakes his head.

I nod in return.

He takes a loud breath, and I know he's pushing himself to do this for me, whether to make up for past regrets or to try to forge something new between us, I don't know, but I reach out and place my hand on his back to let him know I'm behind him—I'll back him up.

He jumps at my touch, but then he nods to himself, and the handle creaks as it gives way in his grip. His eyes widen, and he holds a finger to his lips as if I'm going to suddenly yelp with joy.

After pushing through the door, he sticks his hand back out briefly and beckons for me to follow. I didn't expect what was inside.

Where the outside was old and ancient and worn, the inside is gleaming and bright and new. The room off the back porch appears to be a grand seating area complete with a white mantel fireplace, white bookshelves, and gleaming oak floors. The furniture is done in light, complementing blues, and everything looks very, very pricey. I follow Henry as he leads the way again, down a short hallway of closed doors and into a kitchen that again is white on white and spotless. But on the countertop sits a cheesy cookie jar—a pig holding a giant cookie with a chipped ear and faded paint. Something bubbles in a stainless-steel slow cooker next to it.

Someone lives here. I knew that already, in an abstract way, but seeing that ridiculous pig—the only thing in the house with personality—makes it real. I was the bold one when we were younger, but my plans never affected other people.

Have fun and live adventurously but never at the expense of others. Dad taught me that. He'll ask me what it cost me to become a vampire. I know he will. I just hope he's not ashamed of me for all eternity. I'll leave this part out when I tell the story, but if Henry and I *both* get arrested out here, that might be difficult.

We can't both be the bold ones.

"This is a bad plan," I say.

"No kidding," Henry murmurs, but he doesn't turn around and instead moves forward with a stealth he shouldn't be capable of with those long limbs.

"What are you doing?" I stand in the doorway, gripping the white trim and probably leaving a dozen fingerprints. I let go and pull up the hem of my shirt to try to wipe them off.

"What are *you* doing?" Henry asks.

I let go of my shirt and smooth it back out over my belly. "Getting rid of evidence."

I flush at the way his eyes linger at my navel. After a moment, he shakes himself and holds up a clove of garlic. "Next," he whispers. "We probably need a jewelry box or something for the cross." He glances around the cold, plain interior. "Doesn't look like they're the type of people to keep one hanging on the wall."

"This doesn't feel right."

Henry straightens, slipping out of stealth mode. "I think we're fine. Listen." He pauses and lets the silence in the house close around us. "They probably stepped out and left their dinner cooking."

That wasn't what I meant, but I nod. "Let's go, then. They could be back any moment."

We climb a gleaming staircase and search several sterile guestrooms until we step into one with deep-green walls and an unmade bed. There's not much in here worth noting either, but the mahogany dresser shows signs of life: a photo of a woman holding a baby, an unburned cinnamon candle, a carved wooden box, and next to it a small golden cross with a tiny ruby in the center on a chain.

The woman in the photo watches us, her black hair blowing in an endless breeze. The baby, dressed in yellow overalls, stares up at their mom's face instead of the camera. I pick it up, the silver frame cold in my hand. A cross gleams against her chest.

My stomach turns at the thought of stealing something so personal. I won't be able to lie to Dad about this. We don't lie to each other. I'm foolish if I think for one moment he'd be okay with this. I tell myself anything is worth it, but I can't shake the image of Dad telling me to do the right thing, hanging onto my shoulder like one of those creepy angel/conscience things in cartoons.

"I can't do it," I say way too loudly. I place the photo back on the dresser, making a sharp crack in the silence. "I'll go back to Nicholas. I'll tell him to give me another task."

If I can find him again. Something tells me I won't if he doesn't want me to.

I eye the necklace—why'd it have to be a cross? Dad wears a cross around his neck, tucked under his shirts—passed down from his dad and his grandfather before that. I wonder if Nicholas has me picking up these two things as a joke or if vampires really can't stand crosses and garlic. Dad could live without garlic, but he'd never give up that necklace.

I bite my lip and glance at Henry, who's watching me. His eyes squint. He runs his hand through his hair and then snatches the necklace, sliding it into his pocket without pause.

"Henry . . ."

"No. We're taking it."

Something creaks down the hall in one of the many rooms we'd yet to peek into.

Henry's eyes widen, and then he moves, grabbing my hand and yanking me back toward the bedroom door.

"Hey," a man's voice calls from the other side of the shut door.

I jump. My gut instinct yells for me to scramble backward, but Henry grips my arms. Spinning me to face him, he holds a finger to his lips.

"I thought you weren't going to be home for dinner," the man continues. "I've got khashlama in the slow cooker if you want any."

I widen my eyes, and Henry shakes his head.

After endless deafening heartbeats, the footsteps move away.

Henry squeezes my hand and turns, slowly cracking open the door. We creep out, still holding hands, even though it makes it harder to navigate the stairs.

We are so, so quiet, but when a door slams upstairs, I bolt, yanking free of Henry's hand even though he tries to stop me. I jump the last three steps and skid through the kitchen and out the back door, which slams behind us as we run. I trip over the headless cat, which crashes onto the sidewalk, shattering its tail.

"Wait." Henry grabs my arm and stops me so fast the only thing that keeps me from falling backward is his firm grip. He fishes our stolen goods out of his pocket, shoves them into my hands, and reaches into my satchel, fishing out the camera. Tugging me against his side, he holds it out, and it flashes. Then he grabs my wrist and pulls me out of the yard. The gate shuts behind us with a condemning clank, but we don't let the guilt stop us as we run, leaping over the roots of trees making their own escape from the sidewalk they were buried under.

Eventually we slow to a walk and then stop. Bending, Henry puts his palms on his knees and stays there, panting. I sit on a particularly large tree root.

When he lifts his head, his grin takes me by surprise. "Did you see me in there? I totally saved you."

I can't help but laugh even though I grip the cross so tightly it digs into my palm. "Don't let it go to your head."

"We make a good team," he says.

"We always did." It's the truth. Normally, I'd be the bold one—calm under pressure, keeping Henry at my side—but all it took was for me to be rattled and Henry stepped up and filled the gap I couldn't in that moment. Perhaps we're an even better team than I realized. We're not just two opposite people who even each other out. We're two people who can read what the other person needs and fulfill that need, handling it without question.

That seems rare. Something to hold onto.

I push Henry out of my mind.

The adrenaline rushes through my system, threatening to ruin my composure, and I promised myself I'd remain in control. Thinking about any feeling I might have for Henry would only make me break down again—something I can't afford right now.

I turn my focus to the tiny gold cross in my hand. A birthday gift? A memento from a loved one who's passed on? It doesn't matter. Someone will come home tonight and miss this.

"Hey," Henry says. "We'll make sure he gives it back."

"Yeah," I say, but it doesn't make me feel any better about taking it in the first place. I try to push the feeling away and store it with the others, but guilt is slippery, more like oil than paint.

Henry's still grinning, obviously still pumped up.

I cling to his excitement. Borrowing it like a jacket, I put on a grin to match. I hope I look light, adrenaline filling me to bursting, but inside I let myself deflate.

There's no going back.

—*Underworld*

# *Ten*

After leaving our picture safely tucked in the book and our stolen items safely with Ruth under strict instructions that they get back to where they came from, Henry and I grab a bite of seafood gumbo at a place recommended by Ruth. By the time we return to the bookstore, Ruth's about to close for the night.

"I was worried you wouldn't make it."

I give her a smile, but it's weighted with too many pent-up feelings that have no place in smiles.

"You okay, dear?" she asks.

"Just tired." I honestly hoped there would be no more challenges today. Nicholas was right about one thing—they force me to feel things when I don't want to feel anything at all. Even the last one, which felt safe from happiness, still gave me a moment of joy when Henry grinned at me after escaping. Maybe this would be easier without Henry.

I slip back to the poetry section, pull out my book, and read my poem first because I need a moment to settle before I face whatever task he's come up with.

**The Dead**

I see them,—crowd on crowd they walk
    the earth,
Dry leafless trees no Autumn wind laid bare;
And in their nakedness find cause for mirth,
And all unclad would winter's rudeness dare;
No sap doth through their clattering branches
    flow,
Whence springing leaves and blossoms bright
    appear;
Their hearts the <u>living</u> God have ceased
    to know
Who gives the spring-time to th'expectant year;
They mimic <u>life</u>, as if from Him to steal
His glow of health to paint the livid cheek;
They borrow words for thoughts they cannot
    feel,
That with a seeming heart their tongue may
    speak;
And in their show of life more dead they live
Than those that to the earth with many tears
    they give.
—Jones Very

I sketch a picture in my mind as I read—rough, charcoal strokes on cream paper, a hillside covered in dead trees, branches grasping at the winter sky above, immune to the cold and still standing, pretending to live despite no longer feeling the sap in their veins. Like vampires—dead but still standing. It's ironic that the words he's underlined are living life when the trees are clearly not. Is he warning me? Is this a plea for me to give up my hunt and go on living the life I have? But that's impossible. My life will never be the same after this, one way or the other.

I unfold the note:

*Now that you've delivered your stolen booty, catch a pirate.*

I didn't know there were pirates in New Orleans. Vampires, definitely. But pirates? That's a new one.

"Are there any pirates around here?" I ask Ruth.

"Can't say for sure," she says, adjusting her turquoise-framed glasses. "You two have a good night now."

She ushers us out.

She knows what we're looking for and won't help; it's all over her sweet elderly lady face—the little hint of wickedness. She loves this. I can't blame her.

Henry and I wander the streets for a while like a pirate might suddenly appear and we can nab them and be done. Simple. Easy. I need a break.

Each task gets me closer to what I want, but each one also sets free something inside me: the warm yellow glow of happiness from laughing with Henry, the pulsing purple fear of almost getting caught that so easily shifted to excitement when we weren't. Watercolors leave stains. You can never totally erase the color once it's on the page, and emotions are equally hard to scrub out.

They linger even now, in the bounce in my step, the way my chest is a little lighter when I glance at Henry. If I'm not careful, they'll take over, and I'll lose my grip on the only thing I have control over.

We head closer to the river, since pirate ships are surely rolling down it all the time, but find only the empty, murky water.

"Got any bright ideas?" I lean against the railing, staring down at the steady flow of water—the way it constantly moves but never really changes. Vampires must feel a kinship with it. It might seem boring to some, but I crave consistency now in a way I never used to. Surprises are rarely good.

He shrugs. I can tell from the droop of his shoulders that he needs to rest. "I did the last one—this one's on you."

"Hey, I was there too."

He grins. He's never going to let me forget how I froze. Fair is fair, I guess. I'd be reminding him every ten minutes if the situation were reversed.

With few options, we move on, stopping on a wide platform built between the river and the square. From here, the church rises in the distance as if it's the center of the city. Glowing white in the almost dark, it resembles a castle from a fairytale. A year ago I would have been drawn to it. I'd have sat outside with my watercolors and tried to capture the hope of the worshippers within in the beauty of the exterior. But dreams don't come true in churches. Maybe for some people, but not for me.

An elderly man sits near the old cannon displayed in the center of the platform, playing the saxophone. Pausing to rest on a painted green bench, we listen until the rest of the sun drops from the sky. I try to enjoy the music without being impatient. Time passes quicker for me now, and I am wasting it. But Henry bobs his head and taps his feet to the music, and I want to give him some piece of joy to thank him for earlier.

Perhaps this challenge won't start until night, when the vampires can play too.

So I sit until the song ends.

"Well," Henry says.

"Okay, let's make a move." I walk up to the man as he prepares for another song.

"Excuse me." I drop five dollars into his open case and hesitate, feeling ridiculous, but I am here to hunt vampires, so I go for it. "Where could we catch a pirate?"

He stares at me. "That's a new one. Lookin' for Johnny Depp or something?" His eyes twinkle a little.

I crack a small smile. Johnny Depp's a garbage fire, but if he offered Orlando Bloom . . . I'm tempted to joke with him. Old Victoria would have. New Victoria doesn't have time for jokes.

"Umm . . . I think I'm looking for a real one."

He chuckles. "Well, you could try Pirate's Alley."

Henry and I share a look.

"Pirate's Alley?" I ask.

He jerks a thumb over his shoulder. "Left side of the church if you're facing it."

"Thank you," I yell, because I'm already running down the concrete ramp. Henry grabs my arm before I can run into the street in front of a car.

"Geez. Slow down, will you?" He makes me wait until another car goes by before I can dart across. I slide between two horse-drawn carriages waiting for riders. One horse snorts, and her breath blows against my hair. Henry mumbles apologies behind me, but I don't care. I finally know where I'm going, and my muscles urge me to make up for lost time.

People still walk along the open square in front of the cathedral. A couple makes out on one of the benches directly in front of the looming church, hands wandering boldly. Definitely not the place I'd choose for a late-night rendezvous, but to each their own. Slowing my steps, I approach the alley.

Henry huffs beside me. "How the hell are you so fast? You're really quite short."

I give him a silent glare, and he shuts his mouth.

I slide up and rest my back against the side of the church like some kind of stealthy spy, except my breath wheezes in and out of me like I just ran five miles instead of a short sprint. Henry is annoyingly fine, probably from all his soccer practices.

"We need a plan," I say.

"We don't even know what's around the corner," he says. "Maybe we should look first and then come up with a plan."

Fair point, but I don't like being wrong.

"The plan is we're just another couple walking down an alley at night. We'll see if there's anything suspicious around."

"Is that a thing couples do? Stroll through alleys at night?"

"I don't know. I would. It sounds kinda romantic."

"Somehow that doesn't surprise me."

I point to the couple slowly sliding into a vertical position on the bench in front of the church. "Looks like it worked for them."

"Okay, then." Henry grabs my hand and weaves our fingers together, dragging me around the corner before I can rethink the plan. I've never been one for plans before, but with Dad's life on the line, I'm trying to think before I act—slow down and look at all the angles like Jessica would do.

"Relax," Henry whispers. My hand clenches his so tight it feels like our bones are touching. I loosen my grip, and he smiles down at me like this is the most natural thing in the world.

I force myself to look away from him and scan the alley. Large rectangular stones pave the entire thing, and it's wider than half the streets. The red and yellow buildings lining one side have faded in the dark, and the murky light from a couple of streetlamps does nothing to bring back their life. A black wrought-iron fence holds back the garden behind the church and lines the other side of the alley. Huge palm leaves escape over the top of the fence and reach for us as we pass.

"Nobody's out here." My voice is soft, and I'm not sure why. We've stopped walking.

"Look," Henry says.

Someone tall and slight leans against the far side of one of the streetlamps, blending into the shadows like she lives there.

"What do we do now?" Henry asks.

"Catch her?"

"I'm not sure I'm comfortable with accosting some woman in an alleyway based on instructions we pulled out of a book. What if she has nothing to do with this?"

"Talk to her?"

"Better plan."

We move toward her, trying not to look like creeps.

Finally, she turns her head in our direction, although I get the sense she's been tracking our approach this whole time.

Her braided hair's been pulled back in a low ponytail, and she's traded her white dress for tattered black jeans tucked into knee-high brown leather boots and a brown leather vest a few shades lighter. The vest stops inches above the waist of her pants and leaves her toned arms bare in the heat of the evening. There's no mistaking her. Daniella.

"Took you long enough," she drawls, spinning around the lamppost to face us.

"Sorry?"

"Where else would you go looking for a pirate besides Pirate's Alley? I told him the clue was too simple, but I guess I overestimated you." One side of her mouth twitches up like she's staring at something particularly distasteful. "It's impossibly hot out tonight too." She sighs and kicks at one of the puddles in the middle of the street. "Oh well. It's time for the fun part."

"What's the—"

She turns sharply and darts away.

Henry and I stand there for three solid seconds, still holding hands, before I break free and bolt after her. She's got at least three inches of leg length on me, but she turns her head every once in a while and flashes me a bright smile, so I know she doesn't really want to lose me. She leads me down Bourbon Street, weaving in and out of stumbling, laughing people. I can almost taste the alcohol in the air as I run. She shoves through two people gyrating on the street to the jarring mixture of music pouring out of several bars. I can no longer hear my sharp breathing. Neon signs on all sides of me try to pull my attention, but I keep my focus on her slender back, matching her step for step. She turns down a side street and we're heading back toward the river.

Once we're out of the crowds, I hear the steady beat of Henry's feet behind me. At least I hope it's Henry.

Daniella finally skids to a stop on the empty platform for the train that runs along the water. Henry pulls up by my side, and we take a step forward just as she takes a step back, off the platform, landing gracefully on the gravel below.

"Come on, now. Don't be afraid." She stands on the metal rail of the train track and points her toes as she does a sharp twirl, looking more like a ballerina than a pirate.

The gravel crunches under my feet as I jump the few feet off the platform. It shifts again under Henry's weight as he follows. When I'm close enough to reach out and grab her, she hops back into the center of the track and then up onto the other metal rail, pacing back and forth across it with her arms out like wings.

I don't get any closer. A train rattles in the distance. Lights move along the track.

"What's the matter, Victoria? Are you afraid to die or are you afraid to live? Which one is it?"

The train lets out its first honk. Two sharp lights flash like angry stars coming to wipe out the earth.

I am Michael in *The Lost Boys*, hanging onto the underside of a bridge while everyone else has made the jump, wondering if I should let go and follow or crawl back to my safe life. But the life I used to know is already gone no matter how badly I ache to close my eyes and wake up at home with Dad making blueberry pancakes and laughing. God, I miss his laugh. Letting go and moving forward is my only option.

"Neither," I shout.

She just waits.

When I step over the first rail and into the center of the track, I'm thinking about how quick death would be if I got hit by a train. *Bam*, then nothing. Worse ways to die exist.

The gravel under my feet trembles, afraid for me. The light

from the train turns the night around us into a sepia-tainted dream on the brink of becoming a nightmare. It's cooler here, close to the river and surrounded by gravel and metal and darkness.

I tug my shoulders back, planting my feet directly in the center of the track.

Henry steps up beside me. I guess he's not afraid either.

The horn blares again, closer. Close enough to make me flinch. I watch the approach of the lights out of the corner of my eyes.

Daniella reaches inside the breast of her vest and pulls out a small golden envelope. It glints in the oncoming headlight of the train. I reach for it, but she tugs it back against her chest with a grin.

"Pirates don't give things away."

"What do you want?" The horn covers my voice, and I end up screaming the question again.

"A trade." The rumble of the train vibrates through me. I risk a quick glance to the left. My eyes squint in the lights. Less than a minute until it's on us.

"I don't have anything."

Her eyes slide to Henry.

"No."

"Him for the card."

Henry laughs like this is all a joke, but no one laughs with him, and the train's too close to be funny. He sucks in a sharp breath and falls silent. I can't look at him. I want to reach out and squeeze his hand, but the action might be a promise I can't keep.

"What do you want with him?"

Her lips curl and her mouth parts slightly to show her tongue sliding across her teeth.

"Pick something else," I say.

She waits, cocking her head toward the train. The squeal of metal on metal as it throws on its brakes pierces my eardrums. The horn drowns out my conscience.

"Choose," she yells.

Henry's arm brushes mine. His warmth burns me. I can feel his stare as I shift away from him, refusing to glance in his direction. I bring up the image of my dad in my mind to drown out thoughts of Henry.

When I hold out my hand for the envelope, she grins with victory.

You dress me like a doll.
You make my hair like a doll. Why?
You want me to be a doll forever?
—*Interview with the Vampire*

# Eleven

Henry yells something beside me, but I can't make out the words.

I grip the envelope, smooth and solid in my fingertips, and then a palm shoves me in the center of my chest. My foot catches on the railing behind me, and I stumble backward onto my butt, scrambling to pull my feet off the tracks as the whole ground shakes and the train screams. When I finally look up, Henry's staring at me from the other side of the track, Daniella gripping his forearm and grinning as if she's stolen something precious from me. I feel sick.

Then the train tears between us. The wind from it whips my hair away from my face, and I can barely breathe from the power of it. My lungs burn, and then it's gone.

The other side of the track is desolate and dark.

I pull myself to my feet. My fingers shake as I rip into the envelope and yank out the slender white card. It's too dark to read, so I pull out my phone to light the curving black print:

*Find the dead Southern belle and ask for a dance.*

A simple address would have been nice.

I peer into the dark, longing to ask Henry his advice. They can't have gone far. Perhaps I could find them and take back what I did, but I'm not sure I would—I'm playing a game, after all, and I'm not the rule maker.

I text Henry: **Are you okay?**

I get back an immediate reply: **Henry can't come to the phone right now.**

How the heck did she get his phone from him?

I pray he's okay before I remember prayer let me down recently. I think of the cathedral, invisible from here, just out of sight and always out of reach.

I want to lie down and vomit.

I kick at the gravel as I shuffle back to the train terminal.

"Bad day?" His voice makes me jump, like it usually does. He really likes sneaking up on people.

I'm still a few feet away from the terminal when I lift my head and glimpse Carter's pointed black boots at my eye level. I have to crane my neck to see his smirk.

"I'm peachy."

"You're bleeding."

"What?"

He nods toward my legs, but there's not a single visible drop of blood on the front of them. I can feel the cuts on the back though.

"How—" I cut myself off. I don't need to say it out loud. Maybe he saw me fall and assumed I got cut, but I bet he can smell it.

He smiles.

"You know, my day would get a lot better if you'd just give me what I came for."

He tilts his head like he's actually considering it. "Right now watching you is more fun than eating you."

My pulse jumps.

"Besides," he continues, "this is Nicholas's game. I wouldn't want to steal his fun." He bends over and holds a pale white hand out to me. "The best I can do is offer to help you get back up here. I noticed your legs are rather short."

I grit my teeth. "I'm fine, thanks."

He stands and nods, twisting on his heel before strolling into the night.

It takes me three tries to pull myself onto the platform, but I don't regret turning down Carter's offer. He seems like a vampire that would simply kill me after playing with me for a while. I trust Nicholas a little bit more.

I try to text Henry's phone again: **Tell me he's okay or this is over.**

I know that's a lie, but she doesn't.

How much am I willing to sacrifice for this? Henry's safety apparently.

She takes longer to text back this time: **Don't worry your pretty little head. I'll take good care of him.**

As I walk back toward the square, my phone dings. A picture

of Henry lights up my screen. He frowns at the camera. A pile of beignets doused in powdered sugar sits in front of him.

It makes my choice a little better. He really is safe, but in that moment, when I took the envelope, I didn't know what would happen to him. I didn't even consider it. It looked like the only option in front of me, and I took it with a dangerous, singular focus. Maybe I haven't learned to slow down and plan.

I glance at my other messages—mostly RSVPs to Dad's party. All of them mention how pleased they are to hear he's feeling up to it. I tuck the phone back into my pocket. I'm doing the right thing.

My limbs still wobble from the rush, so when I get back to Jackson Square, I sit for a moment and read the clue again. The cemeteries around here are supposed to be old and beautiful and are probably overflowing with dead Southern belles, but how the hell am I supposed to dance with them? On their grave? The thought turns my already weak stomach. Nobody deserves that disrespect no matter how long they've been dead.

But my dad deserves to live, and if that's what it takes, why stop now? I let Henry almost get hit by a train a few minutes ago. Now he's eating beignets with a possible vampire. I left the moral high ground when I broke into a house.

I search for the closest cemetery on my phone and start walking. I swear Andrew Jackson's judging me as I slink past his statue, like he has any right. That dude was an atrocious human being, and I'm not sure why he gets to sit there on his horse for all eternity. The horse looks pissed, with rounded eyes and veins bulging as it rears back. I'm pretty sure the horse is trying to dislodge the rider. I like the horse.

I give Andrew Jackson the finger and leave him behind, taking the side street so I can avoid Pirate's Alley. Some of the street artists still have their wares set up along the wrought-iron fence surrounding the square, each canvas a small splash of color in the falling night.

I could stand forever and admire all of them. But a watercolor artist draws my attention, each canvas a dripping cascade of colors, so free and wild that at first glance the paintings seem random, but once you embrace the messiness, you can see it—each one captures a different sight in the French Quarter. Watercolor is the perfect choice to capture this city, which bubbles with such vibrant emotions.

But it makes my task harder. How do I keep my feelings at bay when everything I see and touch and smell demands a response? Already, letting myself admire these paintings makes my chest expand like a cheap latex balloon until I fear I might pop.

I force myself to turn away.

A flare of white draws my attention across the street. She sits alone on the two steps leading up to the walkway that runs in front of the shops, dangling a cigarette in one hand, dressed in an overflowing white wedding gown. Black holes suck at the light where her eyes should be. Her blackened lips curve into something like a smile when she catches me staring.

Convenient to find a dead Southern belle in the heart of the Quarter, but I'm not surprised. She stands in contrast to the lit store windows behind her, full of new, expensive clothes, but the buildings themselves are tall and looming, made of bricks older than any of the city's inhabitants. She is one more ghost from the past in a city full of them.

I'm only a little disappointed not to find her in a graveyard.

I take a step forward as she drags on her cigarette.

She beckons me onward with a gloved hand.

Up close, her white, bloodshot eyes flash against the dark makeup painted around her eyelids and under her cheekbones. The dress that looked white from a distance is yellowed with age and torn in spots, revealing bruised skin underneath. The bruises appear startlingly real, but I don't want to ask.

I swallow. "Are you a Southern belle?"

"Don't I look like one, darling?"

She looks like a bride murdered on her wedding day, but I don't say it. Maybe she's both.

A portable record player sits next to her. In front of her, a tattered pink umbrella with ruffles falling off the edges lays overturned in the street. A few dollars float around inside. I dig out a five from my pocket and toss it in.

"May I have this dance?"

She tosses her half-finished cigarette into the gutter and brings the needle down on the record player. A scratchy symphony warbles into the night as she stands and smooths out the tatters of lace cascading from her skirt.

"Do you know how to waltz?"

I shake my head.

"No matter." She grabs one of my hands from my side and places her other hand on my waist. "If a dead girl can do it, so can you."

I almost smile as I place a hand on her bony, cold shoulder. I don't know how she can be so cold in this heat. I'm tempted to ask her if *she's* a vampire, but if she's part of Nicholas's game, I doubt she'll be any more willing to help me than Carter was.

"Follow me," she says. "Forward, side, close. Back, side, close. Repeat."

I obey her commands. My feet fall easily into the pattern, and I'm swirling around the pavement while another thunderstorm rolls in and threatens the sky with flashes of lightning. The whole moment is so macabre—me, a girl with a dying dad, dancing with a dead girl, seconds away from getting struck by lightning. Edgar Allan Poe would have a field day with this.

Dancing can be easy, peaceful even, if you can fall into the repetition of it. If your partner is easy and predictable. The dead girl seems content to dance all night, and the card didn't say how long I had to do this. Impatience makes my fingertips perform their own dance on her shoulders, and I don't even notice until she pauses midstep and places her icy hand over mine.

"Relax," she says.

I suck in a deep breath of the air, hot and humid and electrified by the storm on the brink of eruption. Not exactly soothing. I turn my face up to the sky and listen to the melody, try to lose myself in the melancholy notes—the familiar sadness in them cradles me, helps me focus without demanding my own sadness in return.

I'm dancing, and I don't remember beginning again.

I don't think I mind, but the flash of lightning cracks through my moment of peace and makes me open my mouth.

"So how'd you die?"

"How do you think?" She laughs, and the smell of the cigarette on her breath scratches at my nose. "Lung cancer."

I cringe, but she doesn't notice. I'm tempted to yank away from her or yell at her about how cancer's not the butt of a joke, but she's just a girl trying to make a living. For her, cancer's a bad thing some people die from, something you can laugh about the same way we always laugh about distant fears, but when cancer creeps in and poisons your life, becoming a corporeal fear and not a distant ghost, laughter gets harder.

My dad laughed at first. He joked about how cancer picked the wrong dude to mess with. But as cancer won battle after battle, the joke lost its humor.

"That's not a very poetic way to die. I thought you'd say you drowned in the river or died of heartbreak."

She laughs, and I turn my head slightly to avoid her breath this time. "Honey, nobody dies a poetic death; they just die. Any way you go, you're still dead."

The truth in her words claws at me, forcing me to take them in and hold onto them. Even if I find a way to turn my dad into a vampire, will he still be dead? Will he be like Anne Rice's Louis?

Always struggling to find a way to live again in death? Will I always have to remind him that this was better than the alternative? Will we even like watching vampire movies together anymore? We may not be the same once this is done, but I can't let my thoughts go there. Dad won't be anything at all if I can't do this. A different life has to be better than no life. He'll understand.

"Are you okay?"

I've stopped moving. She lets go of my waist and squeezes my shoulders. I meet her worried eyes, a deep, dark blue that reminds me of sorrow.

A throat clears behind me. "May I cut in?"

The woman's gaze slides past me. Her lips pinch with what I think is concern, but she takes a step away from me before meeting my stare again. "Are you okay?" she asks.

I nod, but I can see she doesn't believe me. She goes back to the silent record player to restart the music. A sadder song whispers out, soaking into my limbs, making them too heavy to keep dancing.

Nicholas clears his throat again. "Victoria?"

I don't want to turn around. I don't want him to see the sadness I'm hoarding beneath my skin. He saw it the other night, and it scared him, made him think I didn't deserve to live forever. I probably don't. I stole a necklace that clearly meant something to someone. I traded my friend for an envelope—I'm selfish. But my dad deserves this. I swallow several times, trying to pull it down, bury it beneath layers of skin and bone in the dark and empty parts of myself where no one else can see it, and I can pretend it's not there even though I feel it like a stone in my gut that I need surgery to remove before it kills me.

I can do it. I can keep it trapped until this is over. I tell myself I am bright and happy and love life, but even thinking those words stirs the sadness in my gut. I need to pretend.

Finally, I turn around.

He scans my face.

I smile.

He shakes his head. "This isn't working. I don't understand. Aren't you having fun?"

I let my smile drop. "You abducted my friend."

He raises a brow. "Abducted is a strong word, is it not?"

"A train almost hit us! Daniella pushed me and dragged Henry to the other side of the tracks. By the time the train was through, he was gone."

The corner of Nicholas's mouth twitches, and I can't tell if it's from a frown or if he's holding back laughter. "She does get carried away sometimes. But you agreed to trade him for the card, did you not?"

"Yes, but—"

"Good." His teeth flash. "And you're both fine?"

I huff. "My legs are cut up."

"Well, we can't have you bleeding out." His mouth curves in a half smile.

I bite my bottom lip. Probably not a great idea to tell a vampire you're bleeding—unless you want to be a vampire, too, which I do, even though some very basic survival instinct tells me to run.

His eyes darken as he stares at my lip in my teeth. I release it with a sharp breath.

"May I see?"

"What?" My face is hot, and my head feels muggier than the air.

"Your wounds?"

I don't know if I've ever heard someone say "wounds" so sexily before. My land, it's a sexy word. His mouth holds the *o* in the middle forever—until I commit the shape of his rounded lips to memory so I can draw them one day when I have an eternity to get them right. He has a face I'd never tire of drawing, and that seems like an okay reason to tie myself to him forever.

I turn around and gesture at the back of my calves.

He gets down on one knee as I watch him over my shoulder. He glances up at me, dark eyes barely visible through the curls falling over his forehead. "May I touch you?" he asks.

"Are you going to lick me?"

"Do you want me to?"

The Southern belle snorts with laughter. My face flushes. I'd forgotten she was even there. I glance toward her, and she shakes her head slightly. I can't tell if it's a warning or amusement.

"I don't think so?" I don't mean it to come out like a question.

He chuckles, soft and low. His breath touches the back of my knee, and I shiver, hoping he doesn't notice but knowing he does.

"I only want to look at it."

"Okay. Yeah. Go for it." I attempt to sound casual. My voice squeaks.

One set of his long fingers slide around my shin, applying just enough pressure to keep my leg still. His other hand brushes across the back of my calf so faintly I lock my knees to stop the trembling. It's too quiet. My own breathing is so loud I hope for more thunder to cover it up. His fingertips probe around my cuts until they touch broken skin, and I wince, straining against his other hand keeping me in place. I mutter "ouch" a few times, but he keeps working, and I let the pain distract me from his touch.

Finally, he stands up, brushing his hands on his slacks as I spin to face him.

"You had a little gravel stuck in the cuts, but I got it out." He smirks. "With my fingers, of course."

He holds out his hand. "Now, about that dance."

I glance at the dead girl. The whites of her eyes widen against the dark. "He's trouble," she says to me.

"What do you mean?" I wonder if she knows what he really is.

"Mind your manners, Elizabeth," Nicholas bites out.

"You know each other?"

"Everyone knows me." He says it matter-of-factly, with just a trace of vanity.

I look to Elizabeth again, but she stares up at the lightning ripping through the sky.

"Fine." I take his hand, and he wraps his arm around my waist, closer and more intimate than the way Elizabeth held me.

"Give us something livelier," he commands.

I don't dare look over at Elizabeth again. Whatever expression she wears now, I'm sure it's not favorable, but after the click of the needle, a few tentative notes sneak out, melancholy for a moment before turning into a peppy tune that makes me feel like a ballerina in a music box, dancing in perfect circles. Painted cheeks always perfectly, falsely, pink.

Nicholas bobs us around with a bounce to his step I can't quite replicate, but I let myself fall into the movement once more, keeping my focus on the tarnished bronze buttons on his vest so I don't have to look at his beautiful face and wonder if I'm happy enough for him—if my steps bounce with enough joy. It takes only a moment for me to match his rhythm, to let him lead me around like I'm that mindless wooden doll, and it feels glorious. Dolls are never happy or sad; they just exist and let others choose their emotions for them.

Nicholas wants me to be alive and happy, so he moves me like I'm alive and happy, and for one second it's easy to pretend I am those things.

Then the lightning finally succeeds in cutting through the canopy of clouds, and as water pours down on us, each drop melts against my skin, washing away the sweat, the gravel, the tension locked in my shoulders. I raise my chin ever so slightly to absorb the way Nicholas's curls dampen and cling to his cheeks. His dark eyes watch my face expectantly, waiting for me to let go in this storm and enjoy it. I need to give in.

*Fake it*, I tell myself. Fake happiness long enough to get what you want. I tilt my head back and grin into the rain. It comes down hard enough to choke me, but I hold my arms out to it while Nicholas keeps his hands on my waist, twirling me like a child.

When I was a kid, Dad would take me outside after a downpour and let me dive into the heavy puddles of mud until my clothes and skin became buried in muck. Those are some of my happiest memories.

The drops soak our skin, splattering and exploding on the unyielding stone we dance on, until the downpour becomes so heavy I'm barely breathing.

Finally, Nicholas laughs, and that's what I'm waiting for, for him to see me as something I was and not what I am. Someone who experiences joy in the rain, not someone who wants to melt into one of the unfeeling puddles gathering at her feet.

He grabs one of my flailing arms and spins me into his chest. He smells like wet cinnamon.

Pulling me to his side, he drapes one arm over my shoulders, shielding me from some of the rain, but I'm already soaked through and through.

"Let's get you out of this," he says.

I laugh. I am the rain—cold and mindless and doing what needs to be done.

He nods toward Elizabeth, who scowls in return. I give her a small wave, and she shakes her head slightly.

We stroll without hurry down St. Peter, everything shining in the dark. People stand in the streets, laughing, rainwater diluting their beers as they drink them. Here the rain isn't something to hide from but one more thrill to be had. Lightning forks in the sky, and nobody flinches. They cheer, encouraging the thunder to join them, to live. The excitement on their faces is enough to make anyone feel alive. Even vampires. Even me. I let my arm drift around Nicholas's waist, mimicking other couples walking together. He pulls a little closer to me. Neither one of us speaks until we stop in front of a bright-yellow building with blood-red shutters.

"This is me," he says. He pulls open a heavy wooden door and waits for me to make a decision. I stand there for far too long, but he doesn't give me any reassurances like *I won't rip out your throat, Victoria. Don't worry, Victoria. I'm a nice vampire.* One side of his mouth is turned up ever so slightly, which someone less observant wouldn't even notice.

No reassurance. But I don't need it. For me, there's only one way forward. I enter the building and follow him up a quiet wooden staircase to the third floor and through another wooden door, which he opens, then motions for me to go first.

Wide-plank wood paneling lines all the walls in his front living area. A fake stone fireplace, bricked off inside and filled with candles, draws the focus to the main wall. On either side of the fireplace, built-in bookcases painted a deep burgundy boast a scattering of old books. A pure white sofa and two matching armchairs take up the center of the room. The splash of white should warm the place, but it glares coldly against the comforting brown.

The door shuts behind me.

"The white sofas are an interesting touch," I say.

His laugh is low and throaty and makes me overly aware that I'm standing in the apartment of a guy I barely know. "This is a vacation rental. You won't find me here tomorrow. We rarely let others into our homes, and you haven't earned that. Yet." When he speaks again, he's closer than before. "But I am partial to white sofas. I like being unexpected."

I shiver. Partly from my rain-soaked clothes growing chillier by the second and partly from the thrill of standing here with damp clothes and a guy who may or may not give me what I want and kill me. My pulse throbs in my throat. I'm afraid and excited at the same time. I forget for a moment why I'm here, what I want, and lean into another desire, the thing that draws me back to those vampire movies again and again—not the carnage of *30 Days of Night*, but the dangerous seduction of Lestat, embracing terror and letting it drown out everything else but lust.

When I finally turn around, he's so close I have to look up to see his darkened eyes. He stares down at me, and I'm not sure he's breathing. Or maybe it's me who's not. No, my breath is there, ragged and uneven, thundering in my ears as if the storm followed us indoors.

He lifts a finger and drags it from my earlobe to the tip of my chin, tilting my head upward. I bite my lip.

Yes. There's his breath, close enough to caress the top of my head. I reach a hand out toward his chest, where his heart should be beating—or *not*—but his other hand grasps my fingers a little too tightly, and I wince. He drops my chin and steps back from me, smirking slightly.

"We need to get you changed." I stare down at my drenched sundress. It feels like I've been wearing it for years.

I shiver now, and it's only from the cold.

"I don't have dry clothes."

He nods at an ornate coffee table with a silver bag on top. The white tissue paper crinkles as I pull it out and unwrap a shiny gold slip dress.

I raise an eyebrow. "Did you plan that thunderstorm to get me into a new outfit?"

"Maybe. I do have connections."

I smile, and he grins back—probably thinking I'm enamored with the dress. I am. It's gorgeous, but more importantly, he handed me another piece of proof: he can control the weather—a lesser-known power that dates back to Norse mythology.

I am so close, and if I thought it would work, I would crack open with the same abandon as the sky and cry and plead for him to turn me so I can save my father. But the vampires in myths and legends aren't known for their sympathy toward dying humans.

And he clearly loves this game we're playing.

The safer route's to keep playing to win.

I keep my smile pasted on until he points me to the bathroom. I drape my wet clothes over the towel rack in the bland white-and-gray-bathroom. The fabric drips like molten gold from the thread-thin straps, pooling seductively right at the edge of my cleavage and stopping a couple of inches below my butt. I admire myself until I get distracted by the mess that is my hair. My normally soft waves have turned into full-on curls from the rain. I always carry a ridiculous amount of bobby pins in my purse though, so in another second I have the mess artfully piled on top of my head with a few almost-dry curls framing my face. Thank goodness my makeup is waterproof.

When I emerge, Nicholas stands in front of a large, curved window. I move closer so I can look out with him. I gasp a little. "You can see the convent from here."

"Does that interest you?"

Of course it does, and he knows why. He's smiling, waiting patiently for me to ask him all my questions.

"It's beautiful, that's all."

He laughs low in his throat. "You look beautiful, too."

"Thanks." My blood warms under his compliment. Maybe that's why vampires seduce their victims first—it's like humans boiling water for tea. I try not to let his words go to my head, but my cheeks must be flushed with pink.

I take in his clothing change—soft caramel-colored slacks and a thin white linen shirt that pops against his brown skin. "Right back at you."

This time his laughter is loud and barking and infectious. I smile automatically.

"Are you ready?" he asks.

"For what?"

"Anything."

*He's a vegetarian. The last thing he'd want to do
is eat a live being or eat blood or eat meat.*
—*What We Do in the Shadows*

# Twelve

Anything ends up being dinner at the oldest restaurant in the United States: Antoine's. Every window's lit, and it glows, warm and welcoming enough for some of the tension to melt off my body. Nicholas has been strolling beside me, hands loosely in his pockets, but he pauses before we go in and offers me his arm. "This place deserves a grand entrance," he says.

"If you say so." I grip his forearm without hesitation. He grins at my willingness to go along with his request as he opens the door for us.

I understand immediately why he gave me a dress to change into. The place is stunning—high white ceilings and white beams lined with soft round lights. Gold chandeliers with white orbs add another layer, casting a golden hue on the pristine table-cloths. Rich wooden chairs save the room from becoming too sterile. Everything is lovely, and the place is filled already with soft chatter and guests waiting to be seated.

"This is going to be a long wait," I murmur.

Nicholas's lips twitch as he glances down, winks at me, and

leads me past the waiting line with a single nod to the maître d'.

"There aren't any open tables."

"They have fourteen dining rooms; it's one of the beauties of this place."

We cross the threshold into another large dining area. This room's darker than the other, with a wood ceiling and rusty red walls accented with wood paneling. It gives off the vibe of a giant pub more than a fancy restaurant, and I relax a little.

"I like this one better," I say.

"Ahh, but we're not stopping just yet." He pats my hand, still resting in the crook of his arm, and then leaves his fingers on top of mine there, and the way he grins down at me, eyes bright with excitement, I bet to anyone watching we appear to be a couple in love. I could imagine walking into my home, introducing him to Dad and Mom, and they'd probably both like him—Mom because he's poised and polished and Dad because *I* like him. But Dad would also ask me what happened to Henry. I think he was more worried about our split than I was.

But it's good that I like Nicholas. If he drinks my blood and I drink his, we'd be bonded forever—although how deeply, I'm not sure.

I consider asking him, but I don't want him to think I'm unprepared or doubting that I really want to be a vampire. It doesn't matter what I want now. What Dad needs is the only thing that matters.

I keep my mouth shut and picture myself curled up on a white sofa with him next to me, reading a worn copy of Edgar Allan Poe—probably a first edition, because we'd have the time and money to track one down, and we'd be sipping a glass of red wine.

But, of course, it wouldn't be red wine, would it?

The thought of drinking blood ruins my fantasy.

I focus on Nicholas's cold fingers instead.

We arrive at the other side of the room, and Nicholas opens a thick white door with gold trim and ushers me inside.

"Wow." I passed through classic rich people dining, to a fancy club, to a room straight out of Versailles. The walls are a rich emerald, accented with gold crown molding and gold trim rectangles with scalloped edges, giving it those lush details only the truly rich have time and money to care about.

A long table that must sit at least thirty guests takes up the center of the room. I cross the lush burgundy carpet to stare at the glass cases built into the walls showing off golden scepters and crowns.

"This room is decorated with Mardi Gras memorabilia," Nicholas says.

I nod. I can't bring myself to speak yet.

He watches me as I trace every detail with my mind. I want to sketch the way the ceiling and the corners of the room curve. Longing pulses through my fingers. I want to live in a world without sharp edges, but it's not my world. This is not mine to sketch. Nobody could draw this without feeling joy. I let my fingers drop from the trim I was petting as I strolled in circles.

"What's wrong?" Nicholas asks.

I try not to wince. I don't want him to see any trace of the sadness in me. I need to be like this room—beautiful and grand and the kind of thing people want to preserve.

"It's gorgeous." I hesitate. "It makes me want to draw again."

It's a lie. I don't want to draw it now, but for a split second it drew me in and made me *want* again. For me, drawing is always about want. Wanting to capture something, and not necessarily something beautiful, but anything that pulls emotion from me, good or bad.

I try not to want anymore. I only have one want anyway, and how do you draw wanting to cheat death?

"You draw?"

"I used to."

He's silent for a moment, and I brace myself, knowing he'll ask for more details, but the waiter comes in with our menus and saves me.

Nicholas gestures to all the chairs. "Where would you like to sit, mademoiselle?"

"No one else is eating in here?"

He shakes his head, smiling slightly.

I stare around at the empty seats, and it seems like such a waste. Someone else could be in here, enjoying this, but here we are, hoarding it for ourselves. I need to not think about it. I need to just be in the moment for this to work.

I plop down at the head of the table, which is so wide that two seats fit side by side. Nicholas nods, approving my bold choice. I smile up at him as he sits beside me.

The waiter leaves our menus and silently slinks away as if he has instructions to leave us alone as much as possible.

I run a finger across the green and gold rim of the plate in front of me.

"How much did this cost?" I know it's a tacky question, but I can't help myself.

Nicholas laughs. "That doesn't matter."

"Only a super-rich person would say that." Tacky again. I should shut up.

His gaze slides in my direction as he pops open his menu.

Being super rich wasn't on my list of signs, but I add it now and check it off. It makes sense. If you're alive for a long time, you'd inevitably acquire plenty of money and a taste for extreme beauty.

I let myself feel a tiny thrill of excitement. I can't wait to tell Henry.

A pinch of guilt punctures my excited bubble.

Nicholas is saying something, frowning a little.

"Huh?"

"I said what do you like to eat?"

"Anything but meat. I eat fish though."

"You're a vegetarian?" His mouth parts slightly. He looks caught off guard for the first time since I met him.

"Well, yeah, except for fish."

"But you want to be a vampire."

"Well . . ." Shit. Of course I don't want to be a vampire. I may love the idea of it in a distant sense, but a rare steak makes me want to gag. Drinking straight-up blood sounds so disgusting my stomach turns at the thought. "I don't like to kill things." I need to explain it in a way that makes sense, that doesn't make me sound like some lost little girl who doesn't know what she's getting into. Besides, Dad loves his steak rare. He could handle the blood. "You don't kill things, do you?"

He opens his menu again. "Do you like crab?"

"Yep." My pulse throbs in my neck. I take a deep breath. I don't want to look like an appetizer—or maybe I do. I glance down at my barely there gold dress. I look more like the main course, and we are in a private room. . . . Just when I'm starting to wonder if the waiter is really going to come back, the door opens, and he walks in.

I count the crystals dangling from the chandelier to calm myself. I need this. But all I can think about is blood.

Nicholas asks if I'd like to order for myself, and I start to shake my head, but then I have an idea, an easy test if I play it right. I tear open my menu again with a little too much force and scan through the ingredients listed below all the dishes I can't even pronounce, but it doesn't matter. I'm looking for one word.

Garlic.

I point at something without even reading the other ingredients. "This sounds good."

Nicholas frowns, arching his brows as he examines me. "Creamed spinach?"

I try not to grimace—nope, it definitely doesn't sound good. "I love spinach." I widen my eyes to convey my sincerity.

"I'm not a fan of spinach . . . or garlic, for that matter." He gently pulls my menu out of my hands. "But perhaps you guessed that already?" He closes both our menus and hands them to the waiter. "Perhaps I should order." He raises a brow, and I smile in return, and there's some realness in it, because that makes five: I've only seen him at night, the weather obeys his whims, he drinks blood, his hands are always cold, and he hates garlic. He's a vampire. There's no debating anymore—even Mom and Jessica would have to look at my percentages and find reason in them.

We wait in silence until the food comes. Nicholas eyes me with a shrewdness that makes me squirm, and I swear he looks a little pleased, like he would have been disappointed if I hadn't tried to test him.

When the food comes out hot and steaming, the butter and spice make my mouth water with longing, and I barely stop myself from diving in and forgetting everything else. Instead, I fill my plate slowly, watching Nicholas in my peripheral vision. I need to know if he eats real food—not as a test but because I want to know how much I'm giving up. Nothing's worth more than Dad's life, but I still want to be prepared. I really, really like food. And even though I'm certain I'll be giving up garlic, it'd be nice to hold onto some things I love.

Nicholas catches me and smirks a little as he spears a piece of flaky fish on his fork and places it in his mouth. I stare as he chews and swallows.

He turns toward me and opens his mouth to show me it's really gone. "Is this what you're waiting for?"

"Yes." I smile. Dad and I always debated if vampires would eat real food or not. I voted no, but he said they would even if they didn't need it to stay alive. I can't wait to tell him he's right.

I gorge myself on fried crab doused in butter, perfectly cooked asparagus, and steamed broccoli drizzled in hollandaise.

"Holy smokes that was good." I lean back in my chair, not quite caring anymore if I'm next on the menu because at least I've had a last meal worth dying for. I cringe a little. I've always joked about death, and Dad laughed with me plenty of times, but now it strikes me as flippant, and I'm caught between continuing to joke or stopping altogether and acknowledging something's wrong. There doesn't seem to be a middle ground.

"Dessert?" Nicholas asks.

"I am stuffed." I run my hand over my distended belly. This dress hides nothing.

He grins at me with all his too-white teeth. "I could go for a little more." But he's not looking at the menu, only me.

"No way, my friend." Maybe if I play hard to get, he'll get tired of his game and bite me right now.

"No what?" His eyes slide to my neck. "I can't enjoy a choco-late mousse?"

"You know what." I keep my voice light, teasing, but his stare on me increases my pulse until it throbs through my skin like a road map with all the best places to eat highlighted.

He may eat real food, but that doesn't make it satisfying.

His smile widens, and he leans toward me.

I fight the dueling urges: most of me, the pure, animalistic survival part of me, says back the hell up and get out of here. Then my rational side tells me this is why I'm here. Let it happen. But another part of me, the part of me that loves a classic vampire/human love story even if they don't usually end well for the human, says lean on in; this could be fun.

"I want to hear you say it," he says.

I lean in the slightest bit, not enough for him to close the gap, deciding to stick with teasing, make him want something from me instead of the other way around. I say the words slowly. "I am not dessert."

His smile breaks, and he tilts his head back and roars with laughter.

"What a shame," he says, and my pulse spikes even more but definitely not from fear. I dust my hands off and toss my butter-stained napkin onto the table to give myself something to do besides look at him.

It was worth a shot. I switch tactics.

"Well." I clasp my hands in my lap like a proper Southern lady to try to get myself under control. "Are we done here? Are you going to give me what I want?"

"I'm not sure yet." He leans back in his chair. "Smile for me."

"What?"

"Smile."

"I can't smile on demand."

"Sure you can. People do it in pictures all the time."

"You're not holding a camera."

He holds out his hand, and I sigh, reaching for my oversize black bag and fishing out the camera. "You better give it back. That was a gift from a guy I used to like."

He smirks and pulls it away from me, making sure his fingers touch mine as he does.

"Okay." He holds it up to his face. "Say cheese."

"Really? 'Say cheese' is what you're going with?"

He lowers the camera and peers at me with his dark-brown eyes. "I tried a simple request, which you denied."

"Maybe because you said 'smile *for me*' like I owed it to you or something."

"Are you always so difficult?"

"Probably."

He sighs and lifts the camera to eye level again, and now all I can see are his lips curving slightly as he watches me through the lens.

"Smile *for the camera*."

"Well, that's an improvement."

"And yet you're still not smiling."

I bare my teeth at him.

The camera flashes, and he pulls out the picture, laying it gently on the table.

"How about another?" He pushes his chair back and stands, eyeing the room like he's an expert photographer on a shoot. "Here." He points at one of the glass display cases built into the wall. The main feature inside is a floor-length strapless gold gown, covered with what must be fifty pounds of beads in an intricate floral pattern. Above it rest two ridiculously ornate golden crowns, and to the side, a collection of three scepters. The top of one fans into a golden sun. I can't imagine the sheer confidence it would require to carry one of those things or wear that gown. You'd have to imagine yourself as a goddess or at least a queen.

"I cannot stand next to this mannequin. She doesn't have a head or arms and she still looks better in that dress than I look in mine."

He raises a brow. "Do you want to swap dresses?"

"Is that an option?"

"Could be."

I don't think I want to find out how he would manage that switch. There's a small keyhole in the golden-framed edge of the glass, but something tells me he doesn't possess the key.

"I'm good."

"Suit yourself." He motions for me to stand in front of the glass. I lean against the two rows of black-and-white portraits beside it and fold my arms behind my back. This time he takes the picture without asking me to smile for him or anything else.

After several shots of me posing about the room, he comes back and puts the original photo on the table, frowning down at the picture of my face in a way that mostly makes me want to slap him.

"What?" I ask after several uncomfortable moments of silence. "Do I have asparagus in my teeth?"

Wouldn't surprise me.

He glances up at me and then back down. "No, it just looks like you're snarling at me more than smiling." He cocks his head. "Almost like you want to bite me."

"Maybe I do."

"Oh—I know you do. That's why we're here, isn't it?"

The reminder sinks into me and turns my stomach like bad seafood. This isn't a game to me, and I shouldn't be forgetting that, not even for a moment. I force a smile to cover my mood.

"Don't do that."

"What?"

"Smile to try to hide what you're feeling."

"Isn't that what you *asked* me to do?"

"No. I wanted a real smile."

"This is real. Who made you the judge of all smiles?"

"I'm not a fool, Victoria."

I don't answer. How can I win in this scenario? Giving him a real smile would be a betrayal of my dad lying in his bed dying of cancer. I don't own real smiles anymore, only cheap knockoffs.

"Can't you just give me immortality?" I ask. "Do we really need to do this?"

"I'm still not convinced you actually want it."

"Why do you get to be the judge of everything?" I can't convince him I want it for myself. The more I think about it, I don't. I can't imagine what that would be like—the boredom of it. Would I even want to draw, knowing I had forever to see anything I wanted again and again? Nothing would be special.

But I'd have Dad. This is my default thought I use to push away all my other fears. I know we'll find a way to be happy.

His chin tilts up, and he stares at the dangling crystals of the chandelier. "I'm trying to help you."

"You're playing with me like this is some game."

His eyes are hard when he looks back down at me. "Life *is* a game. That's the only way to look at it. Otherwise, each play you make has the potential to eat you alive with guilt and regret. Show me you can play."

The unused steak knife glints dully in the dim lighting. I want to lunge for it and plant it in his hand and take his blood by force, but what are the odds I'd be fast enough? Just because I haven't seen him use superspeed doesn't mean he doesn't have it. I'm still trying to navigate which myths are true and which are only modern exaggerations.

"Fine." I throw him another cheap smile. "Let's play."

Out on the street, I let him take my warm hand in his cold one. He doesn't link our fingers, and it makes the gesture old-fashioned in a pleasant way. We end up back in front of the cathedral, where a single portrait artist sits. Only a few people still walk by this late into the evening. All the warm bodies are tucked away in the clubs, heating themselves with dance partners and alcohol.

Nicholas and I are not warm—each in our own way. The empty darkness suits us.

I search the dark to see if Elizabeth is still out here, but Nicholas tugs me in the other direction, toward the artist, and leads me to the wooden stool.

"Oh, I don't think so," I say.

Either he ignores me or he doesn't hear me. He pulls out a wad of bills from his pocket and passes it to the man. "Thank you for waiting," Nicholas says. The skinny artist nods, tucking the bills into his pocket.

My skin tingles. He planned this, too. Every detail of the night has been carefully curated for me. But for what? To make me happier? Why does he care? And why me? I can't be the first person with a troubled life to come looking for vampires—not after the reveal. The only thing that might make me different is the way grief locked away my beautiful watercolors and I became a black-and-white photograph of who I was.

The painter must see it too, because he reaches past his bright chalks for a stick of charcoal as Nicholas moves to stand behind me.

I miss the softness of charcoal against my skin.

Nicholas's fingertips brush the back of my neck as he shifts my hair to one side of my shoulder. I tense, and he leans down to my ear. "Is that okay?"

I nod, fighting a shiver. His fingers drift down either side of my neck until his hands settle on my shoulders and his fingertips fill the hollow above my collarbone. I swallow, and one index finger trails up my neck in answer.

The movement draws all my focus until the artist begins and soft scratching fills the air. Every so often Nicholas's finger moves in time with the chalk, tracing a line up the front of my neck with the sound.

I fight to keep my pulse under control, but I know he must feel it beating like a scared rabbit, or a horny rabbit, or maybe both.

And then there's the art. The artist puts his charcoal to the side and runs a finger along the paper, and I almost feel it with him—the dusty charcoal, smooth as velvet, catching on the rough paper. I want to get up and take over for him, and then Nicholas's thumb traces a circle on the back of my neck, and I forget all about the paper on my skin and think only about the skin on my skin.

Sitting there, the night air still hot enough to make me sticky, I turn into a creature of hunger and want. Half of me wants to lunge forward and rip into the paper with a charcoal pencil until it tears from the force of my vision, and part of me wants to turn and rip into Nicholas or let him rip into me—I am not sure which. Either way, I've never been closer to feeling like a vampire, like someone who just wants to chase their own desire.

Lust is so easy and uncomplicated—primal—not really an emotion to be controlled. You can feel it and still be empty of anything else. I wonder if that's enough.

I tip my head upward. He needs to see me like this. If he sees this moment of desire on my face, he'll believe I can be like him.

His fingers gently grab my chin and pull my head back down. "Not yet," he says, and I don't know exactly what he means with those two words, what he'll give me when the portrait is finished.

Finally, finally, the artist stops moving and leans back to admire his work. I recognize his critical and satisfied look as one I've had many, many times.

"Almost perfect," he says, brushing his lank hair from his eyes. He scratches his cheek, leaving dark marks behind like black blush. In another moment of time, I would want to be friends with him. Instead of spinning it around to show us, he slides it into a white envelope and passes it to me.

"Thank you," I say. I itch to admire his technique, but it seems rude to unmask what he's already hidden. Maybe he doesn't like to see other people's reactions to his work. I can understand that. I can count the people I've let look at my sketchbook on one hand: Dad, Jessica, Bailey, occasionally Mom, and Henry.

*Henry.* I wish he wouldn't pop into my head. Will he be angry with me? I try to remember the look on his face when I took the envelope, but I wasn't even looking at him or thinking about him when I did it. I did what I needed to do.

I push him away, but he lingers in the corners of my mind, judging the way I brush up against Nicholas as we walk.

Nicholas takes us down the quieter side streets, his long legs moving at a languid pace I can keep up with easily. Occasionally his featherlight fingers touch my back, and I want to boldly tell him to leave his hand on me, but on the darkest street corners, little thrills of fear keep me from speaking.

After fifteen minutes of walking in silence, I get the courage to ask where we're going.

"We're here," he says.

The white facade of my building looms above us.

"How did you know where I was staying?"

He barely lifts one shoulder. "I have sources."

My pulse quickens, but I press on. "Well, did I pass your test?"

He's already turning around. "Not yet," he calls without bothering to look back.

"Bastard," I mutter once I think he's out of earshot.

His low chuckle drifts back to me, brushing against my skin like he's standing behind me. I spin in the dark, but I'm alone with only the streetlight. My fingers shake as I open the white envelope and pull out the picture. There I am—all dark shadows and smudges, and I have to admit I look good in black-and-white. Maybe I can live without the color in my life.

But behind me in the picture, where Nicholas stood with his hands on my neck, is nothing but the dark outline of the cathedral.

It'll be you and me.
—*Let the Right One In*

# Thirteen

All the fear, excitement, and yeah, okay, lust, turns to lead in my veins as I climb the stairs to the apartment. Part of me hopes Henry's already back so I can make sure he's okay, and part of me hopes he's not so I can hide under the covers and avoid facing him until morning.

He's there, sitting on the green sofa, elbows on his knees, staring into the unlit fireplace. The fact that these places even have fireplaces is baffling, and I open my mouth to make a joke about it before I press my lips together again.

The whole room is stiff with anger.

The dampness the humidity left on my skin freezes in the air-conditioning, and I desperately want to move past this moment and hop in the shower instead.

He runs a hand through his hair like he always does, leaving some of it sticking up. I shift uncomfortably, scraping the thin point of my heel across the wood floor.

"Are you going to look at me?" I ask.

His gaze slides up my legs and lingers on my short hemline in a way that would normally make me blush. I just feel cold.

"Nice dress."

"Thanks," I say, pretending to take his comment at face value. I know his words are meant to be a dig, but no guy gets to make me feel bad about what I wear.

His eyes narrow, and I imagine blackening one of them with my fist. One condescending look from him makes me angrier than a thousand slights from anyone else. And somewhere in the back of my mind, I understand why, but I focus on the heat gathering in my cheeks instead of unpacking my feelings for him.

"What's your problem?" I wish I could take the question back, but it's out of my mouth before I can stop it.

"Seriously?"

"Yeah." I double down like I don't know why he's pissed, but I'm pissed now too.

"You traded me for an *envelope*. You let me almost get hit by a train and then left me with some strange woman while you did what? Put on a fancy dress and traipsed all around town? Did you even consider looking for me? Did you worry even a little bit?"

"Nicholas said you were fine. I even got a picture of you eating beignets!" I fish out my phone from my purse, pulling up the picture and holding it out as a shield between us.

"Really? You knew I'd be fine when you made the bargain? Somehow I missed that part of the conversation while the train was barreling toward us. Don't pretend you knew or cared what would happen to me." Quietly he adds, "I should have known."

I wince. I know he's thinking about his grandma's death—me

not showing up for him—but it's easier to pretend he's only talking about this moment.

"I did." I drop my phone down to my side. "I stood there and waited for the train to pass so I could make sure you were fine. You were gone. You didn't have to go with her."

He stands up and takes a step toward me. His teeth grind together as he spits out his next words. "She told me I had to play along or the game was off. I went with her for *you*. I didn't even think twice about it or myself. You gave me up for a freaking piece of paper, and all I thought about was doing what you needed." He sighs, rubbing his hand over his face, anger dissipating to reveal the exhaustion underneath. "I'm pathetic," he mutters.

"You're not." I move to close the gap between us but stop halfway. My heart speeds before I can even make sense of what I'm seeing. "What is that?" My voice comes out so hushed and horrified that Henry turns around to see what I'm looking at, but I'm looking at him—and at what's clearly blood staining the collar of his green shirt.

He looks confused as he turns back to me. "What?"

My hand shakes as I step closer and pull on his collar. "What'd they do to you?" I examine his neck, but it looks smooth and perfect.

He grabs his collar from me and pulls it out so he can see. I wait for him to freak out, but he laughs.

I pull back. Henry's laugh usually puts me at ease, but my heart's still thumping.

"It's ketchup," he says.

"I thought you had beignets."

"We did." His voice is slow and calm. "And then we went for fries. She said I had to stay with her for a couple of hours. Turns out the only thing we have in common is that we both love eating."

"I thought—" My pulse mellows. I take a deep breath.

"I know what you thought," he says. "I'm fine. Doesn't mean I'm not mad though."

I'm still shaking a little from my momentary rush of fear. Even though he's fine, it could have happened, and I didn't think about that when I traded him.

He pulls me gently toward him so my cheek presses against his chest. He smells of hours-old cologne and sweat.

"Sorry." I keep whispering the word, like if I say it enough times, it'll be true.

"Just say you won't do it again."

I take the smallest step away, so I'm still in his arms but a chilly few inches exist between our bodies. I want to close the gap, but leaning back in would be something like a promise not to do it again, and I don't break promises—not unless it's life or death, and with so much on the line, I'd rather not make them at all.

"I didn't trade you for the envelope. I didn't trade you for Nicholas." I traded him for my dad, for the mere possibility of getting what I need to save him, and I'd do it again. I pull back even more, so he's forced to end our embrace or follow me. He lets me go, and I pull out the drawing, holding it up for him.

"Look at this. Nicholas was standing right behind me the whole time, but the artist didn't draw him."

Henry's brows draw together. Of course he doesn't understand the significance.

"Bram Stoker mentions painters not being able to capture a vampire's true essence. It's not in *Dracula*, but it is in his notes. He was very well researched. This is proof, Henry. This is why I came."

"To get a portrait done by a street artist who probably got paid not to draw the dude behind you?"

I ignore his condescending doubt.

"I want to save my dad, and I'll do anything to make that happen. I'll let you down again and again." I look him straight in the eyes as I say it, so he can't have any doubt I mean it. Part of me wants to be there for Henry, to tell him what he wants to hear from me, but it would be a lie.

He sighs, closing the gap between us again, so I can lean against his chest without giving up anything, without making any promises. The gesture is his concession, not mine. His chin rests softly on the top of my head. "It's okay," he says.

I wrap one arm around him. My other hand hangs between us, still gripping the drawing—one more sign. Six out of seven— more than I thought I would get.

Henry's not forgiving me, but I don't forgive me either. You've got to be willing to take it back to forgive yourself, and I wouldn't.

"You could use a shower," he says.

"So could you."

We laugh and pull apart. After awkwardly offering the only shower back and forth, he goes first.

While Henry's gone, my home number lights up the screen on my phone. My first thought, the first thought I've had every time I've gotten a call in the past few months, is that something's wrong with Dad. I never used to be reliable at answering my phone, but now I always pick up on the first ring.

"Hello?" My stomach clenches as I answer and wait to know if the thing has happened or not. Those few seconds add up to some of the worst moments in my life.

"Hey, kiddo. Sorry I missed your call the other day."

"Dad." My breath comes out in a painful rush.

"Miss me?" He gives a raspy chuckle, and I smile into my phone. "Are you having fun?"

"I'd rather be here with you."

"I know, honey, but are you having fun? I want you to have fun for me."

My throat swells. I can't stand lying to him, and I'm already out here. Mom can't talk me out of it now. "I didn't come to have fun, Dad. I came to find a vampire."

He stays silent for so long that I start to worry. I want him to say something: confirm he's hoping I'll succeed or tell me to stop, that he doesn't want this. But I also don't want to ask him. Telling me to stop could break me. Telling me he's counting on me could make me crumble under the pressure.

"Well," he finally says, "I know better than to talk you out of that. You're still having a good time though, right?"

I'm not sure he gets it—why I'm looking. This is more than my own fascination, but my throat is too tight to explain it. "Sure, Dad," I say instead.

"Henry looking out for you?"

"I can look out for myself."

"I know you can." I can feel him smile on the other side of the line. "It's just nice to have backup in that department."

"You're my backup in that department," I say.

He pauses for too long, and it gives his next word too much weight. An impossible weight. "Always," he says. "No matter what."

I know what he means by *no matter what*—that he'll be looking out for me when he's dead—but I don't need or want those types of reassurances, because he's not going to die. I fight the urge to tell him what I'm really doing, how close I am, but I haven't won yet, and I don't even know if being a vampire can save him. Maybe it won't work on someone as sick as him, but I don't want to think about that.

I cannot fail. I'll never forgive myself, and Dad won't be around to give forgiveness in my place.

I need to get off the phone. Dad sounds weak and tired, like a man who has less time than the doctor said, and if I think too much about that, I could lose the hope I have to save him, and without that, what would be left for me? I'd drown in all the sorrow I'm holding at bay. I'd be dead, too, and not in the good, immortal way—just a person rotting on the inside.

"I love you, Dad," I say, even though my throat hurts so much I can barely speak. I don't know why it gets harder and harder to say "I love you" to someone you might lose. It seems like it should be easier, but maybe it's because each time you say it, it could be the last. The three words end up carrying more meaning than we're used to.

"I love you too, kiddo."

When Henry comes out of the shower, I'm sitting on the sofa, phone hanging limp in my hand. He pauses across the room, and I sense his assessment, though I don't look up at him. Eventually he sits next to me, close enough for the cushion to dip and cause me to fall into his side. Before I can right myself, his arm slides around me, loose enough to shake off but solid enough to keep me there.

I tell myself a small bit of grief is okay. Nobody will see it but Henry, and it's not grief about my dad's death—not like Jessica wailing after the doctor's last prognosis. I won't grieve something I'm hoping to stop, but I grieve the fact that he's sick while I'm here. We'll never get to navigate eating beignets for the first time together. I shared that moment with someone else. So my grief is for that. It *has* to be.

Henry's dampness from the shower soaks through his T-shirt into my clothes and skin.

A few tears find their way onto my cheeks.

We stay like that until we're both dry.

Oh, yeah.

That's the vampire spirit.

*—Mom's Got a Date with a Vampire*

# Fourteen

In the morning, I shrug off the memory of Henry's arm around me and ignore the ghosts of the tears on my cheeks. Now more than ever is not the time to let too much sadness leak out of me. It would show through my smiles like amateur brushstrokes on a forgery of a priceless piece of art, and Nicholas would see it, and then I would fail. But letting go a little bit felt good.

I leave Henry asleep in his room and walk the Quarter alone, ignoring the smell of hot pastries drifting from more than one corner. My stomach begs to stop, but I hush it. I'm on a mission. Plus, I need to call Mom. I know talking to Dad last night will not get me out of my scheduled check-in, so I'd rather get it out of the way. I bet she's just getting up now, at the crack of dawn, having coffee with way too much sugar and cream. The thought makes me smile a bit. Mom's the type of person you'd think took her coffee black, but she has a major sweet tooth like everyone else in our family. She'd love beignets even if she'd hate the French Quarter. I should tell her about them.

She answers immediately.

"Hi, Mom." I don't bother asking how Dad is yet. He used to be a morning person, but that changed when he got sick.

"Hi, sweetie."

I smile. Mom only calls me "sweetie" in the mornings, when she's always a bit softer around the edges and hasn't turned into a no-nonsense attorney yet.

"How are you?" she asks. It's an open, weighted question that I've never liked answering truthfully—even before.

"Henry and I ate beignets. They're a thousand times better than doughnuts. You'd like them."

"I'm sure I would." She pauses. "Have you drawn anything?"

My chest tightens. If this is her trying to be like Dad again . . . I just can't.

She moves past my silence. "I always wanted to go to New Orleans, back when I had time for art. I used to imagine myself doing portraits on the street." Her voice is soft with what I think is longing, but it's so unlike her I can barely make sense of it. Then she laughs, breaking it. "Can you imagine me as a street artist?"

"Yes," I say, even though I can't really, but I *want* to see that side of her. Suddenly I wonder if deep down she wanted to come on this trip with us all along, but she never said it, and I never guessed.

It makes me sad, but also hopeful, like there's more to us than I thought.

"I hope you start again. I thought a new place might help

you." She almost sounds like she wants me to go to art school, but she probably just wants me back to normal.

"I'm thinking about it." It's not a lie. I am thinking about art in a way I haven't been able to back home, not for a long while now. But I'm not sure it's a good thing. I'm not sure I want to see what comes out of me.

"Jessica said you didn't call her yet."

I wish she wouldn't bring up Jessica in every conversation.

"She could call me."

"She won't. She thinks you're mad at her for showing up at church without warning you first. She might be as upset about that as . . ."

That hurts. I press my hand to my stomach like that will help.

"I wasn't mad," I say, but I was. I hated the way it felt to watch her and Mom accept the unacceptable.

But that wasn't entirely fair.

Hanging onto hope is so, so hard when every turn gives you a reason to let go. I'm shredded with the effort. It's wrong to expect others to put themselves through what I have.

And crying last night into Henry's chest felt needed, like getting out that small grief helped me keep everything else contained.

But everyone can't hold things back as well as me.

"Okay, I'll do it."

"You promise?"

I cringe. "Yes."

"Good," she says.

I'm about to end the call when she says my name.

"Yeah?"

"Draw me something, will you?"

"I'll try." I hang up. Her last question rings in my ears. It didn't sound like her trying to be Dad. It sounded like something she's wanted to say for a long time.

Maybe I'll have it in me to draw again when this is over.

I speed up, skirting around the handful of bright-eyed tourists who turned in to bed early and stepping over the handful of people still passed out in the street who never went to bed at all. Early morning in the French Quarter is probably the one time the two crowds meet—if you can call stepping over someone's legs meeting.

The bell *ding*s as I open the bookstore door. Cool air wraps around me—already ten degrees cooler than the outside. I expect to be the only one here at this hour, but two men in their twenties stand in the back, debating the merits of some author.

Ruth catches my eye and winks as I slip around the corner into the poetry nook.

Nicholas didn't tell me to come here again. Replaying our conversations last night, I realize he didn't reveal much of anything.

But something must be here waiting for me. If not—

I'll hunt him down like I'm the great-granddaughter of Van Helsing himself.

The thought brings a vicious smile to my face.

I tug my little book off the shelf and flip through it. There. A snag in the pages, and a new note next to a new poem.

### We Wear The Mask
We wear the mask that grins and lies,
It hides our cheeks and shades our eyes,—
This debt we pay to human guile;
With torn and bleeding hearts we smile
And mouth with myriad subtleties,

Why should the world be over-wise,
In counting all our tears and sighs?
Nay, let them only see us, while
We wear the mask.

We smile, but O great Christ, our cries
To thee from tortured souls arise.
We sing, but oh the clay is vile
Beneath our feet, and long the mile,
But let the world dream otherwise,
We wear the mask!
—Paul Laurence Dunbar

This one hits home and feels like a warning. I am the one wearing a mask and smiling with my bleeding heart in my chest, and Nicholas knows it. I need to do better. I open my note, fingers shaking slightly as I do.

*Gold suits you, which bodes well for you.
We love wearing gold, after all. But our lives
aren't all glitz and glamour. Time to test your
fangs. Your next challenge: pet an alligator.*

"Hell no," I mutter.

"Good book?" One of the young men stands at the entrance of the nook. He takes in the cover of my book through his overtly trendy black-rimmed glasses and shakes his head, reaching and plucking it from my hands without asking, sighing as he flips it back and forth. "This one's just a tourist trap—spooky poetry for a spooky place. I can recommend something better."

As he moves past me, I grab the book back from him. "I'm good, thanks."

He shrugs, pushing a Walt Whitman collection back on the shelf, like recommending *Leaves of Grass,* the one poetry collection everyone's heard of, would have been impressive. "Your loss."

"Right." He heads back out toward his buddy. "Wait."

He turns back around, eyebrows raised in that anticipating way, like he's about to be right about something.

"Do you know where I can pet an alligator around here?"

He snorts.

His buddy snickers behind him.

I smile sweetly even though I'm imagining what I'd do to him if I really were a vampire.

"No idea." He turns and leaves with his friend, laughing together about tourists.

"Assholes." I turn and find Ruth behind me. "Sorry about my language."

She smiles. "No problem, dear. Undergraduate English majors tend to be a bag of pricks."

I freeze and then laugh until my stomach hurts.

She's back to straightening her shelves when I catch my breath.

"You might try a swamp tour," she says. "I don't think they encourage you to pet the beasts, but they'll get you close enough."

Eighty dollars and one long bus ride later, Henry and I board a rickety metal boat with ten other people and a guide who tells us not to worry—none of their tour boats have sunk in at least a month.

Henry cracks up with half the other people.

The other half and I share a few frightened glances.

"That's not funny," I whisper.

"Sure it is." Henry's grinning like a kid going to Disneyland for the first time. He seems to have forgotten what I did to him yesterday.

"I can't swim, remember?"

"How could I forget?" He laughs even louder, like my drowning takes the comedy level up a notch.

I scowl. He's too bright—too happy—there's an air of falseness to it, like he's the one putting on a mask to hide any lingering hurts from me. I should never have cried in front of him. He's trying to make *me* feel good when I don't deserve it.

He was always the first one to apologize.

"Lighten up. I can swim well enough for both of us."

"I'm not sure that's how that works. You'll be on dry land fast, and I'll still be drowning."

"I would never let you drown." There's a note of seriousness in his voice that lightens my chest so that I no longer feel like a sack of sinkable rocks. He reaches out and squeezes my hand briefly. "Remember?"

His question pulls up the memory of the time we were at another kid's swim party. I would only get in with the safety of an inner tube, but I was walking along the edge of the pool without it when another boy thought it'd be hilarious to shove me in. My head went underwater, but only for a second before Henry appeared, holding me up at the side of the pool as I coughed and cried from the way my nose burned.

I shudder as I remember the feeling.

"You shoved that kid in the deep end afterward," I say.

"I'll still hurt anyone who hurts you." His voice holds no trace of lightness or humor. I know exactly who he's thinking of.

I keep my voice mellow. "Good to know."

And then the boat shoots forward with a speed nobody antic-ipated. My body slides, closing the couple of inches between me and Henry, and I don't immediately correct myself. If the boat does go down, I should be closer to the guy who promised to save me from drowning. That's just solid reasoning.

The thick green grasses lining the murky water become

nothing but a blur. I focus on the white spray ripping off the side of the boat. When we stop, we're in a swamp cul-de-sac, a small, rounded offshoot surrounded by dense green foliage. It feels like a different world than the French Quarter, which is so alive and layered with human history. Out here teems with untouched life—a different kind of vibrancy and beauty.

"Here they come, folks," the guide says.

I don't know when my hand latched onto Henry's biceps, but I squeeze a little tighter as a seven-foot alligator drifts up to the side of the boat.

"I am not touching that thing," I mutter.

Henry laughs. "I don't think that's an option."

I didn't tell him about the next challenge. When I shook him awake this morning to tell him to get ready for the swamp tour, he thought I got the tickets for him. A little surprise for my betrayal from the night before. I didn't correct his assumption.

And now I feel terrible.

I let go of him so he can lean forward and get closer to the rails than I want to be.

"Holy crap." His voice rises on the *a* in crap in a way that makes me a little concerned about his level of investment. "They're glorious. They're like little miniature dinosaurs."

I stare at him like he lost his mind on the ride out here, but he's not looking at me. I could probably take off all my clothes and start nude sunbathing, and he still wouldn't look at me because he's more into the scaly rough look.

He loved dinosaurs as a kid. When we were ten, we holed up in his room and watched the first *Jurassic Park* movie even though I wasn't supposed to watch it yet, and he regaled me with random facts like how long a real T. rex's teeth would be as it chomped into a dude or how a T. rex wouldn't actually be fast enough to keep up with a Jeep going full speed, as if that made it any less scary.

At that point in my life, I much preferred my favorite Disney Channel Original Movie: *Mom's Got a Date with a Vampire*.

"'Pretty cool'?" I say, keeping all my fingers and toes well away from the railing on the boat. Even though eventually I'm going to have to stick my hand out there and go for it.

"Pretty cool." Henry's voice still carries that higher prepuberty pitch as he finally breaks his loving trance with the gator to gape at me. "I don't think you're appreciating this at the appropriate level. Look at those eyes. They're ancient and cold and true killers. I bet they'd eat vampires for breakfast."

"No doubt." The slitted golden eye roves over me like I barely register on its radar of important things in life.

The guide dangles a little ball of something out over the water, and the alligator leaps for it, snagging it in his mouth and then dropping back down.

Henry cheers.

I pull the Polaroid from my purse and snap his picture.

His face falls when I do.

"What?"

"Why'd you bring that thing?" He dips his chin toward the camera like it's some kind of horrible contraption he can't even name. "Is this another task? Are you doing this for him?"

I want to argue. Nothing I do is for *Nicholas*—not really. I thought I made that clear last night.

"I just wanted to take your picture."

"Oh." The alligator makes another leap behind him, and he misses it. "Look." He points down the side of the boat behind me, where a smaller one eyes the show hungrily.

"Will you take my picture?" I ask. I pass the camera to him, trying not to let my fingers tremble, which would be a dead giveaway.

He hesitates but plucks the camera from me.

I lean against the rail and take a deep breath. "Don't take it yet."

"It's going to swim away."

"I want to touch it."

He lowers the camera from his face, suspicion latching onto his expression, tugging down the corners of his mouth. I probably left fingernail imprints in his arm when they swam up to the boat, and now I want to touch one? He isn't buying it.

"My dad will think it's cool." The lie burns my tongue so bad I might need to jump in the swamp to make the pain go away.

"Will he think it's cool when you come home minus three fingers?"

"I'm sure he'll love me anyway. Just take the shot, will you?"

He pulls the camera back up to his eye.

The tour guide and the rest of the people on board focus on the giant alligator snatching his snacks from midair. It's now or never.

I lean closer to the rail, gripping it with both hands. I count my ten fingers and wonder if I'd actually be good with counting only seven. The little gator floats there, eyes focused on the bigger gator getting all the snacks. He really wants a snack too.

I lean back in my seat, feeling queasy.

"I can't do it." I like my fingers. I use them to draw pretty things, or at least I used to. I thought maybe I'd be able to draw pretty things again once I saved my dad, but if I'm missing all my fingers I won't be able to. Then again, some people learn to paint with their toes—I think I read that somewhere. But if I don't save my dad, I'll never draw a pretty thing ever again, just endless black holes.

My face is wet. Am I crying? No—I wipe away one errant tear. Damn it. They're too close to the surface after last night.

"Hey. It's okay. We can take other cool pictures for your dad," Henry says.

"No . . . I can do this." Remembering the weakness in Dad's voice, I let out enough sorrow from my well to drown out my fear. At least I don't have to smile for this challenge. I only need to be brave—channel my inner child who would do almost anything. Almost. How'd that bastard know I don't like anything resembling a dinosaur?

Sucking in a breath, I crouch down by the rails, lean over,

and touch the rough, slick back of the alligator. Then it's gone, and my fingers touch nothing but water. I yank them back and count them.

Henry's grinning at me.

"Did you get it?"

He nods and passes me the still black Polaroid.

"Are you shaking?" he asks.

"Nope. Not at all." I realize our arms are touching again and start to shift away, but he reaches out and grabs my hand, weaving his fingers between mine and squeezing tight enough to stop my tremors. He rests both our hands on my knee, watching me the whole time to make sure it's okay.

It feels nice.

The guide kicks the engine on, and as we speed through the next section of the swamp, I dry up the little bit of sorrow I let out and relax into our surroundings. I achieved my task, and it's not like I can jump off the boat and swim back to deposit my picture any sooner.

The second part of the swamp tour takes us through a narrow passage dense with trees growing straight out of the water, half their roots twisting above the waterline. Everything is green and dark, and you just know something will kill you if you fall overboard. Delightfully creepy.

And then I spot the pack of wild raccoons, smaller with redder fur than the raccoons in the city.

"Ohhhh, they are too cute. Maybe I can pet one of them."

"Gross," Henry says. "They probably have rabies. They're more dangerous than the gators."

One stands up on its hind legs, cocking its head at us as we coast by. I wave at it.

"Did you seriously wave at that rodent?"

I punch him in the shoulder with my free hand. "Don't make fun of me."

"I'm not—it's cute."

I widen my eyes dramatically. "Did you admit I'm cute?"

"I'm pretty sure I admitted that more than once before."

Some of the humor's left his face, replaced by something else I'm afraid to name. Something way beyond physical chemistry. Something I don't have room for in my life. Not now. Maybe not ever again.

The comfort of my fingers between his shifts to something electric—exciting but hard to bear.

We stare at each other until I break my hand free and turn back to the swamp, whose murky water suddenly seems much safer than this boat.

"Holy cow. Would you look at the balls on that boar?" The boar roots through the mud in front of us, and it's impossible to ignore that it's the male of the species.

Henry barks out a laugh. "Well, that's one way to change the subject."

I watch him in my peripheral vision to gauge if he's upset, but he's already smiling slightly, leaning over the bars on the boat, trying to catch a glimpse of the water snake the guide pointed out moments before.

I paste an easy smile on my face and withdraw, letting it do the work for me. If Henry notices I'm not engaged anymore, he doesn't mention it. Occasionally he smiles in my direction, but it carries none of the suggestion from our earlier conversation.

I don't have room for romance in my life right now. It would only distract me from my tasks. I can't help but think of how I leaned into the moment last night—Nicholas's cold fingers tracing the pulse in my neck—but that's different. I'm playing pretend with Nicholas. Henry's real.

When our boat docks again, he offers his hand to help me step up. Even though I certainly don't need it, I take it like a peace offering. Friends help friends off boats.

Everything's fine until we get back on the bus and I register the photograph still gripped in my hand. I lift it and stare at my blurry arm and the dark shadow in the water, which looks nothing like an alligator. You can't even tell I touched it.

My stomach bottoms out, and I almost cry again for the second time in one day.

Thankfully, Henry doesn't notice. He's going full nerd beside me, rattling off fun facts from his phone about alligators, which are apparently his new favorite thing.

When we get back into town, we head to the bookstore under the pretext of getting the next challenge. I shake my head slightly at Ruth when we walk through the door, praying she gets the hint and doesn't mention me being here already this morning.

She's spry as ever in a pink linen dress and a little white shawl, but I catch the crease of worry in her brow as she watches me head back to the poetry section. Henry's safely chatting with her, so I pull the book off the shelf and place my photo between the pages, hoping the blurry action is enough. I don't know what I'll do if I get behind. I don't have the money to postpone our flight, and I worry Dad doesn't have that kind of time. Plus, I've never missed a single one of Dad's birthdays. I'm not going to start now, even if I plan on him having an endless amount of them.

"What are you doing?"

I snap the book shut, but Henry grabs it from me and flips it open to the picture.

His usually warm face goes cold as he closes the book and hands it back to me with two fingers as if it's been doused in poison.

"You lied," he says simply, staring above my head instead of directly at me.

"I really thought you'd enjoy it."

He makes a harsh, angry sound in the back of his throat. "Being lied to?"

"No. The alligators. I would have taken you even without the task." I reach for his forearm, but he backs away from me.

"But you didn't."

"I'm sorry." I shake my head. "I told you I'd do anything to save my dad."

"No—I know that. I'm okay with that or I wouldn't still be here, but you could've told me it was a challenge, and we still could've had a good time. Why did you lie though? What was the point?"

I hesitate, biting my top lip to prevent the truth from breaking out: I wanted to make him happy. When I saw the challenge, I thought of how much Henry would love it. I didn't see it as one more roadblock to overcome in saving Dad. I saw it as a way to make Henry smile. But I can't tell him that—I can't open that door.

I take the easy way out. "Would you have enjoyed it as much if you knew Nicholas was behind it?"

He shrugs, searching my face like he knows there's more to it, but I turn myself into an empty canvas and give him nothing.

"Stop making this about you." My words are cruel, and I deliver them with simple coldness. Perhaps these tasks are also training me to be as vicious as a vampire.

The muscle below his eyes twitches and then he turns away. I let him go. He can't expect me to choose him in this. He keeps seeing this as him versus Nicholas, but Nicholas is nothing but a means to save my father, and when it comes to a choice between hurting Henry's feelings and saving my father, I'll rip apart Henry's feelings with all the ruthlessness of an alligator, and I won't be made to feel regret.

Well, maybe a little. I collect it in my well of watercolor—it's the burning orange of the sun right before it sets.

*I am all in a sea of wonders. I doubt; I fear; I think strange things, which I dare not confess to my own soul.*
—*Dracula* by Bram Stoker

# Fifteen

I don't look for Henry, and he doesn't come back to our place. As I walk to the bookstore later that night, I can't help but notice what a lonely place New Orleans could be. Barely anyone walks the streets by themselves here, and even if you are alone, it's so easy to turn and interact with someone beside you. I can't bring myself to do that, though. There's too much pain inside me to open my mouth and enjoy meaningless conversation. My well won't allow it. Keeping it contained consumes all my thoughts. I count the cracks in the pavement to distract myself but give up after a hundred, because I'm walking too dang slow and the bookstore will close before I get there.

"You look sad."

He doesn't make me jump this time, but my heart still lurches at his voice. I turn and find Carter standing under an ornate gas lantern, shadows playing across his face. I bet he planned that position. He looks extra creepy.

"Are you going to report me?"

He shrugs.

"What are you doing?" I ask.

"Watching."

I sigh. "What do you want?"

"Nothing. Everything. Hard to tell after a while." He looks thoughtful, like he's lost in the past or maybe the future. Maybe it all blends together.

I wonder if I can get something out of him while he's like this. "How long have you and Nicholas known each other? Have you always done his watching?"

His eyes snap back to me, narrowing suddenly in a way that makes my skin crawl.

"Don't all packs of predators have leaders and minions? I do the dirty work." He brings a hand up to his face and inspects his nails like there's something staining them. I can't tell in the dark if there is or isn't, and not knowing is worse.

"We all have our roles," he says. "You should probably continue with yours." He gestures down the street, and I don't wait around this time. I'm not going to ask him again to turn me. If there are bad vampires and good ones, I know which one I'd put in each category.

I glance over my shoulder once as I move away, but he's already gone.

"Hey, Ruth," I call out when I finally slide through the door of the bookshop, mentally preparing myself to explain why Henry's not with me again.

"Expecting someone else?" Nicholas lounges in Ruth's chair,

two of the legs off the floor, his heavy black shoes draped across her desk, keeping him balanced.

"Something tells me Ruth would not like your feet on her desk."

"Are you going to tell on me?"

I don't answer, keeping a little piece of power over him.

He smirks at my silence and drops his legs off the desk, leaning forward to check the empty doorway behind me.

"Where's your man?"

For a second I freeze, thinking he means Carter, but no. I can tell by the tightness in his expression that he means Henry.

"He's not *my* man." I shut the door.

"Ah, excellent." His lips curve in a feral way that makes my stomach drop. I struggle to capture it and drag it back up to sensibility.

"What are you doing here?"

"I like to run the bookstore in my spare time. Immortality gets boring without a purpose."

I sigh.

"I was waiting for you, of course."

"Got tired of the book? Just going to give me the answer?"

"Not quite." He jerks his head toward the poetry section.

"So I still have to play this game with you sitting right there."

"Someone's cranky tonight."

I don't answer. I'm supposed to be full of joy, after all, and whatever's about to come out of my mouth is more like joy that died and came back as a zombie.

I pull the book off the shelf with a little too much gusto, and Nicholas chuckles behind me, because of course he followed me. He's here to see all of his little game in action.

I read the poem first.

**The Ghost**
Softly as brown-eyed Angels rove
I will return to thy alcove,
And glide upon the <u>night</u> to thee,
Treading the shadows silently.

And I will give to thee, my own,
Kisses as icy as the <u>moon</u>,
And the caresses of a snake
Cold gliding in the thorny brake.

And when returns the livid morn
Thou shalt find all my place forlorn
And chilly, till the <u>falling</u> night.

Others would rule by tenderness
Over thy life and youthfulness,
But I would <u>conquer</u> thee by fright!
—Charles Baudelaire

"Ahh, one of my favorites," he says, so close behind me I jump, and he laughs softly in response.

I turn around and glare up at him. "Are you trying to scare me? Threatening to conquer someone isn't exactly romantic."

"Are you scared, Victoria?"

I let a little trickle of fear release within me—a deep, pulsing purple. We're alone in a bookstore after-hours on a side street few people would consider walking down this time of night. But fear is perhaps the easiest emotion to control when you absolutely have to. I push it back down.

"Nope. I'm pretty relieved, actually. I wasn't sure you'd give me another clue. My alligator picture was less than perfect."

"It's the spirit that counts."

"Great. I've got spirit coming out my ears."

"You are too funny."

"I aim to please."

"That's precisely what I'm afraid of." His voice grows suddenly serious.

"What do you mean?"

"I fear you may be showing me what I want to see and telling me what I want to hear without really feeling it in here." He taps me on the chest right below my neck.

"My collarbone?"

"See—humor as a shield again."

"I'm just a funny girl."

"Prove me wrong." He points to the still-folded note in my hand. I open it.

*Lasso Joanie on the Pony.*

239

"What does that even mean?"

"You'll see. That's what I'm here for." He stands with his arms clasped behind his back, waiting for me to commit, but I'm already way past committed.

"Lead the way."

We end up on the streetcar line, and I make Nicholas take the window seat so I can escape the branches trying to kill me. When we pass the house Henry and I robbed, I can't help but squirm.

"Uncomfortable?" he asks.

"You returned that stuff, right?"

"Of course. What do you think I am—a monster?" His teeth flash.

"You'd better be."

He chuckles.

We exit our ride in front of a massive brick church, almost a silhouette against the purpling night sky. I'm afraid for a second that we might be about to steal some holy water, but Nicholas passes the church without even glancing at it, and I worry he can't stand the sight of it.

I stop in front of it though. I'm tempted to test him—invent a reason to go inside—but if vampires can't enter churches, then ignorance will be my best defense against how pissed Dad will be. I don't know for sure what Dad wants, whether or not he was serious when he told me to find him a vampire, but if I make him a creature that can't stand the sight of something so important to him, he could spend eternity resenting me.

Would that be worse? I almost call out to Nicholas—ask him directly.

But it's not like I'm going to turn Dad without his permission, and he'll want to know everything I know. If I don't know anything for certain, then I have a better chance of him agreeing.

Because what happens if I do all this and he says no? If he'd rather die and leave me than be a vampire, how could I live with that? Spend an eternity alone with that haunting me?

"Beautiful, isn't it?"

I didn't hear him slide up next to me, but he's there, staring up at the church with something like reverence on his face.

"I'd take you inside, but they're closed for the night already."

So much relief courses through me, I barely stop myself from crying.

"You were worried about that," he says softly.

"Yes," I whisper, and that one word is more honest than I've been with him yet.

"Those are myths," he says, and then he grabs my hand. "Come."

He leads me onto Tulane University's campus, past a massive stone building worthy of castle status. Lampposts with perfectly round globes on top light everything, so if you squint your eyes, they seem like floating moons.

"It's gorgeous," I whisper. I could spend hours here, drawing until I captured this nighttime whimsy. I'm glancing behind me at the largest building when Nicholas pulls me to a stop.

"Look up," he says, so I do.

I can't help myself. I gasp like a child seeing snow for the first time. Thousands of beads dangle from the branches above me like multicolored vines. A single lamppost sits just beneath the tree, lighting the beads around it with an iridescent glow. I stepped into a fairytale, and it causes a sharp pang in my chest because I'm past the point of believing in fairytales, but for one second when I looked up, I believed again. Maybe I can hang onto that.

"There," Nicholas says. "That was what I was looking for— that look on your face that said anything in the world is possible if you believe." He reaches out and runs a hand down my cheek. "Where did it go?"

"It grew up and flew away like everything else." I point up at the tree. "It went to live in fairyland with all the other beautiful things."

"Well, maybe I can get it back for you." He steps away with a grin, then crouches and leaps straight up at the tree, snagging a set of pink beads from one of the branches. Coming back to me, he places it around my neck. I can't help but smile a little. He cocks his head and scrutinizes my expression. "You need more."

He continues to jog around the tree and jump for the necklaces, capturing those little pieces of magic and dragging them down to earth to be trapped with me. I stare down at all the colors combined against my shirt, and somehow they don't weigh me down like I thought they would. I actually laugh, and they dance with the movement of my chest.

"I don't have to flash you for these, do I?"

He raises a brow. "Well, I wouldn't say no if you're offering."

I laugh again, loud and startling and so right in this little land of dreams. I don't want to go when he takes my hand and starts leading me out, but he promises the night won't be over, and I don't want it to be. With the weight of the beads on my neck, I let some of my own weight go. On the tram ride back downtown, the breeze through the window threatens to blow me away.

I sense Nicholas watching me, and I know he's seeing what he wants, and it frees me from the guilt of feeling momentarily happy, because happiness is a necessary evil. Besides, I'm not really happy. I am still wearing a mask, but one more closely melded to my own skin.

I let myself sink into that false happiness, a bright, unnatural yellow.

We end up walking toward the French Market, past Café Du Monde, to the point where the road splits, leaving an awkward triangular island surrounded by the street.

Nicholas points to the golden statue of a woman on a horse. "That's Joan of Arc. We call her Joanie on the Pony."

I gape. "And you want me to lasso her? With what?"

A devilish grin spreads on his face as he tugs on the beads around my neck, running his fingers over the strands. "I'd say you have about thirty chances."

We cross the street and stand below her. The lights in the

dark give her a molten, fluid look, as if she captured the fire that burned her and used it to forge herself into a god. The banner she holds above her head almost waves in the glow.

"Is this really necessary?" I'm not keen on vandalism. Although it looks like she already wears a couple of necklaces left over from Mardi Gras.

"She's a symbol of perseverance and determination. She deserves to have a little piece of you with her."

"She was burned at the stake."

He shrugs, looking up at her with grim respect. "Sometimes it's not about how someone ends."

His words tighten around my throat, and I remove one of my suddenly heavy necklaces to ease some of the tension.

I pull my arm back and toss it. It clinks against her nose so loudly I wince. I select an orange necklace next. It hits the flagpole and sinks to the ground.

"I can tell you never played sports as a kid," Nicholas says.

"Shut up."

I eye my stack of necklaces. I need one that suits. A color that feels like hope. I choose a spring green even though the beads are weather-worn. That doesn't matter. Hope gets worn out too.

"Hey." I jump. A cop car has pulled up along the other side of the street. The woman leans out of her window. "What are you kids doing?"

Nicholas turns slowly to me. "Last try. Make it count."

I wind back as a car door slams, focus on Joanie's golden head, and let it soar. The beads crown her head for a second and then slip down and rest against her chest.

"Yes!" I jump and pump my fist in the air. My beads jingle.

"We must go now," Nicholas says, grabbing my fisted hand in his long fingers and dragging me after him. We run down the street and through the closed French Market, past stalls draped with tarps, waiting for the next day. Once we get through the other side, Nicholas slows and glances behind us. "I don't think she came after us."

"Did you see that?" I wheeze. I'm not a fantastic runner. My heart beats too fast and my lungs flounder. But there's a thrill in pushing your body to the edge. It gets rid of everything but the physical, burying it beneath the need to keep breathing.

Nicholas is silent. When I catch enough breath to stand upright, he's watching the labored rise and fall of my chest. I try to hold my breath to stop it, but I end up breathing more deeply. Taking a step toward me on our abandoned street corner, he wipes a sweaty piece of hair off my cheek.

"You are beautiful," he says.

And even with my clothes sticky with sweat, I soak in his words and believe them.

His fingertips trail down my warm cheeks to my neck and then lace into the beads dangling there. He tugs them ever so gently toward him, and I follow, getting closer and closer to his chest, which is suspiciously still, given we just sprinted half a mile.

I tilt my head up, and his mouth slides into a smile.

"What do you want from me right now?"

I part my lips to tell him the same thing I've been saying all along. I want him to give me the secret to his immortality. I want to be like him. But the words won't come. I can't find them. His breath warms my face, and my head's a fog with no colors, only weightlessness, and I want to keep it that way.

"I want to kiss you," I say.

He pulls the beads until I'm pressed against him. He lowers his mouth, and I rise onto my toes to connect with him. His lips move slow and soft against mine, gently lulling me. His grip shifts on the beads, tightening, pulling me impossibly closer so I'm aware of how violently my heart beats against his ribcage. I lock my fingers around his neck and pull him closer, biting his lower lip as I do. His hands around my necklaces clench, momentarily squeezing my windpipe so I gasp and break contact.

He drops the beads, and they clink between our chests. Placing his thumbs along my neck, he traces both sides of my windpipe as I stare up into his eyes, almost black in the darkened shadows of the night. His thumbs travel the bottom of my jaw, tilting it up as he bends and places a kiss in the hollow of my throat, lips moving upward as my pulse skitters under his touch, but I don't pull away. Teeth scrape cautiously across the tender part of my neck until his lips rest against the throbbing pulse beneath the corner of my jaw. He lingers. My fingers tighten in his hair, and he draws in a sharp breath as I pull him closer. Closer. He breaks his trance, and his lips travel back down my jaw. The thrill drowns out everything, and when he reaches my mouth again, I dive into him, swimming through his emotions and making them mine.

I am lusting red tinged with purple fear and streaked with yellow happiness—real happiness, not something fake. I only told myself it was fake earlier to make it okay. I've lost control of my well. Nicholas is pulling up buckets of color.

Water splashes us as a car drives through one of the constant puddles on the street, and suddenly I'm back in my own skin, aware of what I've done—I let myself live in the moment. I let myself feel things that have no purpose in my life right now.

His fingers close around my beads again, like he senses me pulling away and wants to hang on, but I'm already stepping away, and the beads stretch between us. He gently lays them back against my chest.

I thought it would be easy to pretend for him, to show him happiness on the outside without any of it existing inside. But I'm not just fooling him. I'm fooling myself. He draws out something real inside me—the thrill of adventure and danger, the erratic pulse of longing. And when my heart started pounding, it drowned out everything else—my bond with Henry. Even Dad. I sketch Dad in my mind, all in smudged charcoal that's fading with age. I hang onto the image, letting it drag me back out of my momentary happiness.

Nicholas was right all along—I *am* capable of feeling true joy through my pain. But I don't want to.

"Can we be done for the night?" I ask.

"Of course," he says. "I didn't mean to make you . . ."

He doesn't finish the sentence, probably because he has no idea what's wrong with me. He doesn't know about my father.

I brush past him and walk into the night. He doesn't speak to me again, but I sense him behind me as I walk. The streets are rowdy, and I dodge more than one group of drunk men, so I appreciate the gesture. When I reach the doorway to the building, I pivot and catch his silhouette turning the corner, walking in the other direction.

Part of me longs to call after him. I tell myself it's only to ask if that was enough—if one minute of betraying my grief will satisfy him—but the traitor within me just wants him close enough to feel those things again.

I turn and take the stairs to the apartment two at a time, moving so fast my muscles burn by the time I reach the door.

Good. I deserve the pain.

"You were out late," Henry grumbles from the couch when I get through the front door.

I almost make a "sorry, Dad" joke, but it wouldn't work, given everything.

I go with silence instead.

Henry sits up, and I get the sense he's inspecting every inch of me. "You look like you had fun," he says, and my stomach clenches. He's not wrong. I did. I felt light and free and alive in a way I haven't felt in months. I let out all the vibrant colors, and now I can't stop the rest from coming with them.

Happiness demands an equal dose of sorrow.

I let myself be bright and pink and golden, standing in the shadows, and now I spiral into a sea of blues I can't separate.

I walk to my room and shut the door.

Sad songs hit the spot, don't they?
—*A Girl Walks Home Alone at Night*

# Sixteen

In the morning, I slink out of bed and to the bookstore, giving Ruth a cheery hello on my way back to the poetry section. She watches me over her glasses, probably sensing something's off, but she's shrewd enough not to ask. I take a picture of the poem and grab the note and don't bother looking at either one until I get back under my hot-pink bedspread.

I'm honestly not sure I can do this anymore, but I've already come so close and sacrificed too much. It's Saturday. Three days left—how much more can he ask of me?

I unfold the note.

> I've never seen anyone so determined. Joanie's got nothing on you. Your story will have a different ending. I want the world to see that determination. Your task for tonight: Sing with a jazz band.

I get terrible stage fright. I wanted so badly to be a performer as a kid, but every time I tried, I froze. But this doesn't even faze me. Fear I can conquer.

A place and time are listed below at the bottom of the note.

I have nothing to do until tonight, and that feels like such a waste. I'd rather have another silly challenge to occupy my mind—something to give me at least the illusion of progress instead of lounging around on vacation while my family needs me.

I open the pictures on my phone so I can distract myself with the poem.

### The World

By day she woos me, soft, exceeding fair:
But all night as the moon so changeth she;
Loathsome and foul with hideous leprosy
And subtle serpents gliding in her hair.
By day she wooes me to the outer air,
<u>Ripe</u> fruits, <u>sweet</u> flowers, and full satiety:
But through the night, a beast she grins at me,
A very monster void of love and prayer.
By day she stands a lie: by night she stands
In all the naked <u>horror</u> of the truth
With pushing horns and clawed and
   clutching hands.
Is this a friend indeed; that I should sell
My soul to her, give her my life and youth,
Till my feet, cloven too, take hold on hell?
—Christina Rossetti

This poem scares me. Is Nicholas the beast, or am I? What if *I'm* the one playing with *him*?

I lay back and close my eyes, but the darkness behind my lids magnifies every thought. They snap open, and I count my heartbeats instead, but that only makes me think of what it would be like to not have one at all—to be undead or just dead. I wonder if God has a heartbeat or if he's like a vampire, feeding off the energy of everyone on earth. I wish I could ask Dad his thoughts about that interpretation, but I don't think he'd like my God-might-be-a-vampire theory.

I move on to counting planks of wood in the ceiling, but eventually I need to face the fact that I let my well open last night, and now emotions trickle under my skin like a leaky faucet I don't know how to fix.

I need to regain control. The only way to win this is to hide my sadness, and to do that, I need to hide everything.

I fortify it by thinking of Dad—not him sick, but all the times he was strong for me, like when I slipped and broke my arm climbing up a slide after my mother told me not to, and while I bawled and my mom screamed, he calmly scooped me up like nothing was wrong and packed me into the car like it was any other day. I actually stopped crying in the face of his calmness, and I can do the same now.

The harder part is containing the emotions that have already seeped through my skin and left watercolor stains. I chase down happiness first, a sharp, translucent yellow—those few moments last night watching my necklaces soar through the air. I picture my dad's once round and jovial face sunken in with pain, and the happiness slinks back without a fight.

Sorrow's harder to draw out. It shifts and changes like the blue of the sea and hides in all the curves of my veins. I'm tempted to let it stay, but letting it stay would be giving up. I squeeze it out by imagining Dad, healthy for all eternity, so grateful that I believed and took this risk for him, and the sorrow scurries back from my determination.

The guilt's the hardest to scrub out—gray and as untouchable as a storm cloud, it refuses to be contained with other colors. It eats at me until my insides become a field of suffocating fog. And because I have no colors to fend it off with, I let it stay. After all, Nicholas said I was too sad to live forever. He didn't mention guilt.

I wallow in it until an hour before I have to go.

I choose a white cotton dress with soft blue vertical stripes, accented in the middle with a large dove-gray bow. My hair embraces the waves the humidity gives it, and I keep my makeup light. I smile at my reflection. I'm the embodiment of air and lightness, and nobody will ever suspect the hole in the center of my chest when I look like this.

When I come out of my room, Henry's gone. I try not to care. I let the fog cover that feeling too.

The jazz club is nothing like the loud, decadent place where I first met Nicholas. The vibe is cool in a simple, effortless way—a classic wooden bar, faded green walls covered in an eclectic array of art I could look at all day, a tiny stage set up in front of the window facing the street, and a couple of small tables and chairs.

I'm surprised to see Nicholas leaning back in one of those wooden chairs in light jeans and a gray T-shirt, a beer in front of him, his normally slick curls soft and natural. When he smiles at me, a little flush of lust, hot and red, flares through my haze. He pulls a single pink rose wrapped in gold tissue paper off the table and hands it to me.

"My favorite color." I wrap a hand around the smooth, thornless stem.

"I thought it might be." His smile is shyer than I've ever seen it. Something holds his normal cockiness at bay.

"Why are you doing this?"

His smile fades. "What do you mean?"

I dangle my flower in front of his face.

"I'm wooing you, of course. Haven't you been wooed before?" His voice is serious.

I think of Henry.

"I guess not. But why?" He could just bite my neck, give me his blood, and be done with it, or tell me to leave and never think of me again.

"Do I need a reason?"

"Everyone has a reason."

"True." He hesitates, eyes narrowing, searching me for something I probably can't give him. "If I turn you, we'll be connected for a very long time. It'd be delightful if we got along."

"Oh. So you kind of like me, then?"

He grins, and it draws out the tiniest bit of joy, which my guilt immediately swallows without mercy.

I attempt to draw on a smile to hide it. But the muscles in my face protest. They are so, so tired.

"Victoria?" He pauses as he's pulling out a chair for me to examine the downturned corners of my uncooperative mouth. His own lips mirror mine.

Shit. Why can't I pretend anymore?

Nicholas starts to say something as someone clears their throat behind me.

I glance back, and there Henry stands, hands stuffed in his pockets, looking like he regrets his decision to come.

His eyes flicker between me and Nicholas.

Nicholas waits with one hand on my chair, face smooth, saying nothing.

"How'd you find me?" I ask him.

Henry's cheek twitches. He glances at his toes and then the band setting up next to us. Whatever reaction he wanted from me, this was not it. "Ruth told me."

Nicholas finally breaks his stony silence behind me and grumbles something about never trusting Ruth again.

I shoot him a glare, and he stops. "Should I pull up another chair?" he asks a little too sweetly.

I turn back to Henry.

"I'm sorry," he says.

"Me too," I answer.

We don't get into what we're sorry for. It reminds me of how easy it was when we were kids, pissing each other off one minute and forgiving the next with no drawn-out apologies.

He runs a finger inside the collar of his white shirt, smiling softly in a way that makes me want to close the gap between us and let his long arms close around me for a second. Then Nicholas clears his throat behind me—or growls—I'm not sure which.

"Add the chair," I tell him.

He grabs one and scrapes it across the concrete floor, putting it a little farther away than the other two chairs. I resist the urge to roll my eyes as I take the center seat and Nicholas takes the chair closest to me while Henry takes the farthest one and proceeds to scoot closer.

Henry picks up the rose on the table and lets it drop again. "What's this?"

"Some of us know how to treat a lady," Nicholas says as he drapes an arm over the back of my chair.

Henry snorts. "By giving her gifts she doesn't want instead of the one she does?" He leans forward, putting himself almost in Nicholas's face. "Or maybe you can't give her that."

Nicholas's arm tenses against my back.

I can't let Henry scare him off.

"Boys," I say, because they're definitely not behaving like men. And if not for my need to complete my next task, I might let them sit here by themselves with all their angst, because it's sure not doing anything for me. "When does the music start?" I ask. The band's set up, poised, ready to go.

"Whenever you're ready." Nicholas grins.

"You're going to sing?" Henry pulls a face halfway between shock and terror. I can relate.

"I sing really well."

"I remember. But when you got the solo in our second-grade concert, they had to restart the song three times before you would actually go through with it."

"Gee, thanks for the reminder."

He bites his lower lip and then laughs. "Sorry. What I meant to say was, I totally one hundred percent believe in you."

"A little over the top, don't you think?"

He wraps his hand around mine and gives it a quick squeeze as Nicholas grabs my other hand to lead me over to the musicians and introduce me to Jaeda on the drums, Patrick on the saxophone, and Denzel on the bass.

"What songs do you know?" I ask.

"You name it and we can play it," Denzel says, smiling widely and strumming a few notes on his bass.

Jaeda shakes her head behind him, and I like her immediately.

I turn to consult Nicholas, but he's already back sitting at the table with Henry, my empty chair between them. This is all me.

I chew my lip for a moment. "'She's Not There' by the Zombies?"

Naturally, Dad and I both love and listen to the Zombies. After all, zombies are only a quick slide down from vampires, so we've been known to watch a zombie movie or five as well.

"Nice," Jaeda says, nodding.

I beam, telling the guilt inside me to back off—I'm doing this for Dad, not for myself. The guilt whispers back, telling me

I'm lying. I've been having fun all along. This was never about Dad—it was a thinly veiled attempt to escape watching him die.

I shake, and not from stage fright.

But when the deep hum of the bass picks up, I manage to turn around, grasping the cold mic in both my hands. The saxophone jumps in and echoes the tune while the drum beats in rhythm behind me. And when the saxophone drops out, I know it's my time to come in, and I do. My singing voice's always been an octave lower than my speaking voice, and it always bothered me, but I embrace it now. I have enough things to fear, and being onstage can't be one of them right now.

The first line trembles out. Some people at the bar turn to watch, but I'm too caught between staring at Nicholas and Henry. They both smile, but tension tightens their jaws, straining the edges. My stomach flips.

I close my eyes and sink into the song until I get to the line about the girl not being there even though she looks fine on the outside.

Because I'm *not* here. The real me exists six months ago, before Dad got sick. All that's inside me right now is the guilt, and I'm afraid to let go of it and risk letting anything else in.

I stop singing, and the saxophone slides back in and covers the melody like this was always part of the plan.

Cold fingers wrap around my hands, still clenching the microphone. I open my eyes and stare into Nicholas's worried ones.

"Dance with me?" His voice is low and soft. I nod, and he puts a hand on my waist as I step down. He doesn't give me time to think; we just move together, faster and sweeter than when we danced at the club—an easy rhythm of movement and forgetting. I don't know how Nicholas always makes me forget, but I end up letting out a strangled giggle. And drops of happiness and sorrow threaten to burst out again. But the guilt cackles and swallows them, and I stumble from the force of it, and I try so hard to smile, but my lips refuse to do anything but grimace. The guilt won't even let me pretend. And I'm so close to falling to my knees that I need to do something, *anything* to regain control.

I need something rooted in the physical, something to pull me out of the violent thunderstorm growing inside.

His kiss made me weightless last night. Before I let it get too far, too real, it was blissful nothingness. I need that and nothing else.

The next time Nicholas spins me, I slam into his chest at the end, lace my fingers against the back of his neck, and pull his lips down to mine, releasing a red, wicked heat that burns through the fog and leaves me feeling okay for a single moment.

But his lips against mine tease out more than the burning red of desire. Whatever draws us together flickers with traces of yellow and blue like a true flame—complicated and indescribable.

He pulls back, surprised, breathing heavily. For a second his expression is chaotic and vulnerable, as if he also has emotions that have broken free of the coffin he stores them in.

And then he shuts the lid, face smoothing.

"You don't have to do that," he says. "The other night, you—I didn't want you to think you had to kiss me to get what you wanted."

"No—I wanted to kiss you. I just got scared."

He grins down at me, his dark curls dangling over his eyes, not bothering to hide the relief in them. He looks younger now, and I wonder if he's younger than I originally thought.

The heavy wooden door of the club slams, and I jerk.

Henry.

I unwind myself from Nicholas and run after Henry without looking back.

"Henry, wait!" I call as I race outside.

The back of his white shirt glows in the dark as he moves farther and farther away from me.

"Damn it, Henry. Wait," I yell, chasing him. Even with him walking, I'm slower in my white kitten heels.

But he spins and strides back toward me.

His face is contorted and angry. "I'm trying here."

His words catch me off guard. What's he trying? I don't like that he's placing the blame on me like we didn't both hurt each other in the past.

"What exactly are you trying, Henry? I didn't come here for us—to rekindle whatever we had before."

"What are you really here for, Victoria? To save your dad or to screw some guy with a vampire complex? And why did you bring me?"

His words stake me through and through, and every single dig and splinter in them cuts me. He still has no faith. He still doesn't believe in vampires or me. The second part hurts worse than anything else. The stake in my heart poisons me as effectively as it would any vampire as the guilt returns. I become nothing but hollow bones, and he watches me with cold eyes.

No, not completely cold. Regret flickers in them and then gives way to pity. His pity makes me reshape myself with fury, building new, tougher skin, but my bones still hurt, because he's not wrong. I let myself enjoy those tiny moments, kissing Nicholas, losing myself in his touch. It gave me a tiny island in a sea of grief. But that island was nothing but a shipwreck of true emotion. A way to keep from feeling.

How dare he push me off of it? Why can't I stop swimming for one second?

"I didn't ask you to come with me. You decided you could be some kind of knight—bring some sanity back to the deranged girl who believes in vampires. But I don't need you here to save me from the things that go bump in the night. *I'm* the hero in this story. I'm the one saving someone. If you can't deal with that, then get the hell out of my life."

His eyes grow impossibly sad. "Forget I said anything."

My chest pounds. I can't breathe around the anger and sadness and guilt. The combination is more than the human body was meant to handle. I wonder if vampires deal with emotion better than people do. Maybe they can turn it off like in *The Vampire Diaries.* Nicholas said it didn't work like that, but I want to feel nothing. I breathe deeply and push everything down, but something in my well has broken, and I can't seal it over again without drying out first.

"Just leave," I say.

Henry wavers, leaning toward me, so I turn to the side and stare at the empty street. I stand like that for a long time, until another voice searches me out.

"Are you okay?" Nicholas asks.

I glance back to where Henry used to be and find nothing. He listened, then. "I'm fine. I needed some air."

I don't turn to him.

Nicholas wants me to feel happy. Henry wants me to feel sad. And *I* want to feel nothing. I want to stop worrying about what reaction seems appropriate and go back to just existing.

I listen as Nicholas walks closer and leans against the building behind me.

"You're sad," he says.

"No," I lie.

"It's okay. You can be happy and sad at the same time."

"That's an oxymoron."

"No, they're emotions, and emotions are complicated."

"Not my emotions. Mine don't work like that."

He sighs like I'm a student who simply doesn't get it even after years of study, but I don't trust him—this is a challenge, and he's not really my friend. Admitting I'm sad would be game over.

"Do you want me to take you home?"

"Your place or mine?" I ask boldly.

"Yours."

"No. I want to dance again." I force my mouth into a smile—he can take it or leave it.

He accepts my answer without trying to know what's best for me. I turn around and grab his hand and pull him back through the door.

They say that vampires' hearts are cold and dead.
Definitely dead. But I don't know,
I think I still feel things inside it.
—*What We Do in the Shadows*

# Seventeen

*I*n the morning, Henry waits for me on the couch, and seeing him there makes my chest ache, but whatever's really between us is too complicated, too big for me to sort through. It would require more than I can give. If that makes him hate me, so be it. Maybe one day he'll understand.

I try to walk by him without acknowledging him. My hand is on the doorknob when he decides not to let me.

"What happens when he fails you, Victoria?" His voice is so soft I almost don't hear him. "I'm not sure I'll be here for you."

My hand tightens, squeezing until my fingers turn white and red against the copper knob.

"I won't fail." I don't turn around. The shine of pity in his eyes would be too much.

He sighs. "That's not what I said."

I know it's not, but I can't think like that. Allowing myself for one moment to consider the possibility that Nicholas won't come through for me in the end would leave me curled up in a shaking, sobbing ball.

My phone rings, and I'm relieved at the chance to get out of this conversation until I see that it's Jessica's name lighting up the screen.

I pick up. "I was going to call you," I say.

"Well, I win then," she says, and I smile a little. We made everything a competition as kids—even who could brush their teeth fastest. Luckily, Dad caught us at that one and made us stop.

"You win for now," I say, which was always our answer.

She clears her throat. We can only hide for so long behind our childhood games.

"I shouldn't have surprised you at church like that," she says. "I should have told you I was coming. I just . . ." Her voice warbles, and the sound makes me want to throw the phone across the room to escape whatever's coming. "I wanted us to be on the same page for once."

She's sniffling now. I can hear it. My own throat tightens in response, and I wonder if all my hatred for her crying wasn't about her giving up but instead about the way it made me want to let go and cry too.

I take a deep breath, keeping my voice steady. "I'm not ready." My eyes sting. I have to clear my throat to keep going. "But I don't hate you if you are."

She sobs openly now. I stand there, listening to her hiccuping, wet breaths, and I cannot stop my own eyes from going wet in response, but I don't join her. She's crying because she believes Dad will die. I don't. I glance at Henry and then away again. His look of sympathy isn't going to help.

Finally, she draws a long breath and stops.

"I love you," she says.

"I love you too." My voice is strong. I end the call and tuck my phone in my pocket.

A few traitor tears slip from my eyes, and I reach up to banish them, but then Henry's in front of me, cupping my hands inside of his.

"What are you doing?" One tear has made it down my cheek. I try looking to the side to hide it.

"Don't," he says.

"What?" I step back. He follows me, hands soft against mine but firm enough to hang onto me. I know he'd let me go if I really pulled away from him, but I like the way my hands disappear inside his, like someone else is in control if only for a moment.

The tear drips off my jaw and stains my baby-blue shirt with an ugly dark splotch just above my breast.

"Damn it." I blink. I let one renegade out, and now they all want to be free.

"It's okay," Henry says.

"No." I shake my head, taking another step as he follows. "It's okay for some people. It's okay for Jessica." And I really believe that now—she's doing what she has to do to survive. Like I am. "It's not for me." My voice cracks. This time I do pull free, but as soon as I do, he reaches up and cups my face on either side, and I can't wipe my tears without tangling my arms in his.

"Let it out, Victoria."

"No."

"It helps. I promise."

"How would you know?" I'm mad now. It's hard to rein in my emotions when I can't even erase the physical evidence from my cheeks.

His eyes slide away from me, and his fingers twitch against my face before he looks back at me. "I can't tell you how many times I lost it at my grandma's funeral. I couldn't keep it together." His voice hardens. "But you wouldn't know that, would you?"

Henry still doesn't know that I *was* there, but I guess it doesn't count that I was. I didn't stay. It was a few days after we kissed and he ran away from it. I walked into the church and saw him sitting there with Bailey. I don't know what I expected—for him to have broken up with her and be waiting there for me? Clearly that wasn't the case. And suddenly I was afraid that Henry wouldn't want me there at all, so I left. But he's right. I didn't see him cry at the funeral.

I fear he'll walk away now, pay me back, but his fingers press harder into my cheeks instead.

"I'm sorry," I say.

He shakes his head like he doesn't want or need those words. "My mom held everything in, and now she's a ghost. I can't watch you become that. You already are, and I can't stand it. I just got you back."

He leans down, and I hold my breath, but he only presses his forehead into mine.

"Please," he whispers.

I'd do almost anything for him in this moment.

"Cry," he says. "Let it out."

But not that. I can't cry for my dad like Henry cried for his grandma. Dad's not dead.

"I *can't*," I say, even as a tear slips out and travels the maze of his fingers.

"Why? Make me understand." He pulls back to look me in the eyes.

We're so close, like the night we kissed. It makes me want to be vulnerable again.

"I won't mourn something I plan on stopping."

"You can cry because he's sick. He's sick right now, Victoria. You can feel that, at least."

I *am* crying. The tears come hot and fast, but I shake my head, forcing Henry's fingers to slip on my wet face, yet he hangs on. Dad's sick. Even when I heal him, we'll always have the pain of these last few months.

I let myself cry for that.

"Cry for what you're losing if you succeed in what you're doing," he says. "Because you'd still be losing something, wouldn't you?"

Yes. So many things. And Henry will probably be one of them. Right when I finally have him back.

I sob now, and Henry lets go of my face to squeeze me into his chest.

After a minute I pull back to look up at him.

"I was there."

"What?" His brow furrows.

"At your grandma's funeral. I came, but I walked in and saw you sitting with Bailey, and I assumed she was who you wanted—that you didn't need me, too, so I left. I should have stayed and just lived through the embarrassment of loving you when you clearly loved someone else."

Henry furrows his brow and shakes his head, then laughs a little in a way that cuts through some of my pain. "What about our past makes you think I didn't love you?"

"Let's see . . . maybe you dating my other close friend?"

He shakes his head. "I'm talking about before that. Dating Bailey—" He shakes his head again, cringing a little like he doesn't want to say what's coming next. "I liked her, but I was trying to get over *you*. I was trying to move on finally."

I step back from him. "Move on from what? When did we have a chance to be anything?"

"Are you serious? *I* kissed *you* first. You literally fled to the woods to get away from me."

"You surprised me!" My voice has gone up an octave. "You clearly regretted it. You apologized about fifty times. And you're the one who came up with the ridiculous pact." I point my finger at him, but he grabs it and ends up gripping my hand awkwardly between us.

His voice goes down an octave. "I didn't want to lose you. I said those things to save our friendship. I thought you'd come around eventually."

"I thought you said those things because you regretted it."

"Not for a second."

"Why didn't you say anything later? In all those years in between?"

"I thought I was. I used to make up excuses to sit too close to you. I made sure our fingers touched every time I passed you something." He runs a hand through his hair. "I stared at you so often, I bet I could close my eyes and draw your lips perfectly from memory, and we both know I'm not an artist. But you were always the one who looked away or moved away."

"We had a pact," I mutter.

He ignores me, which is fair. It seems silly now, but I thought the pulling away was mutual. How did I not notice it was me? That I was just too afraid of seeing that look of regret on his face when he found me in the woods and apologized for that first kiss.

Henry shifts his hand that's awkwardly holding my fist and eases open my fingers with his until only our fingertips are touching. "Every single time I touched you and you hesitated before pulling away, I thought, this is it. This is the moment she reaches to hold my hand instead of running. But you pulled away every time. It got harder and harder to watch you—the way you smiled up at a blue sky like there was something there the rest of the world couldn't see. The way you could paint a night sky and still make it feel warm. The way your eyes brightened when you looked at me. All those things started to kill me. And then you said yes to going to junior prom with Peter." His voice rises on that last part, and then he mutters, "I was going to ask you. I already had it planned out. I was going to make a fairy ring in the woods where we first met and spell out 'prom' in the middle with flowers."

My mouth is dry. I did say yes to Peter, who was part of our larger group, but *we* were going as friends. I even clarified that *before* I said yes. I assumed Henry would stick to the pact and not ask me unless it was just as friends, and going platonically with Henry when I wanted so much more would have been miserable.

Henry took Bailey.

My stomach hurts thinking about memories that will never be mine now. "You could have told me," I whisper.

He sighs. "I thought you guessed."

"Why did you run, then? When I kissed you?"

"All I wanted was to let go. Fall into you and forget about everything else. But it wasn't that simple, was it? You can't tell me you didn't think of Bailey."

I don't answer. Of course I thought of Bailey—after. Not in that moment though. I only thought of how it had been way too long between kisses.

"I ran because I didn't want to acknowledge what was between us before I ended things with Bailey, and if I stayed anywhere near you, I wouldn't wait. But then my grandma died, and everything was such a mess, and I thought you weren't there. That the kiss was such a mistake you didn't show up for my grandma's funeral." He shakes his head again. "I was hurt."

His fingertips move across my palm. "Why didn't you stay or

reach out? Even if I had stayed with Bailey—you couldn't get past that? You couldn't be there for me anyway?"

His eyes are wet, and I can barely stand to look at him. I did that. I added to his pain. I owe him the truth.

"I *couldn't* reach out. I thought I took advantage of you. I thought you only kissed me back because you were hurting. I thought you had to hate me. *I* hated me." I choke a little on those last words. I've been carrying around this shame, this regret, under so much other grief that I'd forgotten it was there. Now it rips open, fresh and overwhelming.

I'm crying again.

His fingers shift from my palm and travel up my arm slowly, as if asking permission with every inch until his hand rests on the back of my neck. He pulls me a tiny bit closer to him.

"I could never hate you," he says. "Being hurt by someone isn't the same as hating them."

"I know." I smile, trying to lighten the mood. "We never should have made that pact in the first place."

He smiles sadly. "Technically we kept it. We graduated."

We've been talking about the past, not the present—not what we feel in this moment—but his warm hand on the back of my neck is happening right now. And the way he's staring down at me, eyes sliding between my eyes and lips, makes my heart thud. I'm not crying anymore, but then he dips down, pressing his lips to mine. It's so soft, holding so much caution and past hurt that it makes the tears come again.

I've been letting out more and more little griefs, but Henry's lips threaten to tear me wide open and leave nothing buried. I still need to fool Nicholas. I still need to save Dad.

So I pull back and wipe my eyes. Henry lets me go.

"We can't wreck our friendship right now. I need you." It's a weak excuse—we've already survived so much, but I can't explain that I don't want to kiss him because he's too real. He's not a game. And right now I need to be a player.

Hurt crosses his face before I watch him force it away with a nod. Neither one of us is running, but neither one of us is going to fight for this either.

He steps back as I move for the door. "Want me to come?" he asks.

I shake my head. "I need a minute."


Ruth's helping customers today and doesn't notice me come in, and somehow it makes it seem like the universe is punishing me for kissing Henry again when I needed to focus. I was looking forward to seeing her.

The poem today makes me ache too.

### Cobwebs

It is a land with neither night nor day,
Nor heat nor cold, nor any wind, nor rain,
Nor hills nor valleys; but one even plain
Stretches thro' long <u>unbroken</u> miles away:

While thro' the <u>sluggish</u> air a <u>twilight</u> grey
Broodeth; no moons or seasons wax and wane,
No ebb and flow are there among the main,
No bud-time no leaf-falling there for aye,
No ripple on the sea, no <u>shifting</u> sand,
No beat of wings to stir the stagnant space,
And loveless sea: no trace of days before,
No guarded home, no time-worn resting place
No future hope no fear forevermore.

—Christina Rossetti

This poem captures the place I've existed in since my dad got sick—the emptiness. But now I feel things. And even as I rein in some of those emotions, part of me doesn't want to go back to the nothingness of the poem.

Perhaps Nicholas understands me better than I realized. Maybe he doesn't want me to feel happiness. Maybe he really wants me to feel everything.

I unfold his note.

*Do something you love, and do it for yourself, not for a clue.*

A crisp hundred-dollar bill sits like a bookmark between the pages. I pull it out. The edges are perfectly pointed without a single bend or tear, like mine are the first human hands to hold it.

The first thing that pops into my mind is curling up in the brown leather chair at home, taking the heavy cream blanket usually draped over the back of the chair, covering my bare knees to fight off the air-conditioning, and turning on *Underworld*.

And, of course, Dad watches with me, and he feels well enough to sit up and gripe at all the gunfights in a vampire versus werewolf movie while I defend them and say they just don't want to get their fangs dirty, and then my dad laughs like I haven't cracked that joke a thousand times before. We never get tired of each other's silliness.

But even if I were home, this wouldn't be possible. The last time I turned on *Underworld*, Dad fell asleep, and his rattling snores underscored the moments we used to laugh at and pretend to argue about. I can't stand the thought of doing that again—sitting there, wanting to cry but not, in case he woke up and saw me.

I drown the memory. Maybe one day I can resuscitate it, but not today.

Henry then. He's here, and I've loved him all my life—the easy, uncomplicated kind of love some people might brand as soulmates, but what he feels, what *I* feel, is too much to handle.

The guilt tries to tell me I don't deserve to love anything right now. Love's a distraction. But I love Dad—that's the only reason why I'm here. *I love Dad*. I repeat the words again and again, and slowly, very slowly, the fog starts to dissipate, replaced by that vicious, single-minded love until I'm whole, breathing deep, muscles ready for a fight.

But a fight would be easy.

I need to love *something* besides Dad, but I'm afraid to. Love for Dad is my fuel, and I burn through it so quickly I barely feel it. Nicholas is asking for more. He wants me to slow down and experience it, but once you let out an emotion like love, how do you hold back all the others? It's like taking out one brick in the dam and thinking you'll be able to put it back again despite the power of the water.

It's why I don't draw anymore. Drawings without emotion are flat. I couldn't hold back the dam and still create something worthy of existing.

I know what I need to do.

Fifteen minutes later I stand across the street from my favorite house in the French Quarter—the one with mismatched flowers—holding an overpriced sketch pad in one hand and a stick of brand-new charcoal in the other. Most artistic people experience anticipation staring at an empty page—promise, even—but for me right now there's only anxiety, a fear of what might come out once I start. Because I'm no longer strong enough to stop it.

I rub my fingertips against the infinite grain of the charcoal, begging it to be kind; then I press it against the paper and let the first dark line mar the innocent page. I move tentatively at first, then in quick, sharp strokes, capturing the wide stones and each slat of the shutters. I force myself to slow on the balcony, noticing the soft curves of the edges, fashioned like vines combined with the geometric rectangles and squares forming the rails. Each shape is unique, and yet together they create one glorious piece. I add in the dangling balls of fern and the planters blooming with flowers of every color. I almost add a girl standing on the balcony, waiting for someone to save her, but instead I sketch the trashcan on the sidewalk, sharing the same space as the quaint black streetlamp because it belongs there as much as the beautiful things, and it makes the picture complete.

Each pull of the charcoal against the paper drags a piece of me onto the page, and I worry there may be nothing left of me when I'm done. I may be nothing but a shell, walking around and carrying all my feelings on a few pieces of paper. But somehow that sounds good too—to have them out, to have them distant. Maybe then I'll be free.

When I finish and stretch my arms out in front of me to take in my picture, I smile, and the ache in my chest opens as I do.

I wander and end up sitting next to the other artists who sell their emotions every day to make a living. I don't know how they get the strength for it, but I join them there and try to steal some of their confidence as I stare up at the cathedral, fingers already stained dark from the last picture, a fresh cream page in front of me.

But the cathedral is too white, too perfect. How do I capture it when I only have darkness to work with? I roll the charcoal in my hand, tempted to toss it onto the cobblestones with the cigarette butts.

"What are you working on?"

The artist next to me has shuffled over, abandoning her stall of bright portraits. She must be at least seventy and wears bright-pink pants and a top with blooming red roses. Only a true artist would pick up on the slightest traces of pink in those roses and pair it with those pants. I can't help but give her one of my sad smiles.

"Nothing yet." I gesture at my blank sheet and then at the church. "This one might be beyond my talents."

"My dear, talent's got nothing to do with it."

"No?" I point behind her at her work. "What do you call that?"

"Desperation."

Her answer catches me off guard, and my mouth can't form an answer.

She laughs at herself or at me, I'm not sure. "Don't we all draw because we're desperate to relieve something inside of us?"

"Don't some people just want a pretty picture?"

"Do you?" she asks.

I shrug and go back to staring at my blank page and the cathedral.

She watches me.

"It's too pure," I say. "Maybe I need watercolor or something."

Laughter cracks out of her so loud I drop the charcoal, and it hits the white page, leaving an ugly black scar.

I move to fold the ruined sheet back.

"Leave it," she says.

My hand pauses, gripping the paper in the air like this is a major decision. One of the things I love about drawing is the control it gives me—if something doesn't turn out the way I want, I can throw it away and try again. I like fresh starts.

"If you think anything is perfect, you're not seeing it. Look for the shadows and build it from there." She walks back to her stall.

I turn to the cathedral, searching for the splotches against the expanse of white, and then I begin to see them—the darkening behind the pillars in the front, the traces of shadows under each overhang and each decorative curve and corner of the stone. And finally I notice the other imperfections—the worn surfaces where the off-white stone has darkened, the way some of the slats and shutters have bent, the stains around the roman numerals of the white-faced clock.

Once I've captured every little imperfection, the cathedral glows off my page.

I hold it back from myself, and it's perfectly imperfect. For a second I think God might like it too, even though we're on the outs, but maybe I've been looking at him the wrong way. Maybe he's an artist who smudges things and has to leave them because that's the way they're supposed to be. Doesn't mean I like it, and it doesn't mean I won't look for another way, but maybe I've been wrong to abandon something Dad loves.

I smile, and the ache in my chest grows, taking up more space than ever before.

I glance around and find the elderly woman watching me again. I hold up my drawing in her direction, and she applauds.

And because the church was almost too much, I head to the

river, the dull, murky Mississippi, and lean against the rail. This time it's easy to start. I draw that rippling, endless water and make it stand still on the page for me, and then I move on to the bridge rising toward the sky. I spend hours capturing the peaked pattern of all the metal rods, losing myself in the monotony of the movements, hoping the mindlessness will numb the pain.

Finally, I pull back and take in my work—the restless water, the bridge crossing the entire page with no end in sight, and the clouds. I don't remember drawing them—two thick and heavy with unshed rain in the foreground and one fluffy and white in the distance, so, so far away.

And the sorrow inside me leaks out because I let my heart bleed into the sketches with each and every stroke. Tears break from my eyes and splatter the water drawn on my picture, smearing it, somehow making it even more lifelike. I gulp, fighting the incoming flood, but love and pain always walk hand in hand. Haven't I watched *Buffy* enough times to understand that?

*Be strong like Buffy*. But maybe I've been wrong about what that means. What if it isn't about not feeling at all? What if it's about letting go of control sometimes, letting it *all* go—not just the pieces you think are okay—so you can be in control when it counts? If I want to win this game with Nicholas, I need to let go.

A few more tears travel down my face, dripping onto the picture.

They're for my dad. For what might happen.

When I'm done, I rip the three pictures out without the care

I'd normally give one of my drawings, folding them once, twice, three times over so I won't be tempted to view them again. Then I walk back to the bookstore and tuck them into the pages, but at the last minute, I pull the cathedral out and put it in my pocket. For Dad. Then I take the house. For Mom.

I only walk around the block before stopping back in the bookstore and slinking past Ruth to grab my book. I suspect she's the one who changes out the notes, and I must be right. The sun's still out, but my pictures are gone, and a new note sits in the pages.

> *Kiss someone in a thunderstorm in a graveyard.*
> *I'll be in the Lafayette Cemetery at 10 p.m. if*
> *you'd like that someone to be me. Find me with*
> *a beautiful uptown lady.*

I am so close. He knows I leave tomorrow, so tonight must be the last challenge, and I'm prepared to feel whatever I need to.

Ruth's reading at her desk when I come back out.

"Are you the one putting the notes in? I was gone only ten minutes before I came back. No way he was that fast."

She glances at me over the top of her book. "You're a lovely artist." She smiles and goes back to reading.

I laugh softly and then stop as I step back onto the cracked sidewalk outside.

*If you kiss me right now, will I live forever?*
*—Byzantium*

# Eighteen

I'm not up-to-date on the required attire for kissing vampires in a graveyard, so I decide to recycle the white dress I wore the first time I met him. Tonight, I put on the heavy black eye shadow I bought and pair it with my favorite pink gloss. I let my hair stay long and in tangles.

"The note says someone," Henry says in the doorway behind me.

I jump and glare at him in the bathroom mirror, and then flinch at the note unfolded in his hand. I left it on the kitchen table.

"It doesn't have to be him."

*It could be me* hangs unsaid in the air between us, but he won't say it. I pray he doesn't say it.

Kissing Henry is too much. He's seen me fall backward off a swing and cry so hard I blew snot bubbles. I've seen him puke after eating too many hotdogs at my eighth birthday party.

And he knows about my dad.

Kissing Henry *means* something.

That's hard.

Kissing Nicholas is easier, even though it gets harder each time. But when I turn to move around him, the pull between us, the one we've ignored for so long, forces me to halt in front of him, my nose inches from his chest. His heart beats too hard under his shirt, and mine charges forward to match, and all I need to do is lift my chin.

But I need this one thing to be simple, and Henry's a complex variable. The safer route to ensuring I get what I want is Nicholas.

I'm careful not to let our fingers touch as I take the note and leave him behind.

I love graveyards. Since I was as old as I can remember, I'd ask to stop at them anytime my family traveled, and Dad and I would get out of the car and search for the oldest headstone while Mom and Jessica stayed behind, probably discussing how weird we both were. Sometimes I wonder if Dad is really strange like me, or just pretending so I won't be the odd one out. It doesn't matter. Either way I love him for it.

I swallow the thought and focus on the graveyard as I approach, breathing in the always-wet air tinged with the faintest scent of citrus.

It's glorious. A high wall surrounds it—the gray plaster breaking off in places, revealing the faded brick underneath. Small ferns sprout from every crack, and I run my fingers through the damp softness of them as I edge around the perimeter. A rusted chain weaves between the bars of the main gate, but I walk on until I find a smaller, unlocked gate. It creaks as I push through it like any graveyard entrance worth its salt would do.

In New Orleans, they bury their loved ones aboveground to protect against flooding, and it turns an otherwise simple graveyard into a miniature city for the dead. In a plain old Californian graveyard, I'd be able to look across almost the whole thing and spot another person. Here the tombs rise well above my head, creating a maze lined with the homes of the dead amid thick magnolia trees.

"Nicholas?" I take a tentative step deeper in, where the air turns thicker with a lingering fog and the smell of wet green things and dead leaves. I call his name again and get no answer from the living or the dead. Or anyone who's both.

*Find me with an uptown lady.* I thought that was a role for me to play, but it could be a clue, and searching for him is part of the game.

I choose the path in front of me, the one with the biggest crypts. Many crumble with age, forgotten somewhere along the generations, or maybe there's just nobody left to care. Others are clearly updated with recent years of death listed. I read the names and dates—the least I can do for them since I'm intruding on their evening.

I stop at one that lists five children, all dead young, and the parents many years later.

The next one shares a first name with my dad. I cannot bring myself to read the inscription. I turn away before the soft ground beneath my feet swallows me.

It is not a sign.

Moving on, I trace my hand along the cold, rough surfaces. I sense Nicholas here, listening, watching, enjoying his game, which forces me to face the parts of myself I'd rather keep hidden.

A shadow moves to my right, and I squeeze through the narrow gap between two tombs, almost freezing in the abnormally cold air trapped between them. I break free into another empty aisle full of names asking to be read. My skin crawls with the memories of the dead that must be buried here.

"Nicholas." My voice comes out soft, singsongy, as if I'm the ghost begging to be heard.

I reach a corner darker than the rest, hidden under the heavy leaves of a magnolia tree blocking out the moon.

My first name catches my eye.

VICTORIA ANN FINES

A LOVELY UPTOWN LADY

One of the shadows resting against her tomb unfolds into a man dressed in black.

"Found me."

I twirl toward him, playing the part he wants, and my white dress flares.

"You look like a haunted spirit." He steps closer, mouth curling.

"You look like my shadow."

"Do spirits still have shadows?"

"Probably not." And I don't know why, but this makes me sad, and that tiny trickle of sadness threatens to set free an entire stream

I'll never be able stop, so I say, "Are you going to kiss me or not?"

And this is both part of the game and not. I do want him to kiss me.

It dawns on me that I'm using Nicholas as a bandage in all this, a quick fix to prevent me from feeling anything real. I crave these moments of pretend.

But I don't think he realizes or cares. His teeth flash in the darkness. "I'm waiting for something."

"What?"

He points up just as the thunder rips the sky, and five seconds later huge drops of water pelt my skin and leave me gasping for air. My dress clings to my body as lightning flashes above, illuminating for the briefest moment the hunger on Nicholas's face.

He reaches for me, fists clinging to the damp material on my hips. He tugs me forward, and I drift toward him like the ghost I am. And we stand there for a moment, his fingers folded in my skirt, the only part of him touching me, and I drink in the air, growing denser with moisture, thick with the lemony scent from the white blossoms dripping above us, and decide I can't wait anymore. I close the gap between us until my wet body is flush with his, and we stand like that for another minute, my nose pressed against the wet fabric of his shirt before I finally lift my mouth for his.

As his lips find mine, his hands tighten on my dress, pulling it taut against the back of my thighs and butt, and suddenly it's like we can't get close enough.

He spins and backs us up, our legs tangling together. I gasp and tilt my chin up as he breaks away and runs his teeth down my neck. I'm pressed against the dead Victoria's tomb, which seems so wrong at first but then fitting. Maybe this will be the moment he turns me. The moment I die so my dad can live, and I'm ready. Whatever comes next, I'm tired of being human. His kiss makes me feel like something more animal than girl. I can't imagine what his bite will do.

But he doesn't break my skin. Instead, he breaks my soul as he reaches my lips again.

There's an urgency in the way our lips move and our hands grasp. He's pouring something into our kiss that's more than pure and simple lust, and I answer him.

The rain goes hot on my face.

I'm crying.

Just like that, my carefully crafted well shatters, and I become a swirling mess of the red lust for Nicholas's lips, the comfortable honey yellow of being with Henry when we're not fighting, the bright magenta thrill of lassoing Joanie, the hot-pink embarrassment of being covered in powdered sugar, the deep-blue cascade of grief I can't hold back any longer, and finally, hope—blazing like the first green of oak leaves in the spring—that this will be enough for him.

I'm everything I kept back let loose all at once.

I break our kiss and push against his chest, and he immediately takes several steps back.

I stare down at my pure white dress, clinging limp and tired to my body, expecting it to be splattered with color. Nothing. Nobody can see what's swirling inside me.

I tremble from the heat between us and the wet.

"Hold me," I say.

"Are you sure?"

I nod, and he steps back toward me, wrapping his long arms around me and resting his chin on top of my head. I'm surprised to find his body trembling too. His heart thuds against my cheek.

"You do have a heartbeat."

"You can have a heartbeat and still be dead."

His words ring true.

I would know. I've been walking around like the living dead already, and my heart works fine.

But I'd hoped he didn't. It was one of my signs of his vampire status, but not the only one. I still have my five out of seven, and right now it comforts me that the speed of Nicholas's heartbeat matches my own.

I hope his embrace lets me press my well back together.

It doesn't.

He tugs at the ends of my wet hair and looks down at me.

"What just happened?" I ask.

"We lived," he says. "I felt alive for a moment, didn't you?" He reaches out and wipes a thumb under my eye like you would for someone who'd been crying. But how could he tell? His own eyes appear a little red in the dark.

"Yes," I say, and my voice cracks with more emotions than I could possibly name.

"I was wrong about you needing to be happy and never sad to live forever. You need both. You need everything. You showed me that." He runs a finger down my cheek. "I see everything in you now. It's beautiful."

His face is shadowed and dark. Rain drips from his cheeks to mine. "But it hurts," I tell him.

"I know," he says, squeezing water from the tips of my hair. "I know."

I twist my head to reveal the vulnerable skin of my neck. "Will you give me what I want?"

"Tomorrow," he promises. "I want to see you one more time before you go." He bends and brushes his lips across my wild pulse.

We met, and we talked, and it was epic,
but then the sun came up and reality set in.
—*The Vampire Diaries*

# Nineteen

Monday morning comes harsh and bright. This must be how vampires feel when someone opens the lid of their coffin during the day. I don't know what time I came in last night, but when I rip back my covers, I'm still dressed in my white sundress, damp and stained with hints of mud and streaks of moss. I brush back my tangled hair as I stumble to the bathroom. My once gorgeous eye shadow runs like dark tears, as if I've been crying guilt, releasing the last bits that held me back.

I wash my face until my makeup has that artful *had a wild night but still look great rolling out of bed* look and change into cutoff jean shorts and a sunny-yellow tank top.

And once I've finished with the outside of me, I turn to the inside.

But there's no point. My well broke beyond repair last night, and now every color ripples under my skin and I can't decide which one to focus on.

Excitement beats back the sorrow, telling me the sorrow will be gone soon anyway.

Today's my last full day. My flight leaves tomorrow at 6 a.m., giving me plenty of time to see Nicholas after the sun goes down. Today I get what I want, and then tomorrow I'll be home, saving my dad and living happily ever after for eternity.

Henry's dressed and waiting at the kitchen table when I leave my room.

He looks up from a comic book he probably bought from Ruth as I smile at him, my nervous excitement beating out the tentative way he takes in my appearance.

"I did it," I say. "I won. Today's the day."

He cringes, and I know he's thinking about what I did to win the game, the sacrifices I may have made, but he doesn't get it—I *wanted* to do those things, not just to win, but because they let me live a little while part of me was dying. They made me feel things even when I fought not to. And I craved that even as I feared it.

My limbs shake with all the released emotions.

"I'm going to the bookstore," I say.

Henry pushes back his chair.

"You don't need to come with me."

"I want to be there," he says, standing. "For you. As your friend."

"I'd like that," I say, and the brightest yellow fills me, turning my limbs light, and I don't need guilt or sadness to chase it away anymore. I won.

Ruth sits at her desk with a fresh plate of beignets in front of her and an open book of Sylvia Plath poetry in her hand. She smiles as I walk in and offers me the plate with a wink. "Want one?"

I can't help but laugh. "I've had enough powdered sugar for a lifetime."

"You only live once," she says.

I pause at her words. How much does she know about Nicholas and what I want from him? I'm afraid to ask, so I nod and move past her without touching the food. Henry can't resist. He munches as he follows behind me.

"I'm really going to miss the food here," he says.

"On that we can agree."

I grab the book and pull it off the shelf, holding it pressed to my chest for a moment, feeling my heart pound against the cover. It's like holding a letter from a college you're waiting to see if you got into, except this is life and death.

I flip the book open, and it lands immediately on a page with a sealed envelope, and a note written on the top. *Solve the puzzle and open the envelope. No cheating!* Below are the blank spaces, spelling out a phrase.

E _ _ _ _ _ _ _   _ _ _ _ _ _ s   _ _ _ _ _ _   _ _ ,
a   _ _ _ _ _ _ _ _   _ _ _ _ _ _ _   _ _ _   and   _ _ _ _ _ _
_ _ _ _ ,
the   _ _ _ _ ,   _ _ _ _ _   _ _ _ _ o _   of   _ n _ _ _ _ _
_ _ _ _ t.

My   m_ _ _ _ _   _ _ _ _ _   _ _ _   l_ _s .

My   _ _ f _   is   a   _ l_ _ _ _ _ _   _ _ _ _ _ .

Do   not   _ _ _ _   for   _ _ _ _ _ _ _ _ _ _ _ .

S_ _ _ _   at   the   _ y_ _ _ _ _   of   _ _ i_ _ _ _ _

_ _ _ _ _ _ _ _ .

_ _ _ _   of   _ _ss_ _ _ _   and   _ _rr_ _ .

_ _ _ _ _ _ _   _ _ _ _h   by   l_ _ _ _ _   in   the

_ o _ _ _ _ _ .

"Just open it," Henry says. "He won't know."

"He might." I pull out a pen and start writing the words I've collected at the bottom of the envelope so I can see where they fit.

I start with the ones underlined in my final poem and work out from there.

### The End

If I could have put you in my heart,

If but I could have wrapped you in myself,

How glad I should have been!

And now the chart

Of <u>memory</u> <u>unrolls</u> again to me

The course of our journey here, before we had

    to part.


And oh, that you had never, never been

Some of your selves, my love, that some

Of your several faces I had never seen!
And still they come <u>before me</u>, and they go,
And I cry aloud in the <u>moments</u> that intervene.

And oh, my love, as I rock for you to-night,
And have not any longer any hope
To heal the suffering, or to make requite
For all your life of asking and despair,
I own that some of me is dead to-night.
—D. H. Lawrence

This poem drags at all the loose emotions inside me, forming a painful swirl of them in my center. I swallow, and it burns my throat. I may have been using Nicholas, and he was probably using me, but it ends now. We weren't in love, but attraction can be missed too. The poem suggests we'll never see each other again. Clearly, I am the girl with many faces. I thought we would be bonded forever—that I might come back here eventually and introduce Dad to the boy who saved him. I frown—even Nicholas hinted he would remain in my life after the transformation. But I can let go of him as long as I am dead tonight too.

I fight to compose myself. I don't want Henry to see how much I actually started to care about Nicholas. Because I care about Henry more.

But Henry will not want me as a vampire. He's too serious, too set in what he wants to believe about the world to not see me differently. He will leave me. I've known this all along, but now it hits me in the stomach, and I fight back nausea. I might be left with no one else, but I'll have Dad.

Fingers shaking, I turn back to my puzzle and start counting the lengths of words and putting them where they might work.

"This seems a little melodramatic even for a vampire," Henry says as I struggle to make sense of the words.

"Shut up and help me," I say, but I grin. He referred to Nicholas as a vampire. And if Henry can say it out loud, it must be real. He starts giving directions to me, laughing when I place a word where it can't possibly go.

"I think we got it," I finally say.

A poem. He turned the words into a poem, and I'm not surprised at all.

> Eternity unrolls before me,
> a sluggish setting sun and falling moon,
> the ripe, sweet horror of unbroken night.
> My memory grins and lies.
> My life is a bleeding dream.
>
> Do not stop for immortality.
> Smile at the mystery of shifting twilight.
> Sing of passions and sorrow.
> Conquer death by living in the moments.

"What the hell does that even mean?" Henry asks.

But I know. I've been reading poems all week. I know how to

piece together the unexpected images to form a complete picture.

Every color inside me drains away, and I'm empty again for one second as I flip the envelope over and drag my finger under the seal so fast I get a paper cut that leaves a harsh red streak on the pristine white envelope. I empty the contents onto the green rug I'm sitting on.

Pictures. Me with powdered sugar on my chest. Henry and me, rushed and blurry, holding a clove of garlic and a gold necklace. Me baring my teeth in a not-quite-smile at Antoine's. Scattering them around the floor, I search for something, anything else. Another clue. One last set of instructions I know I won't find. His poem told me all I needed to know—eternity sucks, and he wants me to live.

Henry's grim face looks down on me.

"He played with you," Henry says slowly. "It was all just a game. He was never going to help you—if he even could." He says it like he's known this since the beginning but hoped it wasn't true.

Hearing the words he's been saying all along, this time with the weight of proof behind him, breaks me. I bend at the waist until my forehead rests on the pile of photos, each one a representation of what I gave up to get here. Nicholas made me chip away at my well while he chronicled it and then disappeared once the floods broke. A sob shudders through me.

Henry's hand rests between my shoulder blades, and it's enough to make me draw a breath and stop another sob in my throat.

"It's all right," he says.

"No." I push myself up off my knees, shrug away his touch, and rush out to where Ruth sits with her empty plate covered in powdered sugar.

"Where is he?" I ask.

She has the nerve to look startled.

"*Who* is he, really?" I don't know which question's more important to me. My hands clench the edge of her desk as if I might flip it over if she doesn't answer me.

Ruth closes her book slowly, eyeing me like I'm a starved and rabid cat and she can't decide if I need to be put down or fed. I think she might lie to me, keep up the charade, but she sighs. "He's the son of a wealthy real estate investor. You can't throw a stone in the Quarter without hitting something his father owns." She gestures around the shop. "He owns this place. Nicholas isn't a bad kid, but he gets away with a lot ever since . . ." She shakes her head. "He pays me in cash to play his games using my shop."

Games. Plural.

"How many times has he done this?"

"You're the sixth one who's been in here. There were a couple of boys before you and a few girls before that."

My stomach bottoms out. "Did he . . . ?" I stop and look away. I want to ask if he seduced the others too—if the connection we had was just as fake as his vampire status, but I can't ask that without admitting I *was* seduced. And I can't say that in front of Henry, even if he already knows.

Ruth seems to sense what I'm not saying anyway. Her expression softens. "He's never asked me to let him meet the person in my bookshop before. That was new. You were different."

That doesn't answer my question, but I still feel some relief, and that makes me angry. Why should I care if his feelings were real or not? The most important thing was a lie.

"How could you—" Something dark and dangerous and worthy of a vampire builds in my chest, and I can't speak anymore without fear of yelling. That darkness travels upward. My face burns as I fight to control it. I swallow, and it's like swallowing coal, but I do it again and again until I trust myself not to lash out. None of this is Ruth's fault. I push down the fire, but I don't snuff it out. The effort releases a few tears from my eyes, and I step back from the desk to wipe them away.

"I thought it was all fun and games," Ruth says quietly.

I almost spill open right there and tell her about my dad and how this was my last shot to find a way to keep him, but she doesn't deserve that burden. And suddenly I can't say the words out loud. I'm acutely aware of how foolish they will sound. And then she'll have the look—the one Henry had when I first told him, the same one as the woman and the security guard at the convent.

"It's okay." I lie instead. "Just tell me where he is."

She looks away. She may want to tell me, but she won't—not if it means risking her shop. No wonder Nicholas had access to everything. Everyone seemed to know him and be a little afraid of him, but that fear was really for his father.

Henry says my name, and I turn around. He has the stack of photos in his hand. He holds one out to me: me and Nicholas together at the restaurant, his arm draped across my shoulder, leaning toward me like he might tell me a secret we both know he never will.

"I don't want to see those, Henry."

"Look at his neck."

I peer closer, where his shirt stretches farther open than normal as he leans in, revealing a small golden cross with a ruby center.

Henry holds up the other, blurry photo of our thieving selves. They look the same.

"He kept it," I say. He's a liar, why not a thief, too?

"Unless it was already his."

I swear my heart skips a beat at that. "Let's go," I say, but first I rip the pictures out of Henry's hands and set them on Ruth's desk. "Leave them." I hold out my hand to Ruth and give hers a little squeeze, adding a broken smile on top so she knows I don't blame her for any of this, and then I'm gone, with Henry close behind me.

*I just feel like all the sand's at the bottom
of the hourglass or something.*
—*Only Lovers Left Alive*

# Twenty

This time, when we go through the side gate, we don't creep around the back. We climb the worn-down porch and ring the doorbell.

A handsome man in his early fifties with warm brown skin and graying curly hair answers the door. He has dark circles under his eyes, like we've just woken him from an ancient sleep, and he seems startled to see actual people on his front porch. He stares past us for a moment, probably at the still-chained front gate, before making eye contact.

"Can I help you?"

All the ways I could answer that question flood my mouth, and I flounder to pull out a single word.

Henry finally speaks up for me. "Nicholas home?"

"Nick?" He looks behind him and then at us again. "He's upstairs in his room."

"Can we come in and say hello?" Henry reaches out and shakes the man's hand. "I'm Henry, by the way. We met Nick in town earlier this week and he mentioned we could stop by."

Henry gives that winning smile of his that frequently got us out of trouble when we were kids. I say a silent prayer of thanks that he's still as smooth as ever at manipulating adults. I could never get my scowl at getting caught to go away long enough to do the same.

"Sure." The man steps back, opening the door wider.

"Great. Thank you," Henry says, and we're in.

Walking through the house as an invited guest instead of a burglar is a different experience, but I'm not in the mood to appreciate the opulent wealth today. I head right up the stairs and toward the bedroom I know Nicholas must be in. Henry speeds up at the last minute and beats me to the door like he doesn't quite trust what I'll do once I'm on the other side.

Nicholas lies on top of the dark-brown bedspread, eyes closed, hands behind his head, earbuds in, his phone on top of his chest. He wears gray drawstring sweatpants and a white tank top, and he looks younger than I've ever seen him—just another guy a couple of years out of high school still living with his parents. There's a softness in the slightly upturned corners of his mouth that I can't make fit with the shadowed smirks and grins I remember. He crosses his legs at the ankle. So innocent—not like a vampire at all. Did he ever look like one, or did I see what I wanted to see?

He smiles at whatever he's listening to, and that does it. I dart past Henry and rip an earbud out.

His eyes widen, and he jerks upright, phone sliding off his

chest and thumping softly on the bed. I'm tempted to pick it up and hurl it into the mirror above his dresser. He pulls the other bud from his ear. His mouth opens and closes, and I wait for him to find the words even though I know they won't help me. The window across the room opens to the morning sunlight, which makes his warm brown skin glow with obvious life. I scan the room, searching like a fool to find bloodstained carpet or a dead, drained body—*any* sign to override the ones breaking in front of me. I struggle to breathe as I realize I was still holding onto the smallest splinter of hope that I would come here and find him in a room blacked out with heavy burgundy drapes, and he'd take me into his arms and suck enough life out of me so I could live forever without any of the pain of being human. But all I find is a half-empty cup of coffee on his bedside table.

"What are you doing here?" he finally asks.

"I don't know," I spit out. "What are you doing here? Don't you belong in an attic sealed in a coffin during this time of day?"

He lets out a nervous chuckle, much higher in pitch than those sexy ones in the dark corners of the night. His fingers pull at the neck of his T-shirt as if he's a nervous boy with a girl in his room, and he's trying to remember how to be cool. Every move he makes shatters another piece of the illusion I've been feeding on. He shifts on his bed, smoothing back his hair so the sun catches the little bits of red in it. I hate that he's still so attractive—someone I would definitely say hi to in a coffee shop—but without the night surrounding him, it strips away

an air of mystery. Who was the creature I kissed last night in the graveyard? Because it is not this boy.

"You're joking, right?" he asks. He runs his hand through his curls, and the gesture reminds me of Henry. Nicholas never touched his hair before—he never made a single move that wasn't silky with confidence. He'd be an excellent actor. He *is* an actor.

I don't know him at all, and that thought brings a fresh hurt, like getting a paper cut on your finger when your arm's already broken.

It still stings. I blink slowly. He seems to be waiting for a response, but I don't give one.

"Of course I'm not a vampire. I thought we were just having fun. Pretending." He doesn't meet my eyes as he says it. He knows it was his game and not mine. He's trying to fool *himself* now—probably trying to get rid of the guilt of fooling me.

Still, his words rip through me. *Just having fun.* That last drop of burning green hope gets swallowed by other, hot and angry colors. My limbs shake. My fingers clench as the rage crashes through my system.

I failed. Dad is fading. I felt it in my gut when I talked to him on the phone, but I ignored it because I convinced myself I was so close to saving him when really I was just playing games with a boy I liked kissing. I bend at the waist and try not to hurl.

Sorrow tries to flood its dark blue through my veins to blend with the violent red, but I fight it. I'm afraid of turning into a pulsing purple thundercloud that rains without ceasing, and I

can't do that yet. I need to face Dad. I'll still need to be strong and hold his hand at the end without adding my pain to his.

I try to embrace my hate and ignore everything else fighting to surface, but perhaps the worst part is that I'm not just angry at him. I *did* have fun. There was hard evidence in those photos I left behind in the bookshop. Those smiles were never 100 percent fake even when I told myself they were.

I had fun while my dad is dying.

And suddenly I want Nicholas to feel that kind of pain. I pull myself up to face him and all the mistakes I made.

"You're a liar. You knew this was more than fun to me." I choke on the words and look away. Henry's silent, but I feel him right behind me, close enough for me to turn and crash into his chest if I need to.

"What else could it have been about?" He still refuses to look at me—still insists on playing.

"*Everything.*" I push the word from my mouth like it will mean something to him. Even now, I can't bring myself to tell him the truth. If he laughs or looks at me with pity or simply doesn't care at all, I might turn to dust like a vampire staked through the heart, and then Dad will never see me again because I won't resemble his daughter. I'll be a pile of ash—the leftovers of a girl who felt more than she could handle.

Nicholas shakes his head, finally looking at me and facing my pain, but he seems confused, like he can't quite understand it, and why would he?

"Immortality isn't everything. There's a difference between living and existing," he says.

"But you can't live if you don't exist." How much longer does Dad have to exist? He's already beyond the point of living—that's what drove me here.

"But you *do* exist. You're standing right here." He reaches toward me, and I back into Henry's chest. Henry's heart beats hard against my back, as if he's ready to lunge forward at any moment.

Nicholas drops his hand without touching me.

"I'm sorry, but do you know how many silly people come out here looking for vampires, wasting their time trying to find immortality when they should be living their own life to the fullest? Nobody's seen a real one since they went back into hiding. I believe they exist, but they don't want to be found. It's such a waste, wanting to leave behind family and friends and real connections, and for what? To live forever? People who want to live forever usually don't deserve to. I took one look at you and thought, 'There's a girl who doesn't know how to live. Maybe I can help her before it's too late.' You should be thanking me. I did you a favor. Don't you feel more alive?"

I do. I'm painfully, excruciatingly alive, and I will be long after my dad's dead.

I finally look back at him. He slid off the bed during his little speech to stand in front of me. He waits, mouth pressed in a thin line as if he doesn't know how this will go—will I hug him and thank him for our fun game or slap him in the face? I lean toward the second option, but my limbs are too heavy for the movement.

"It wasn't for me," I whisper. "I swear this wasn't for me."

"What?" His voice sounds far off and confused.

I realize I've sunk to the ground at Henry's feet. My hands touch dark-blue carpet, which matches my dominant emotion. Oh God, the grief. It washes away everything else until I'm drowning in it.

"Her dad's dying, you asshat." Henry's voice lashes out above me. "Cancer. They ran out of treatment options. She thought you could save him."

The silence in the room is unbearably heavy. It settles on me, squeezing a few more tears from my eyes.

"No." Nicholas repeats the word over and over again like he's the broken one. A hand touches my shoulder, and then it's gone. When I lift my head, Henry's pushed Nicholas away, and Nicholas leans around Henry trying to get to me. "Please let me," he says as they grapple. "Please." And then he says the only words that could make me listen. "My mom died. A year ago. A car crash."

The room freezes. Henry stops trying to shove him farther away from me, but he doesn't let go of his arms.

I push myself to my feet. Everything hurts.

Everything in this whole room hurts, and maybe everything in the whole world, and it is too much for any one person to bear.

I walk over to Nicholas, and Henry lets go of him and steps away, looking between Nicholas and me like he can't quite decide what will happen or what he wants to happen.

Nicholas's head drops to his chest so I can't see his face. I don't need to. I know the kind of grief I'll see there—I'm not sure how I didn't see it before.

I slide my arms under his, hanging by his side, and hug him. His chest heaves, and then his arms wrap around me, and we stand there—two twin pools of grief finally understanding each other. His tears wet my shoulder, and somehow it's easier to handle my own grief when faced with someone else's. In this moment, grief is perhaps the only thing that could bring us together.

"I'm sorry," I say.

"I never would have done it if I'd known," he says. "I knew you were sad. I tried to turn you away because I thought you might drag me into my own sadness again, but when you came back, you had this spark in your eyes like all you needed was a little purpose to pull you out of it. I could relate. I thought I could help you." His arms tighten around me as if he still wants to save me. "I thought you'd lost someone too. I never imagined . . ."

He clings to me until I release him and his pain and step behind him, to the photo of the woman and child that caught my eye before. His cross necklace sits beside it. I run a finger along the frame, warm from the morning sun catching it. Above it, taped to the mirror, is my drawing—a shrine to our shared grief.

Nicholas moves to stand beside me—our arms touch, and I

don't pull away even though his closeness makes my chest hurt. "My mom was so outgoing, so alive, always pushing me to get out of my comfort zone and really live." A deep, aching kind of love warms his voice and makes my own throat burn for his loss. "When she died, I knew she'd want me to keep living. I just didn't know how. I used to work in one of those vampire-themed souvenir shops, and people would come in asking questions, wasting their lives looking for something that might kill them if they found it, so I decided to give them something else—a game to turn their focus on actually experiencing the city." His arm shifts against mine as he shrugs. "I thought it would help them. I thought it might help me, too."

"Did it?" My voice is so soft that for a second I'm not sure he heard.

He shifts to face me, and I look up into his dark-brown eyes and the deep grief there I could have seen if I weren't so focused on pushing away my own. He hinted that first night in the club of its existence, but I was only seeing what I wanted to see—in more ways than one.

"Not at first, but you were different. You made me feel again, so much that I almost ended things sooner because I was so afraid I'd need you to keep living, and you'd be gone, and I'd be worse off than before. But I don't deserve happiness." His throat constricts, and I can almost feel the pain he's swallowing.

I reach out and squeeze his hand, still as cold as ever, but some people just have cold hands. "You deserve to live," I say.

And living means joy and pain and everything in between. He showed me that. "Everyone should get to live."

But everyone doesn't get the chance.

And then I let go of him and step back. I can't heal his grief. Nobody can. And I can't use it as a distraction for my own.

"Goodbye, Nicholas."

He lifts his chin, blinking red eyes.

I turn and walk from the room and out of the house without looking back. I don't stop until I'm off the porch, past the broken animals in the yard, and out on the cracked and wounded sidewalk, and there I finally lose it.

I slip to my knees, fingers grasping at the cracks, and I cry. My grief has flooded me, and there's no place for it to go but out. Henry kneels beside me and folds his arms around me, and it makes me cry harder. When someone outside of your grief holds you, everything comes loose. Strength isn't necessary, and your tears won't soak into them—they can handle them. Henry's always been able to handle my emotions, and that's exactly why I've been afraid to be close to him this whole time. I knew he could deal with them and keep going like he did when we were kids. I knew he would break those emotions free again and again. Because he's known all this time that I needed to let them out.

I cry until I'm empty, and then, before I can refill again, I stand, and Henry does too, facing me, keeping his hands lightly on my shoulders in case he needs to pull me back to him again.

I always thought of him as the kind and sweet one—I was the

brave one, always jumping in headfirst. But maybe it's braver to be kind time and time again, even when people push you away.

"Kiss me," I say. I used Nicholas's kiss to try to drown out my grief, and now that I'm cried out, I want to refill with something real, something brighter, if only for a moment.

His eyes widen, and his mouth frowns. His fingers twitch on my shoulders like he wants to pull me in but doesn't.

"Not like this," he says.

"Like what?"

"You're sad. I don't want to kiss you just because you're sad. I don't want to do that to you."

"You're not doing anything to me. I'm tired of people trying to tell me how to respond to my emotions." I start to pull away from him. "If you don't want to kiss me, fine, but if you do want to kiss me and you think you know what I need better than I do, you're no better than him."

I jerk out of his touch and spin, catching my toe on a root breaking through the sidewalk and stumbling onto my hands and knees. Henry's there in a second, pulling me to my feet, but instead of letting me go, he cups my face in both hands and holds me there, eyes wandering over every inch of my face as if he's the artist, sketching this moment for eternity, and then he kisses me.

Kissing Henry's like setting memories on fire and burning them into something new. His kiss is the same red lust as Nicholas, but an undercurrent of sweet golden honey runs with it, turning it into something more alive, more whole. Something that can exist *with* my sadness instead of drowning it out and bringing back the guilt. I press into his kiss, hungry for it. His hands slip into my hair, cradling my head as our connection deepens. When he pulls back, we both stand there with aching grins on our faces.

He grabs my hand and links our fingers together.

"Let's go home," he says. "Forget about vampires."

I take one step with him before I freeze, forcing him to stop too because our hands are still linked.

Vampires. Plural. Nicholas was never the only option, and I still have hours before my early flight. I twist back toward the house. "I need to go back."

Henry's face falls. "Why?"

"I just need to. I need to say one more thing to him."

"Fine," he says, taking a step to follow me, but I place a hand against his chest.

"I need to do this part alone."

His fingers tighten around mine for a long moment, but then he lets go, nodding like he doesn't quite trust himself to speak.

I turn and run back. This time I don't bother knocking. I take the back steps and dart up the stairs, pulling open Nicholas's door. He's standing in front of his dresser, staring at my drawing. He wipes at his eyes when he sees me and cringes, like maybe I came to my senses and rushed back here to scream at him after all.

I don't have time for yelling. "The others. Your vampire coven or whatever. Are any of them real?"

He jerks back at my question, shaking his head. "Daniella's a friend from high school, and Marcus is her cousin. Carter is . . . I don't know. He showed up with Daniella one day and wanted to play?"

Carter.

I remember the fear that quivered through me the first time I met him. Instinctual. Primal. Different from what I felt with Nicholas. Carter has been on the edges of this the whole time. He smelled my blood from five feet away.

Plus, he's the one with the name linking him to a legend.

Nicholas steps toward me. "I wish I knew one for you."

"Maybe you do," I whisper.

"What?"

"What were you drinking in the club the first night I met you? It looked like blood."

He grins a little, like he's happy to give up his secrets. "Diluted corn syrup we dyed red. We pour it into old wine bottles. Kind of gross, but we don't have to sip much, and it fools everyone."

I shake my head. "I smelled blood. But it was Carter's cup I picked up that night."

Nicholas goes still. "It's not possible," he says, but his eyes narrow, and his lips bend into a frown. "He always brought his own bottle—said something about being allergic to the dye. I think he used some type of tomato juice instead. . . ." He trails off.

"Nicholas. Where do I find him?"

He's shaking his head. I have to reach out and touch his arm to get him to stop.

His eyes focus and meet mine. "Don't, Victoria. It's not worth the risk. What if . . . ?" He swallows. "I don't know anything about him. I've never even seen where he lives."

I let go of him and take a step away. I'm not surprised, but I know where to look without his help.

"Victoria," Nicholas says as I turn away from him. There's fear in his voice, but I don't turn back, and he doesn't come after me.

*Only those prepared to die will find eternal life.*
—*Byzantium*

# Twenty-One

I tell Henry I need some time alone in the city before we leave. Time to mourn. He doesn't like it, of course, but he understands grieving better than most.

But I'm not dressing in black just yet.

The convent is unchanged—still dimly lit and glowing softly in the dark, still simple and unassuming. It hasn't suddenly revealed itself as a secret den of vampires, but that's okay. I'm not here for the convent. I don't need the vampires in their attic, if they're there at all. I need the one who's been watching this game from the beginning. I'm banking on the fact that he's still watching.

I wrap my hands around the metal bars of the closed door. The chipping paint chafes my skin in a way I didn't notice the first time I stood here. Every part of me feels a thousand times more sensitive, more alive at the possibility of dying. My grip tightens as I fight the urge to look over my shoulder every few seconds. He likes sneaking up on me, so I'll let him believe he is.

My heart throbs with anticipation. I try taking deep breaths to calm it, but eventually I give up and let it race unchecked.

I don't have to wait long this time. He's expecting me.

A shoe scrapes faintly against the sidewalk behind me, and my muscles tense, but I don't turn yet. I'm still playing a game, just not the one I thought.

"You figured it out," he says. The exhale of his breath brushes the back of my neck. As I jerk in surprise, a rough piece of metal on the bars pricks my finger. I didn't expect him to be so close. Not yet. I'm not ready. I wish I had called my dad one more time—in case this doesn't end the way I want it to. Too late now.

I spin to find myself chest to chest with Carter. Coldness reaches out from him and turns my skin to goose bumps. He wears black leather pants and a lavender tank top that bares plenty of his pale skin reflecting the moonlight, and he's close enough that he has to tilt his chin down to look at me. His stringy blond hair keeps his face shadowed, but his eyes are bright.

Instinct takes over, and I step back the few inches I can so my shoulders scratch against the metal bars.

His gaze drifts down to my finger, where a tiny drop of blood gathers. I shift it behind my back as he raises his eyebrows in a look that says this won't help me.

My chest heaves like a cat cornered by a pack of wild dogs. I need to regain some type of control. I tell myself he's only one vampire, but somehow that doesn't help.

"You told me it was you from the beginning." I try to sound bold and confident, but it comes out in a squeak.

"I did."

"You could have been a little more specific."

His lips peel back into a smile. "Where's the fun in that?"

"So this has always been your game. Nicholas thinks it's his, but he's a pawn."

He sighs. Even pressed against the gate, as far away from him as I can get, his breath brushes the hair around my face. "That fool almost ruined it. He wanted to back out after catching *feelings*. He's only human, though, so I can hardly blame him."

"You don't have feelings?"

His eyes drift to where my bleeding finger hides. "I feel all kinds of things."

I swallow. I need to know if all vampires are like this—callous and calculating, treating people like playthings. That would be worse than death for someone like my dad, like me, but I doubt I will get a straight answer.

"Do they all figure you out in the end?"

"The smart ones. The ones who know the legends and recognize my name. Nicholas is an excellent decoy, though. He might be a better vampire than I am." He laughs, and the sound is surprisingly light, but his eyes don't crinkle around the edges, and when he stops abruptly, I can't fight the shiver that runs through me. "Maybe I should make him one. What do you think, Victoria?"

I don't answer. Something tells me showing the slightest care for Nicholas is the wrong move. I don't like where this is going.

"Why bother with him at all? Why not play your own games?"

"I've played lots of games before, but a game within a game? That's something new. I heard about Nicholas's little ruse, and then I found his weak link. I love the weak. They don't taste good." He frowns a little, then smiles. "But they're easily bought."

My mind stumbles over itself, connecting everything. "Daniella. She knows what you are?"

He nods. "Her mother has considerable medical debt. People will do a lot for their families. Like I said, weak."

"That's not weak," I blurt without thinking. I respect her for it. She's doing what she has to—just like I am.

He shrugs, watching me as if he's waiting for one more thing to click.

Then it hits me. "She had Henry alone."

He leans forward, voice dropping so low it barely registers. *"I had Henry alone."*

My heartbeat stutters. "No. He would have told me."

He beams, rocking backward on his heels, waving a hand like this is nothing. "He'll never remember. A drop of my blood can heal, and the right word can erase memories."

The stain on Henry's shirt—the one he insisted was ketchup.

This time I bend over at my waist, fighting the urge to vomit. *I* did this. Henry paid a huge price to get me here, and he doesn't even know it.

I can't let that cost be for nothing. I straighten. Carter looks like he's growing bored.

I try to swallow, but it lodges somewhere in the back of my

throat, and I can barely get out the next sentence. "So you are one of them."

"Yes."

"You kill people."

"I give them what they want." He smiles wistfully, like he's in the midst of a sweet memory.

"I want to be a vampire."

"So you say."

"Will you do it?"

"I haven't decided yet." His tongue brushes his top lip. "I can't decide until I taste you—until I feel the rhythm of your heart as the life bleeds out of you and into me. Will your pulse race with fear until the very end, with the desire to keep going, or will it slow, surrender, accept what it really wants, which isn't eternal life but the sweet bliss of nothing at all? I give people what they desire."

"Sounds like a terrible deal."

"It's my only offer. Give yourself to me, and I decide."

"Does anyone actually go through with this?"

"Some."

"How many people have you actually turned?"

He smirks. "Some."

"What happens to the rest?"

"You know who I am."

I do. One of the Carter brothers. A serial killer. A *vampire*.

I stare at him, expecting to find the same cruelty twisting his

lips reflected in his eyes, but they're empty, and somehow that's worse.

But I've got hours before I need to leave for the airport. I don't have time to find a nicer vampire. I don't know if a nicer one exists.

"Do it," I say.

His eyelids flutter, and the faintest flicker of life finally reaches his cold, dead eyes as he closes the gap until only a centimeter separates us.

Even a human could hear the sound of my heart beating.

He brushes the hair away from my neck, and then his hands reach to grip the bars behind my head. His face leans down beside mine.

"Hold still or this will hurt," he whispers, and then he strikes, and it's not slow or sensual. It's how I'd imagine a snake bite would feel—sharp and angry and painful.

My body convulses with the urge to yank away. He's not holding me. His arms cage in either side of my head, but the only part of him that touches me is his mouth and teeth buried in the side of my neck.

Perhaps this is part of the test, standing here when I could jerk away at any moment.

I bite the inside of my cheek and taste blood—thick and coppery—and try not to gag. I wonder if it tastes better to him. I can't imagine drinking it to live. I can't imagine killing another person so I could keep going forever and ever. He fed on Henry and didn't kill him, but taking away someone's memory might be worse—the sickest violation. There must be other ways. Animals. Blood bags. I need to know. I should have questioned him more. I should have found out more. I still don't know what it means to be a vampire—everything Nicholas showed me was fake. I'm assuming it's better than death, but the only vampire I've met is a serial killer, an empty shell of a person. The only emotion I've seen reach his eyes was when I agreed to let him possibly kill me.

What if vampires feel nothing at all? Dead on the inside as well as out. A week ago, this may have been appealing to me, but now? I just got my emotions back. I just started feeling alive again. I don't want to go back to existing instead of living.

Is my pulse slowing? I can't tell. *Keep fighting. Be brave. Be strong like Buffy.*

Something hot touches my cheeks, and for a second I think he's bitten me somewhere else, but no. I'm crying.

Dad wouldn't want this life. He wouldn't want me to risk this.

Buffy knew when she had to lose someone—when there was no other option.

This might be a choice, but it's not a good one. At worst, I'm dead. At best, I'm a vampire and Dad's a vampire, and we live forever fighting the urge to take lives, to hold onto our humanity, slowly feeling nothing inside. Nobody's ever been more human than Dad. He's too good for this.

"No," I mumble. When did I start to sag? The door behind me holds most of my weight.

Carter hums in response but doesn't move.

"No," I say louder. I lift my hands to his chest and push. His fangs strain against the skin of my neck as he budges the smallest amount.

He's not stopping.

I swear his lips smile against my neck.

He gave only two outcomes: vampire or dead. Backing out was never a choice.

I let a sob rip through me. I let my grief flood my system, and then I let my legs collapse out from under me as I finally let go of hope and accept my fate.

He doesn't expect this, and since he wasn't holding me, I drop, and his fangs rip away from my neck before I hit the ground like an empty sack of flesh.

He runs the back of his hand across his mouth as he glares down at me. "That wasn't part of the deal."

One of my hands goes to my neck, presses against the wet, hot life leaking out of it. I dig the fingers of my other hand into one of the cracks in the sidewalk and try to pull myself out from under his shadow. He crouches and watches me drag myself away inch by inch. My limbs are made of nothing but water and grief, but I force myself to keep crawling.

"You've just voided our agreement," he says. The soft giddiness in his voice strengthens my next push away from him. "Do you want to know what I would have chosen? Do you want to know if you were going to live forever or die? Not that it matters now."

I'm too weak. I pull myself to the rough wall of the convent and lean against it as I sit with my legs tucked to my chest. I've put only four feet between us. Not nearly enough. My vision blurs.

Carter crawls toward me on his hands and knees like something out of a horror movie.

He *is* a horror movie.

I kick a leg out at him, and his hand latches around my ankle. I sense him squeezing, but I barely feel the pressure.

"Do you want to know what I chose?" he asks again, because this is his game. My despair is his prize.

"I'm choosing life." My voice comes out clearer than I expect.

"I don't think so, my dear." He lets go of my ankle. He doesn't need to hold it. I'm not going anywhere alone. But I don't need to.

I hear voices. I can't see them yet, but they sound close enough to reach me in time.

So I let out a bloodcurdling, vampire-movie-worthy scream.

Carter's eyes widen. He shakes his head at me like I'm a very naughty child who deserves both admiration and punishment for their wicked ways. He bites into his hand, wiping his blood across the wound on my neck. And then he's gone.

Worried faces blur in front of me as I pull out my phone and point to Henry's number.

*Come. We have not much time left before sunset.*
*—Mark of the Vampire*

# Twenty-Two

I'm on my flight. I don't remember much before getting here. I remember Henry crying though.

He swore a lot too. Some of it was directed at me. Some of it at himself.

We're not sitting together, but Henry uses the bathroom about ten times, and I'm sure it's so he can check on me as he passes by.

At least he believes in vampires now. I didn't tell him what really happened to him. I'm not sure he should be the one to carry that if I can hold it for him. Perhaps I'm wrong, but that's the decision I've made. I wonder why Carter didn't take my memory too in those final moments, but I bet he wanted me to live with it, for it to haunt me. I decide not to let it.

He healed my neck, at least. When I got back to Henry and wiped the blood from my skin, there was nothing, no trace of where the fangs tore my flesh. The people who helped me assumed I was drunk, that I'd cut my hand and touched my neck. When Gerald first appeared, people had wondered why there had never been signs of vampire attacks in the hospitals.

That makes sense now. I didn't go to the hospital, even though Henry wanted me to. I had no proof. Besides, I need every second I have left with Dad.

I spend the flight on any vampire message board I can find, leaving warnings about Carter and the convent, but then I go back and take down my posts. I don't want more desperate people to seek him out like I did.

I also spend the flight getting used to feeling again. I can feel other things besides sorrow and my sorrow won't be any less, and that's okay. There's no more guilt left in me. I tried. Sometimes acceptance is the only choice.

Then the plane lands.

And my phone lights up with multiple missed calls from my mom and sister.

The wet, blue sorrow catches me and drags me out to sea and drowns me so I'm left gasping for air, fingers shaking, other passengers staring as Henry pries my phone from my clenched fingers.

Despair has its own calms.

—*Dracula* by Bram Stoker

## Twenty-Three

Not dead. My dad is almost dead, but he is not dead. Not yet.

*That's what family is. It's the people you're born to
and the people you choose who stand
beside you when things get hard.*
*—The Originals*

# Twenty-Four

**M**y dad is asleep when we get home. Henry offers to sit
with me, but my family needs me more than I need
him.

I run into Jessica in the hallway, and when I move to walk
around her, she steps in front of me again. I stare at the flip-flops
I almost never see her wear and brace myself.

She should yell at me. She should be angry. I left her alone
to plan for the memorial instead of being strong for her, too. I
should have been strong for all of them—not just Dad. That
meant accepting their pain and sharing mine.

"Why didn't you tell me?"

"What?" I finally look at her.

"Dad told me. The whole vampire-hunting thing. I think he
thought you were sharing one of your inside jokes, but I know
you. I know how fiercely you believe. I remember hunting those
damn fairy rings and every other thing you read about."

I stare up at her wet eyes, the dull red of someone who's forgotten what it's like to not cry.

It brings back the guilt. I should have given her a chance. It bubbles in my throat, and for a second I fear it might destroy me right there before I can even get to see Dad, but then she reaches out and squeezes my hand, and the strength of her fingers forces it away.

She gives me her strength when I thought she needed mine.

"I would have helped you," she says.

I don't know what she means exactly: if she would have gone with me or if she would have tried to help me see reason, but it's enough.

I'm thankful she's still gripping my hand when I remember what day it is. "Today's Dad's birthday. I . . ." I choke on the words. I need to call everyone and cancel, and every call will be a torturous round of questions: How Dad's doing? Why did I plan a party in the first place? Where have I been?

Jessica shakes her head. "Aunt Becky ratted you out a few days ago. I took care of it."

Relief crushes me. But my sister's hand in mine keeps me together.

*I would tell you that it's okay to have hope . . .
because sometimes that's all that keeps me going.*
*—The Vampire Diaries*

# Twenty-Five

The bed shifts, and I bolt upright.

I spend most of my time in Dad's room, head resting on the sliver of empty space on the hospital bed, so I'll know if he stirs.

He moans a little, and I reach for the liquid morphine on the bedside table. He's not really conscious anymore. We give him so much morphine now that he never wakes up. It's the price to keep the pain away. A price everyone agrees we should pay.

I won't get to say goodbye to him, not really, just his unconscious body.

That will be my price for trying to save him, and whether I can live with it or not, I pay it.

He moans again.

"Okay, Daddy." I call him Daddy sometimes, like when I was little. I hope he hears it and it gives him perfect memories. "I'm going to give you a little more medicine."

"No," he moans, and I freeze. His eyes open and close again.

"A little more, Daddy," I choke out.

"No, no, no." His no's are mixed in with more moans, so I can't tell where one ends and the other begins.

Shaking, I put the medicine back on the table. I grab his hand, and he squeezes. We sit like that, him moaning, sleeping, waiting for the morphine to wear off a little more.

My mom pokes her head in the room an hour later and hears him. She rushes in the door.

"You didn't give him his morphine?" Her voice is sharp, almost panicked.

"He said no. I heard it."

She reaches for the bottle.

"I don't want it."

Mom's face pinches at Dad's voice, fingers going white around the bottle.

Dad lets go of my hand and reaches for hers, squeezing, and I watch my mom's face soften in a way I never really see.

"Give us a minute, Anna," he says, and Mom bends down and kisses his gray fingers before she leaves. On her way out, she touches my shoulder, and I think it's a reprimand at first, but there's something else in it, a passing of strength.

*Be strong*, it says.

I am. Stronger in a different way than when I left.

I take his hand in mine again.

"Kiddo," he says. His eyes are foggy with pain, but they find mine.

"I'm here now, Dad."

"I know. You've been here all along."

"I wasn't. I'm sorry I left you, Daddy. I shouldn't have gone." I lay my head against the bed for a second, discreetly wiping my tears on that old blanket before sitting straight up again. It's hard not to fall back into old habits. It's hard to let him see me and all my emotions.

"Honey, I'm glad you did."

"It was a mistake. I should have been here with you. We could have watched more movies together." My voice shakes on the word "movie," and I have to draw in a ragged breath.

"You lived our movies. It gave me courage to think of you out there." He tries to smile. "Did you find one?"

I hesitate. I don't want to tell him about Carter. I don't want him to feel guilty that I almost died for him, but I don't want one of the last things I say to him to be a lie.

"Yeah." I try not to cringe as I answer.

He doesn't notice, but something bright flickers in his eyes. "What were they like?"

"Sad," I say, because I'm not thinking about Carter at all. I'm thinking about Nicholas, and the way we held onto each other in our little sea of shared grief without even realizing what we were doing. "He was sad," I repeat, "and lonely."

"You're still human, then?"

"Yeah." I shrug. I can't tell if he believes I really met a vampire or not, but he doesn't need to. "It didn't work out."

"Doesn't matter," he says. "We would have made a pretty cool father-daughter vampire team, though."

I give him a wide smile, so real it breaks me in two. "I already had matching leather outfits picked out."

And then I laugh, really laugh like before, and as I do, tears stream down my face.

He chuckles, and the rattle of death hangs onto the sound, but I keep smiling, and so does he. He lifts a shaking arm and brushes a tear from my cheek. "There's my girl." His smile goes softer, more real than I've seen it in months.

And I know now this is strength—showing emotions as you feel them, counting on others to be able to share the burden of them with you.

He's dying. I can say that now without giving up. I've shifted my hope the same way Dad has, to something else, something less concrete that demands more faith. I'm strong enough now—I wasn't before.

"Did you take pictures?"

I pull out my drawing of the cathedral.

He stares at it for a long time, and then he says, "You're going to be okay, kiddo."

I nod, even though I'm not sure how he can tell from the drawing.

He asks for Mom next, but I can't find her, so I send Jessica instead.

"I think I saw your mom go out back," Henry says from his place on our couch. He sits there all the time in case I need him. I don't yet, but one day soon I will. He doesn't push me to need him. He knows better than that now. Somehow, impossibly, we're back to where we were before, and maybe even stronger. We've both hurt each other, but he's still there on my couch when I wake up every morning, and I let him stay.

He watches me go out the back door, but over the edge of his comic, like he's not really keeping tabs on me. Before, I would have hated that, but now it feels good to have someone I can run to when I need it.

"Mom?" I call.

No answer.

I step off the porch and onto our perfectly trimmed grass. I used to love freshly trimmed grass against the soft arches of my feet. I don't take the time to enjoy the sensation, but maybe another day when I need to feel alive, I will.

I find her around the corner of the house where Dad built her planter boxes last year so she could grow fresh strawberries for her morning smoothies.

Her back is to me. Her shoulders shake, and for a second, I think she's laughing, because the alternative doesn't make sense.

"Mom?"

She freezes, taking two deep breaths before turning.

"What are you doing out here?" she snaps, but it lacks her usual bite.

Red laces her eyes. Her nose runs, and she wipes her hand across her face, leaving a trail of dirt behind. She's been weeding the garden.

If I can hug the boy who led me all around New Orleans hunting something he never had, then I can hug my mother. I eliminate the gap between us and close my arms around her. She goes stiff under my touch. I can't remember the last time we hugged. I always belonged to Dad and Jessica always belonged to Mom, and we were okay with that, but it seems impossibly silly now.

After a moment, she hugs me back, and then she begins to cry into my shoulder. I can take it. I can absorb her sorrow because I'm letting go of some of mine too, trusting that she can feel my tears on her and still be strong, like I can. Crying doesn't make either one of us weaker.

When she pulls back, I grab my other drawing from my pocket. She unfolds it and stares at the simple little picture of a French Quarter balcony. Finally, she smiles. "This might be your best work yet." She looks up at me. "You're going to shine at art school."

Just like that, I'm a little bit lighter. I've wanted to hear those words from her for so long, even when I told myself they didn't matter.

"Do you regret not going?" I've been wondering ever since she mentioned wanting to see the street art in New Orleans.

She glances down at my picture again. "Sometimes, but not really. I wanted certainty more than anything. You're braver than that, braver than me. Even if it doesn't work out, you'll know you took the chance. You'll live your life knowing you tried. That's the thing I miss."

I'm not sure she's talking about art anymore, but I don't need to press her. She's proud of me. I can feel it.

She moves to hand my picture back to me, and my stomach drops, because maybe they were only words and she doesn't really want it, but then she says, "Find a place to hang it by my desk, will you?"

I take it back, feeling that warm yellow happiness spread through a tiny bit of space between my ribs.

I nod. "Dad wants to see you."

She smiles and nods and blinks a couple of times to clear her eyes, then tries out a calm smile on her face, and by the time we walk back into the house, I know she has a well too. I got it from her, and knowing we share that helps.

I don't know what's coming next. But I do know
it's gonna be just like this—hard, painful.
But in the end, it's gonna be us.
—*Buffy the Vampire Slayer*

# Twenty-Six

My mom asks me to sit by Jessica at the funeral since I'm the strong one, and I know what I have to do— but it's not to build up my well again. I take Jessica's hand, and we both sob, each of us taking turns squeezing the other's fingers a bit tighter. We share our grief, spread it between us, carrying more when the other needs it, and other times breaking down completely. Sometimes we laugh through the pain too, like when they play the slideshow tribute and show the picture of me and my dad on Halloween when I was eight: he was Dracula and I was a bat. The laughing hurts—*everything* hurts, and will for a long time, but in that laughter is a promise, too, that even though I'll carry this loss around forever, I'll be able to feel other things as well.

The reception's harder. Dealing with so many people who don't share the entire weight of my grief is overwhelming. They expect smiles and bravery, but I've used all that falseness up.

I'm looking for an escape when Bailey steps in front of me.

I flinch. I didn't even realize she was here, and for a moment I brace myself, half expecting her to say something to hurt me, but that's not who she is. Silently, she wraps her warm arms around me and holds me for a second before letting go and heading toward a group of friends I assumed didn't care enough about me anymore to come. I give them all a grateful nod as I head for the door.

I don't know if I can repair the damage I caused to my friendships, but Bailey's hug gives me hope.

Finally, I find a quiet place to hide in the church parking lot between a tree trunk and the neighbor's fence.

Dead leaves crunch behind me, but I don't bother turning around.

A throat clears softly.

I look over my shoulder at Henry, chewing on his lower lip like always, glancing down at me and then away like he's counting the knots in the wooden fence. He grips a small pink box in his hands.

"You realize this isn't a birthday party, right?" I snort a little, like I'm cracking a joke, but the words ring out crueler than I intend.

He ignores them and climbs into the dead foliage, kneeling next to me. "I want you to have this."

"I can't do this today."

He holds the box out to me, hands steady as he waits.

I take it. What I want in this moment is to be alone in this one dark corner on an otherwise brutal sunny day, and if I take his box, maybe he will go.

He doesn't. He shifts so he's cross-legged next to me, pulling deeper into my collection of shattered leaves and lost sticks. He doesn't realize all this brokenness is for me. I need a moment to wallow. I can't have a whole person here with me. He does not fit.

I open my mouth to try to explain it, to at least tell him to go. He shakes his head like he knows what I'll say before I say it. He used to when we were kids. We always tried to jinx each other by finishing a sentence at the same time. He always got me. He knew me better than I knew myself.

"I'm not a little girl anymore." The words don't make sense, and I don't know why I say them. I haven't been a little girl in some time.

"I know you're not," he says simply. He doesn't ask me to explain myself. I don't need to with him. The realization jerks me with some kind of emotion I don't have the capability to feel in this moment, but I save it for later. One day I'll bring it out and let it flood through me.

"Open it," he says.

My fingers are steel as I untie the white ribbon and lift the lid off the pink cardboard box. I'm proud of how strong I am. My fingers don't start to shake until I pull out the pictures—me grinning with Joanie on the Pony, me jerking back from the alligator, me smiling in a room of gold. The photos slide from my fingers, and I press my chest into my knees, gasping, fighting to keep the summer air in my lungs.

I want to cry. I crave the release now after denying the need for so long. But the funeral has drained me.

"Why would you keep those?" My question comes out harsh and accusing.

But Henry remains steady. "Your dad thought you might want them."

"My dad saw them?" I bury my face in my knees. "Oh God." I haven't cried out to God in a long time. I did it a lot when he first got sick. Now it feels right again.

"Wait, Victoria. Listen to me." Henry's hand rests gently on my back between my shoulder blades. I want to lean into his touch and yank away from it all at the same time. I end up going still from too many conflicting desires. He leaves his hand there and keeps talking. "I brought them back home because I thought you might want them someday. Your dad asked me if I had any photos of the trip, so I showed them to him. I should have checked with you first. I'm sorry."

And then he says the most important thing of all. "He wrote you a note and asked me to give it to you later, when the time was right."

My dad probably didn't mean wrap them up like a present for his funeral, but I don't care. He'd probably laugh at Henry's timing. My shaking fingers scrape at the bottom of the box, pulling out a simple piece of binder paper folded four times over.

I start to unfold it. Slowly, so slowly.

"Do you want me to go?" Henry asks.

I'd already forgotten he was here. His hand on my back belongs there.

My voice is somewhere stuck in my throat, so I shake my head.

"I'm here," he says.

I unfold the note.

"This isn't my dad's handwriting."

Henry clears his throat. "He dictated it to me."

I expect a flush of bitterness that Henry got to hear my dad's note ahead of me, but instead I get a warm rush of comfort, an easing of the pressure. I don't need to pretend anything with Henry. He already knows what the letter says. He probably knows how I'll react to it.

"I need to read it in the sun," I say, even though I know the thought is not rational. Dad was always telling me I needed more sun—that I was turning into a vampire simply by staying inside too much with my sketchbook. I can't read his last words to me in the heavy shadow of a dying tree.

Henry holds out a hand for me, and I let him help me to my feet. We walk into the sun hand in hand, and I don't let go for a long moment.

Finally, I release him and lift the note, blinking against the harsh glow of the sun on the white paper. Henry's chunky black script blurs in my vision.

Kiddo,

Henry showed me the pictures of you on your trip. I loved them. I wish I could have gone there with you, but seeing you there is enough for me. Don't hate Henry for keeping them. I can tell he's worried. He knows how mad you can get. Keep that boy in line, but forgive him once in a while too. He's worth it.

Kiddo, you are the bravest person I know. My fight's done, but yours isn't. I know this will be hard for you. But don't stop fighting, for me and for yourself. Keep living, really living. I know you have it in you. I saw it in those pictures.

And I don't want you to ever stop believing in vampires or God or unicorns or anything else in the world that gives you hope, even if you never get to see or touch them. Because that's what belief really is, a hope in something outside of yourself, and hope can never be a bad thing. Even if you think it fails you in the end, did it really fail you if it carried you through the toughest parts of your life? I don't believe so.

Thank you for hoping for me. Never think it was a waste. It wasn't.

Keep hoping.

Love always,

Dad

Henry's staring up at the sky. When I rustle the paper as I fold it back up, he glances down at me. His eyes glisten, but he's not crying. He's waiting for me.

I step into his arms.

I cry until I'm so empty it seems like I might float up into the sun and combust if Henry lets go of me. I actually move away from him to see if it will happen. Nope. I stand in the sun as he watches me, waiting.

I am empty, but not broken.

Empty things can be filled again.

# Acknowledgments

I have been drafting these acknowledgments in my mind for the past year, but now that I'm typing them, there doesn't seem to be enough words to contain the love I have for the people who helped me achieve this dream. But I shall do my best.

Thank you to my wonderful agent, Rebecca Podos. I had a feeling from the moment I read your comment on my Pitch Wars entry that you were going to understand my weird little book about grief and hope, and I'm so glad I was right. Thank you for championing it and for being totally on board with my can-I-add-a-vampire-to-this brand.

Thank you to the amazing Sarah McCabe, who saw straight to the heart of this story and pushed me to dig deeper than I thought possible. It's been an absolute delight to work with you. I'm always excited to open your edit notes because they never fail to get my mind spinning with new possibilities.

Thank you to the whole team at McElderry: Justin Chanda, Karen Wojtyla, Anne Zafian, Nancee Adams, Elizabeth Blake-Lin, Chrissy Noh, Devin MacDonald, Karen Masnica, Cassandra Fernandez, Brian Murray, Anna Jarzab, Emily Ritter, Annika Voss, Lauren Hoffman, Lisa Moraleda, Lauren Carr, Christina Pecorale and her sales team, and Michelle Leo and her team.

## Acknowledgments

Thank you to artist Jeff Östberg and designers Jess LaGreca and Sonia Chaghatzbanian for giving me the perfect cover for this story.

I'm so grateful for Pitch Wars—especially the 2017 and 2018 classes. This program helped me to become a better writer and gave me something just as valuable: a community. Thank you Dawn Ius and Kimberly Gabriel, the best mentors anyone could ask for. Your passion for my story kept me going. Thank you for being willing to tell me a thousand times that I can't just say my character has emotion, and I need to actually describe a specific emotion. Who knew? I'm eternally grateful for your love and support. To Angela Montoya, my 2020 mentee, you're awesome and talented, and I'm so excited to have another writing friend in my life.

I always thought writing would be me alone with my cat, and a lot of times it is that, but in reality it opened up a world of online friends I wouldn't want to be without. To my writing critique group, Jeff Wooten, Eliza Langhans, Melody Steiner, Ryan Van Loan, Brook Kuhn, and Emily Taylor, our monthly chats are always a delight—I'm so thankful for all your advice and support. A special thank you to Emily Thiede, a sentence wizard, who gave this book the extra shine it needed before querying. Tala Shannak, thank you so much for reading and cheering me on. Your kind words and love for this story were just what I needed. Jess Creadon, I am so thankful that we became friends because every writer needs that person they can turn to with any worry or excitement. I know I can always count on you for encouragement and advice.

This book would not exist without Portia Hopkins. How many friends will hop on a plane with you and take a weeklong trip to New Orleans to chase a book idea and do a tiny bit of vampire hunting? This book was only a concept before that trip. I'll always remember buying tickets to visit the museum in the Ursuline Convent. The ticket lady looked at us and told us quite sternly that there was nothing supernatural inside, and if that's what we were there for, we shouldn't bother. I guess I looked like a girl in need of a vampire. Thanks for doing all the talking and assuring her we really did want to learn about the nuns, which was true in your case even if my motives were a tiny bit different.

Christy Cooper, thank you for being an unwavering support for me on so many levels. You always know just when you need to call me or when I need a surprise package of tea to get me through the week. Bailey Gillespie, I've lost track of how many adventures we've been on. Your attention to the little details in every single moment has rubbed off on me and made me a better writer. Thanks for not letting me die that one time. Stephanie Garber, thank you for always answering my many, many publishing questions and for being so generous with your time and advice. And thank you for giving the absolute best book recommendations. Cameron Wilson, thank you for our many chats about storytelling and for all your support and encouragement.

To my former professors, thank you. I would never have had

the confidence to actually start writing without your kind words and the classes that fed my passion.

To all my former students, thank you for cheering me on. Many of you saw all the highs and lows of my publishing journey. I'll never forget the parties you threw for me at each milestone. Teaching you made me a better writer. I can't wait to see my name in your acknowledgments one day.

To all my family that have encouraged me and put up with my weird comments at every family function, thank you. Thank you to my sisters who always have my back. Thank you to my parents for letting my imagination run absolutely wild as a kid and then putting up with the fact that I never grew out of it. I would not be typing this if you hadn't supported my dreams. Thanks, Dad, for the many, many funny lines you've given me for my stories. Thanks, Mom, for listening to me ramble on and on while working out my story ideas, and for somehow understanding what I'm trying to say. Lucas, Liam, and Gabriel, the wild stories you three spin rival my own imagination. You're the light in my life. Love you.

To Nana, Bampa, Grammy, Papa, and Marge: I know you're all so proud of me. Miss you.

## About the Author

Margie Fuston grew up in the woods of California, where she made up fantasy worlds that always involved unicorns. In college, she earned undergraduate degrees in business and literature and a master's in creative writing. Now she's back in the woods and spends all her time wrangling a herd of cats and helping her nephews hunt ghosts, pond monsters, and mermaids.